CONFESSIONAL

Jack Higgins lived in Belfast till the age of twelve. Leaving school at fifteen, he spent three years with the Royal Horse Guards, serving on the East German border during the Cold War. His subsequent employment included occupations as diverse as circus roustabout, truck driver, clerk and, after taking an honours degree in sociology and social psychology, teacher and university lecturer.

The Eagle Has Landed turned him into an international bestselling author, and his novels have since sold over 250 million copies and have been translated into fifty-five languages. Many of them have also been made into successful films. His recent bestselling novels include *The Judas Gate, The Wolf at the Door, A Fine Night for Dying, Dark Justice, Toll for the Brave, Without Mercy* and *The Valhalla Exchange*.

In 1995 Jack Higgins was awarded an honorary doctorate by Leeds Metropolitan University. He is a fellow of the Royal Society of Arts and an expert scuba diver and marksman. He lives on Jersey.

JACK HIGGINS

CONFESSIONAL

HARPER

Harper
An imprint of HarperCollins*Publishers*
77–85 Fulham Palace Road,
Hammersmith, London W6 8JB

www.harpercollins.co.uk

This paperback edition 2010
1

First published in Great Britain by William Collins Sons & Co. Ltd in 1985

A catalogue record for this book is
available from the British Library

Hb ISBN: 978 0 00 723477 6
Pbb ISBN: 978 0 00 737236 2
Pba ISBN: 978 0 00 723478 3

Set in Sabon by Palimpsest Book Production Limited,
Falkirk, Stirlingshire

Printed and bound in Great Britain by
Clays Ltd, St Ives plc

Publisher's Note

Confessional was first published in the UK by William Collins Sons & Co. Ltd in 1985. It was later published in paperback by Pan Macmillan but has been out of print for several years.

In 2009, it seemed to the author and his publishers that it was a pity to leave such a good story languishing on his shelves. So we are delighted to be able to bring back *Confessional* for the pleasure of the vast majority of us who never had a chance to read the earlier editions.

FOR MY CHILDREN
Sarah, Ruth, Seán and Hannah

PROLOGUE

1959

When the Land Rover turned the corner at the end of the street, Kelly was passing the church of the Holy Name. He moved into the porch quickly, opened the heavy door and stepped inside, keeping it partially open so that he could see what was happening.

The Land Rover had been stripped down to the bare essentials so that the driver and the two policemen who crouched in the rear were completely exposed. They wore the distinctive dark green uniforms of the Royal Ulster Constabulary, Sterling submachine guns held ready for instant action. They disappeared down the narrow street towards the centre of Drumore and he stayed there for a moment, in the safety of the half-darkness, conscious of the familiar odour.

'Incense, candles and the holy water,' he said softly and his finger reached to dip in the granite bowl beside the door.

'Is there anything I can do for you, my son?'

The voice was little more than a whisper and, as Kelly turned, a priest moved out of the darkness, an old man, in shabby cassock, his hair very white, gleaming in the candlelight. He carried an umbrella in one hand.

'Just sheltering from the rain is all, Father,' Kelly told him.

He stood there, shoulders hunched easily, hands thrust deep in the pockets of the old tan raincoat. He was small, five feet five at the most, not much more than a boy, and yet the white devil's face on him beneath the brim of the old felt hat, the dark brooding eyes that seemed to stare through and beyond, hinted at something more.

All this the old priest saw and understood. He smiled gently, 'You don't live in Drumore, I think?'

'No, Father, just passing through. I arranged to meet a friend of mine here at a pub called Murphy's.'

His voice lacked the distinctive hard accent of the Ulsterman. The priest said, 'You're from the Republic?'

'Dublin, Father. Would you know this Murphy's place? It's important. My friend's promised me a lift into Belfast. I've the chance of work there.'

The priest nodded. 'I'll show you. It's on my way.'

Kelly opened the door, the old man went outside. It was raining heavily now and he put up his umbrella. Kelly fell in beside him and they walked along the pavement. There was the sound of a brass band playing an old hymn, *Abide with Me*, and voices lifted, melancholy in the rain. The old priest and Kelly paused, looking down on to the town square. There was a granite war memorial, wreaths placed at its foot. A small crowd was ranged around it, the band on one side. A Church of Ireland minister was conducting the service. Four old men held flags proudly in the rain, although the Union Jack was the only one with which Kelly was familiar.

'What is this?' he demanded.

'Armistice Day to commemorate the dead of two World Wars. That's the local branch of the British Legion down there. Our Protestant friends like to hang on tight to what they call their heritage.'

'Is that so?' Kelly said.

They carried on down the street. On the corner, a small girl stood, no more than seven or eight. She wore an old beret, a couple of sizes too large, as was her coat. There were holes in her socks and her shoes were in poor condition. Her face was pale, skin stretched tightly over prominent cheekbones, yet the brown eyes were alert, intelligent and she managed a smile in spite of the fact that her hands, holding the cardboard tray in front of her, were blue with cold.

'Hello, Father,' she said. 'Will you buy a poppy?'

'My poor child, you should be indoors on a day like this.' He found a coin in his pocket and slipped it into her collecting tin, helping himself to a scarlet poppy. 'To the memory of our glorious dead,' he told Kelly.

'Is that a fact?' Kelly turned to find the little girl holding a poppy timidly out to him. 'Buy a poppy, sir.'

'And why not?'

She pinned the poppy to his raincoat. Kelly gazed down into the strained little face for a moment, eyes dark, then swore softly under his breath. He took a leather wallet from his inside pocket, opened it, extracted two pound notes. She gazed at them, astonished, and he rolled them up and poked them into her collecting tin. Then he gently took the tray of poppies from her hands.

'Go home,' he said softly. 'Stay warm. You'll find the world cold enough soon enough, little one.'

There was puzzlement in her eyes. She didn't understand and, turning, ran away.

The old priest said, 'I was on the Somme myself, but that lot over here,' he nodded to the crowd at the Cenotaph, 'would rather forget about that.' He shook his head as they carried on along the pavement. 'So many dead. I never had the time to ask whether a man was Catholic or Protestant.'

He paused and glanced across the road. A faded sign said *Murphy's Select Bar*. 'Here we are, then. What are you going to do with those?'

Kelly glanced down at the tray of poppies. 'God knows.'

'I usually find that He does.' The old man took a silver case from his pocket and selected a cigarette without offering one to Kelly. He puffed out smoke, coughing, 'When I was a young priest I visited an old Catholic church in Norfolk at Studley Constable. There was a remarkable medieval fresco there by some unknown genius or other. Death in a black hood and cloak, come to claim his harvest. I saw him again today in my own church. The only difference was that he was wearing a felt hat and an old raincoat.' He shivered suddenly.

'Go home, Father,' Kelly said, gently. 'Too cold for you out here.'

'Yes,' the old man said. 'Far too cold.'

He hurried away as the band struck up another hymn and Kelly turned, went up the steps of the pub and pushed open the door. He found himself in a long, narrow room, a coal fire burning at one end. There were several cast-iron tables and chairs, a bench along the wall. The bar itself was dark mahogany and marble-topped, a brass rail at foot level. There was the usual array of bottles ranged against a large mirror, gold leaf flaking to reveal cheap plaster. There were no customers, only the barman leaning against the beer pumps, a heavily built man, almost bald, his face seamed with fat, his collarless shirt soiled at the neck.

He glanced up at Kelly and took in the tray of poppies. 'I've got one.'

'Haven't we all?' Kelly put the tray on the table and leant on the bar. 'Where is everyone?'

'In the square at the ceremony. This is a Prod town, son.'

'How do you know I'm not one?'

'And me a publican for twenty-five years? Come off it. What's your fancy?'

'Bushmills.'

The fat man nodded approvingly and reached for a bottle. 'A man of taste.'

'Are you Murphy?'

'So they tell me.' He lit a cigarette. 'You're not from these parts.'

'No, I was supposed to meet a friend here. Perhaps you know him?'

'What's his name?'

'Cuchulain.'

The smile wiped clean from Murphy's face. 'Cuchulain,' he whispered.

'Last of the dark heroes.'

Murphy said, 'Christ, but you like your melodrama, you boys. Like a bad play on television on a Saturday night. You were told not to carry a weapon.'

'So?' Kelly said.

'There's been a lot of police activity. Body searches. They'd lift you for sure.'

'I'm not carrying.'

'Good.' Murphy took a large brown carrier bag from under the bar. 'Straight across the square is the police barracks. Local provision firm's truck is allowed through the gates at exactly twelve o'clock each day. Sling that in the back. Enough there to take out half the barracks.' He reached inside the bag. There was an audible click. 'There, you've got five minutes.'

Kelly picked up the bag and started for the door. As he reached it, Murphy called, 'Hey, Cuchulain, dark hero?'

Kelly turned and the fat man raised a glass toasting him. 'You know what they say. May you die in Ireland.'

There was something in the eyes, a mockery that sharpened Kelly like a razor's edge as he went outside and started across the square. The band were on another hymn, the crowd sang, showing no disposition to move in spite of the rain. He glanced over his shoulder and saw that Murphy was standing at the top of the steps outside the pub. Strange, that, and then he waved several times, as if signalling someone and with a sudden roar, the stripped Land Rover came out of a side street into the square and skidded broadside on.

Kelly started to run, slipped on the damp cobbles and went down on one knee. The butt of a Sterling drove painfully into his kidneys. As he cried out, the driver, who he now saw was a sergeant, put a foot hard on Kelly's outstretched hand and picked up the carrier bag. He turned it upside down and a cheap wooden kitchen clock fell out. He kicked it, like a football, across the square into the crowd which scattered.

'No need for that!' he shouted. 'It's a dud!' He leaned down, grabbing Kelly by the long hair at the back of the neck. 'You never learn, do you, your bloody lot? You can't trust anybody, my son. They should have taught you that.'

Kelly gazed beyond him, at Murphy, standing on the steps outside the bar. So – an informer. Still Ireland's curse, not that he was angry. Only cold now – ice cold and the breath slow, in and out of his lungs.

The sergeant had him by the scruff of the neck, up on his knees, crouched like an animal. He leaned, running his hands under the armpits and over the body, searching for a weapon, then rammed Kelly against the Land Rover, still on his knees.

'All right, hands behind you. You should have stayed back home in the bogs.'

Kelly started to get up, his two hands on the butt of the Browning handgun he had taped so carefully to the inside of the leg above the left ankle. He tore it free and shot the sergeant through the heart. The force of the shot lifted the sergeant off his feet and he slammed into the constable standing nearest to him. The man spun round, trying to keep his balance and Kelly shot him in the back, the Browning already arcing towards the third policeman, turning in alarm on the other side of the Land Rover, raising his submachine gun, too late as Kelly's third bullet caught him in the throat, driving him back against the wall.

The crowd were scattering, women screaming, some of the band dropping their instruments. Kelly stood perfectly still, very calm amidst the carnage and looked across the square at Murphy, who still stood at the top of the steps outside the bar as if frozen.

The Browning swept up as Kelly took aim and a voice shouted over a loudspeaker in Russian, booming in the rain, 'No more, Kelly! Enough!'

Kelly turned, lowering his gun. The man with the loudhailer advancing down the street wore the uniform of a colonel in the KGB, a military greatcoat slung from his shoulders against the rain. The man at his side was in his early thirties, tall and thin with stooped shoulders and fair hair. He wore a leather trenchcoat and steel-rimmed spectacles. Behind them, several squads of Russian soldiers, rifles at the ready, emerged from the side streets and doubled down towards the square. They were in combat fatigues and wore the flashes of the Iron Hammer Brigade of the elite special forces command.

'That's a good boy! Just put the gun down!' the colonel called. Kelly turned, his arm swung up and he fired once, an amazing shot considering the distance. Most of Murphy's left ear disintegrated. The fat man screamed, his hand going to the side of his head, blood pumping through his fingers.

'No, Mikhail! Enough!' the man in the leather overcoat cried. Kelly turned towards him and smiled. He said, in Russian, 'Sure, Professor, anything you say,' and placed the Browning carefully down on the bonnet of the Land Rover.

'I thought you said he was trained to do as he was told,' the colonel demanded.

An army lieutenant moved forward and saluted. 'One of them is still alive, two dead, Colonel Maslovsky. What are your orders?'

Maslovsky ignored him and said to Kelly, 'You weren't supposed to carry a gun.'

'I know,' Kelly said. 'On the other hand, according

11

to the rules of the game, Murphy was not supposed to be an informer. I was told he was IRA.'

'So, you always believe what you're told?'

'The Party tells me I should, Comrade Colonel. Maybe you've got a new rule book for me?' Maslovsky was angry and it showed for he was not used to such attitudes – not from anyone. He opened his mouth to retort angrily and there was a sudden scream. The little girl who had sold Kelly the poppies pushed her way through the crowd and dropped on her knees beside the body of the police sergeant.

'Papa,' she wailed in Russian. 'Papa.' She looked up at Kelly, her face pale. 'You've killed him! You've murdered my father!'

She was on him like a young tiger, nails reaching for his face, crying hysterically. He held her wrists tight and suddenly, all strength went out of her and she slumped against him. His arms went around her, he held her, stroking her hair, whispering in her ear.

The old priest moved out of the crowd. 'I'll take her,' he said, his hands gentle on her shoulders.

They moved away, the crowd opening to let them through. Maslovsky called to the lieutenant, 'Right, let's have the square cleared.' He turned to the man in the leather coat. 'I'm tired of this eternal Ukrainian rain. Let's get back inside and bring your protégé with you. We need to talk.'

* * *

The KGB is the largest and most complex intelligence service in the world, totally controlling the lives of millions in the Soviet Union itself, its tentacles reaching out to every country. The heart of it, its most secret area of all, concerns the work of Department 13, that section responsible for murder, assassination and sabotage in foreign countries.

Colonel Ivan Maslovsky had commanded Department 13 for five years. He was a thickset, rather brutal-looking man, whose appearance was at odds with his background. Born in 1919 in Leningrad, the son of a doctor, he had gone to law school in that city, completing his studies only a few months before the German invasion of Russia. He had spent the early part of the war fighting with partisan groups behind the lines. His education and flair for languages had earned him a transfer to the wartime counter-intelligence unit known as SMERSH. Such was his success that he had remained in intelligence work after the war and had never returned to the practice of law.

He had been mainly responsible for the setting up of highly original schools for spies at such places as Gaczyna, where agents were trained to work in English-speaking countries in a replica of an English or American town, living exactly as they would in the West. The extraordinarily successful penetration by the KGB of the French intelligence service at every level had been, in the main, the product of the school he had set up at Grosnia, where the emphasis was on everything French, environment, culture, cooking and dress being faithfully replicated.

His superiors had every faith in him, and had given him *carte blanche* to extend the system, which explained the existence of a small Ulster market town called Drumore in the depths of the Ukraine.

The room he used as an office when visiting from Moscow was conventional enough, with a desk and filing cabinets, a large map of Drumore on the wall. A log fire burned brightly on an open hearth and he stood in front of it enjoying the heat, nursing a mug of strong black coffee laced with vodka. The door opened behind him as the man in the leather coat entered and approached the fire, shivering.

'God, but it's cold out there.'

He helped himself to coffee and vodka from the tray on the desk and moved to the fire. Paul Cherny was thirty-four years of age, a handsome good-humoured man who already had an international reputation in the field of experimental psychology; a considerable achievement for someone born the son of a blacksmith in a village in the Ukraine. As a boy of sixteen, he had fought with a partisan group in the war. His group leader had been a lecturer in English at the University of Moscow and recognized talent when he saw it.

Cherny was enrolled at the University in 1945. He majored in psychology, then spent two years in a unit concerned with experimental psychiatry at the University of Dresden, receiving a doctorate in 1951. His interest in behaviourist psychology took him to the University of Peking to work with the famous Chinese psychologist, Pin Chow, whose speciality was the use of behaviourist techniques in the interrogation and conditioning of British and American prisoners of war in Korea.

By the time Cherny was ready to return to Moscow, his work in the conditioning of human behaviour by the use of Pavlovian techniques had brought him to the attention of the KGB and Maslovsky in particular, who had been instrumental in getting him appointed Professor of Experimental Psychology at Moscow University.

'He's a maverick,' Maslovsky said. 'Has no respect for authority. Totally fails to obey orders. He was told not to carry a gun, wasn't he?'

'Yes, Comrade Colonel.'

'So, he disobeys his orders and turns a routine exercise into a bloodbath. Not that I'm worried about these damned dissidents we use here. One way of forcing them to serve their country. Who were the policemen, by the way?'

'I'm not sure. Give me a moment.' Cherny picked up the telephone. 'Levin, get in here.'

'Who's Levin?' Maslovsky asked.

'He's been here about three months. A Jewish dissident, sentenced to five years for secretly corresponding with relatives in Israel. He runs the office with extreme efficiency.'

'What was his profession?'

'Physicist – structural engineer. He was, I think, involved with aircraft design. I've every reason to believe he's already seen the error of his ways.'

'That's what they all say,' Maslovsky told him.

There was a knock on the door and the man in question entered. Viktor Levin was a small man who looked larger only because of the quilted jacket and pants he wore. He was forty-five years of age, with iron-grey hair, and his steel spectacles had been repaired with tape. He had a hunted look about him, as if he expected the KGB to kick open the door at any moment, which, in his situation, was a not unreasonable assumption.

'Who were the three policemen?' Cherny asked.

'The sergeant was a man called Voronin, Comrade,' Levin told him. 'Formerly an actor with the Moscow Arts Theatre. He tried to defect to the West last year, after the death of his wife. Sentence – ten years.'

'And the child?'

'Tanya Voroninova, his daughter. I'd have to check on the other two.'

'Never mind now. You can go.'

Levin went out and Maslovsky said, 'Back to Kelly. I can't get over the fact that he shot that man outside the bar. A direct defiance of my order. Mind you,' he added grudgingly, 'an amazing shot.'

'Yes, he's good.'

'Go over his background for me again.'

Maslovsky poured more coffee and vodka and sat down by the fire and Cherny took a file from the desk and opened it. 'Mikhail Kelly, born in a village called Ballygar in Kerry. That's in the Irish Republic. 1938. Father, Sean Kelly, an IRA activist in the Spanish Civil War where he met the boy's mother in Madrid. Martha Vronsky, Soviet citizen.'

'And as I recall, the father was hanged by the British?'

'That's right. He took part in an IRA bombing campaign in the London area during the early months of the Second World War. Was caught, tried and executed.'

'Another Irish martyr. They seem to thrive on them, those people.'

'Martha Vronsky was entitled to Irish citizenship and continued to live in Dublin, supporting herself as a journalist. The boy went to a Jesuit school there.'

'Raised as a Catholic?'

'Of course. Those rather peculiar circumstances came to the attention of our man in Dublin who reported to Moscow. The boy's potential was obvious and the mother was persuaded to return with him to Russia in 1953. She died two years later. Stomach cancer.'

'So, he's now twenty and intelligent, I understand?'

'Very much so. Has a flair for languages. Simply soaks them up.' Cherny glanced at the file again. 'But his special talent is for acting. I'd go so far as to say he has a genius for it.'

'Highly appropriate in the circumstances.'

'If things had been different he might well have achieved greatness in that field.'

'Yes, well he can forget about that,' Maslovsky commented sourly. 'His killing instincts seem well developed.'

'Thuggery is no problem in this sort of affair,' Cherny told him. 'As the Comrade Colonel well knows, anyone can be trained to kill, which is why we place the emphasis on brains when recruiting. Kelly does have a very rare aptitude when using a handgun, however. Quite unique.'

'So I observed,' Maslovsky said. 'To kill like that, so ruthlessly. He must have a strong strain of the psychopath in him.'

'Not in his case, Comrade Colonel. It's perhaps a little difficult to understand, but as I told you, Kelly is a brilliant actor. Today, he played the role of IRA gunman and he carried it through, just as if he had been playing the part in a film.'

'Except that there was no director to call *cut*,' Maslovsky observed, 'and the dead man didn't get up and walk away when the camera stopped rolling.'

'I know,' Cherny said. 'But it explains psychologically why he *had* to shoot three men and why he fired at Murphy in spite of orders. Murphy was an informer. He had to be seen to be punished. In the role he was playing, it was impossible for Kelly to act in any other way. That is the purpose of the training.'

'All right, I take the point. And you think he's ready to go out into the cold now?'

'I believe so, Comrade Colonel.'
'All right, let's have him in.'

Without the hat and the raincoat Mikhail Kelly seemed younger than ever. He wore a dark polo-neck sweater, a jacket of Donegal tweed and corduroy slacks. He seemed totally composed, almost withdrawn, and Maslovsky was conscious of that vague feeling of irritation again.

'You're pleased with yourself, I suppose, with what happened out there? I told you not to shoot the man Murphy. Why did you disobey my orders?'

'He was an informer, Comrade Colonel. Such people need to be taught a lesson if men like me are to survive.' He shrugged. 'The purpose of terrorism is to terrorize. Lenin said that. In the days of the Irish revolution, it was Michael Collins's favourite quotation.'

'It was a game, damn you!' Maslovsky exploded. 'Not the real thing.'

'If we play the game long enough, Comrade Colonel, it can sometimes end up playing us,' Kelly told him calmly.

'Dear God!' Maslovsky said and it had been many years since he had expressed such a sentiment. 'All right, let's get on with it.' He sat down at the desk, facing Kelly. 'Professor Cherny feels you are ready to go to work. You agree?'

'Yes, Comrade Colonel.'

'Your task is easily stated. Our chief antagonists are America and Britain. Britain is the weaker of the two and its capitalist edifice is being eroded. The biggest thorn in Britain's side is the IRA. You are about to become an additional thorn.'

The colonel leaned forward and stared into Kelly's eyes. 'You are from now on a maker of disorder.'

'In Ireland?'

'Eventually, but you must undergo more training in the outside world first. Let me explain your task further.' He stood up and walked to the fire. 'In nineteen fifty-six, the IRA Army Council voted to start another campaign in Ulster. Three years later, and it has been singularly unsuccessful. There is little doubt that this campaign will be called off and sooner rather than later. It has achieved nothing.'

'So?' Kelly said.

Maslovsky returned to the desk. 'However, our own intelligence sources indicate that eventually a conflict will break out in Ireland of a far more serious nature than anything that has gone before. When that day comes, you must be ready for it, in deep and waiting.'

'I understand, Comrade.'

'I hope you do. However, enough for now. Professor Cherny will fill you in on your more immediate plans when I've gone. For the moment, you're dismissed.'

Kelly went out without a word. Cherny said, 'He can do it. I'm certain of it.'

'I hope so. He could be as good as any of the native sleepers and he drinks less.'

Maslovsky walked to the window and peered out at

the driving rain, suddenly tired, not thinking of Kelly at all, conscious, for no particular reason, of the look on the child's face when she had attacked the Irishman back there in the square.

'That child,' he said. 'What was her name?'

'Tanya – Tanya Voroninova.'

'She's an orphan now? No one to take care of her?'

'Not as far as I know.'

'She was really quite appealing and intelligent, wouldn't you say?'

'She certainly seemed so. I haven't had any dealings with her personally. Has the Comrade Colonel a special interest?'

'Possibly. We lost our only daughter last year at the age of six in the influenza epidemic. My wife can't have any more. She's taken a job in some welfare department or other, but she frets, Cherny. She just isn't the same woman. Looking at that child back there in the square made me wonder. She might just fit the bill.'

'An excellent idea, Comrade, for everyone concerned, if I may say so.'

'Good,' Maslovsky said, suddenly brightening. 'I'll take her back to Moscow with me and give my Susha a surprise.'

He moved to the desk, pulled the cork from the vodka bottle with his teeth and filled two glasses. 'A toast,' he said. 'To the Irish enterprise and to . . .' He paused, frowning, 'What was his code name again?'

'Cuchulain,' Cherny told him.

'Right,' Maslovsky said. 'To Cuchulain.' He swallowed the vodka and hurled his glass into the fire.

1982

1

When Major Tony Villiers entered the officers' mess of the Grenadier Guards at Chelsea Barracks, there was no one there. It was a place of shadows, the only illumination coming from the candles flickering in the candelabra on the long, polished dining-table, the light reflected from the mess silver.

Only one place was set for dinner at the end of the table, which surprised him, but a bottle of champagne waited in a silver ice bucket, Krug 1972, his favourite. He paused, looking down at it, then lifted it out and eased the cork, reaching for one of the tall crystal glasses that stood on the table, pouring slowly and carefully. He moved to the fire and stood there, looking at his reflection in the mirror above it.

The scarlet tunic suited him rather well and the medals made a brave show, particularly the purple and white stripes of his Military Cross with the silver rosette that meant a second award. He was of medium height with good shoulders, the black hair longer than one would have expected in a serving soldier. In spite of the fact that his nose had been broken at some time or other, he was handsome enough in a dangerous kind of way.

It was very quiet now, only the great men of the past gazing solemnly down at him from the portraits, obscured by the shadows. There was an air of unreality to everything and for some reason, his image seemed to be reflected many times in the mirror, backwards into infinity. He was so damned thirsty. He raised the glass and his voice was very hoarse – seemed to belong to someone else entirely.

'Here's to you, Tony, old son,' he said, 'and a Happy New Year.'

He lifted the crystal glass to his lips and the champagne was colder than anything he had ever known. He drank it avidly and it seemed to turn to liquid fire in his mouth, burning its way down and he cried out in agony as the mirror shattered and then the ground seemed to open between his feet and he was falling.

A dream, of course, where thirst did not exist. He came awake then and found himself in exactly the same place as he had been for a week, leaning against the wall in the corner of the little room, unable to lie down because of the wooden halter padlocked around his neck, holding his wrists at shoulder level.

He wore a green headcloth wound around his head in the manner of the Balushi tribesmen he had been commanding in the Dhofar high country until his capture ten days previously. His khaki bush shirt and trousers were filthy now, torn in many places, and his feet were bare because one of the Rashid had stolen his suede desert boots. And then there was the beard, prickly and uncomfortable, and he didn't like that. Had never been able to get out of the old Guards' habit of a good close shave every day, no matter what the situation. Even the SAS had not been able to change that particular quirk.

There was the rattle of a bolt, the door creaked open and flies rose in a great curtain. Two Rashid entered, small, wiry men in soiled white robes, bandoliers crisscrossed from the shoulders. They eased him up between them without a word and took him outside, put him down roughly against the wall and walked away.

It was a few moments before his eyes became adjusted to the bright glare of the morning sun. Bir el Gafani was a poor place, no more than a dozen flat-roofed houses with the oasis trimmed by palm trees below. A boy herded half a dozen camels down towards the water trough where women in dark robes and black masks were washing clothes.

In the distance, to the right, the mountains of Dhofar, the most southern province of Oman, lifted into the blue sky. Little more than a week before Villiers had been leading Balushi tribesmen on a hunt for Marxist guerrillas. Bir el Gafani, on the other hand, was enemy territory, the People's Democratic Republic of the South Yemen stretching north to the Empty Quarter.

There was a large earthenware pot of water on his left with a ladle in it, but he knew better than to try to drink and waited patiently. In the distance, over a rise, a camel appeared, moving briskly towards the oasis, slightly unreal in the shimmering heat.

He closed his eyes for a moment, dropping his head on his chest to ease the strain on his neck, and was aware of footsteps. He looked up to find Salim bin al Kaman approaching. He wore a black headcloth, black robes, a holstered Browning automatic on his right hip, a curved dagger pushed into the belt and carried a Chinese AK assault rifle, the pride of his life. He stood peering down at Villiers, an amiable-looking man with a fringe of greying beard and a skin the colour of Spanish leather.

'*Salaam alaikum*, Salim bin al Kaman,' Villiers said formally in Arabic.

'*Alaikum salaam*. Good morning, Villiers Sahib.' It was his only English phrase. They continued in Arabic.

Salim propped the AK against the wall, filled the ladle with water and carefully held it to Villiers' mouth. The Englishman drank greedily. It was a morning ritual between them. Salim filled the ladle again and Villiers raised his face to receive the cooling stream.

'Better?' Salim asked.

'You could say that.'

The camel was close now, no more than a hundred yards away. Its rider had a line wound around the pommel of his saddle. A man shambled along on the other end.

'Who have we got here?' Villiers asked.

'Hamid,' Salim said.

'And a friend?'

Salim smiled. 'This is our country, Major Villiers, Rashid land. People should only come here when invited.'

'But in Hauf, the Commissars of the People's Republic don't recognize the rights of the Rashid. They don't even recognize Allah. Only Marx.'

'In their own place, they can talk as loudly as they please, but in the land of Rashid . . .' Salim shrugged and produced a flat tin. 'But enough. You will have a cigarette, my friend?'

The Arab expertly nipped the cardboard tube on the end of the cigarette, placed it in Villiers' mouth and gave him a light.

'Russian?' Villiers observed.

'Fifty miles from here at Fasari there is an airbase in the desert. Many Russian planes, trucks, Russian soldiers – everything!'

'Yes, I know,' Villiers told him.

'You know, and yet your famous SAS does nothing about it?'

'My country is not at war with the Yemen,' Villiers said. 'I am on loan from the British Army to help train and lead the Sultan of Oman's troops against Marxist guerrillas of the D.L.F.'

'We are not Marxists, Villiers Sahib. We of the Rashid go where we please and a major of the British SAS is a great prize. Worth many camels, many guns.'

'To whom?' Villiers asked.

Salim waved the cigarette at him. 'I have sent word to Fasari. The Russians are coming, some time today. They will pay a great deal for you. They have agreed to meet my price.'

'Whatever they offer, my people will pay more,' Villiers assured him. 'Deliver me safely in Dhofar and you may have anything you want. English sovereigns of gold, Maria Theresa silver thalers.'

'But Villiers Sahib, I have given my word,' Salim smiled mockingly.

'I know,' Villiers said. 'Don't tell me. To the Rashid, their word is everything.'

'Exactly!'

Salim got to his feet as the camel approached. It dropped to its knees and Hamid, a young Rashid warrior in robes of ochre, a rifle slung across his back, came forward. He pulled on the line and the man at the other end fell on his hands and knees.

'What have we here?' Salim demanded.

'I found him in the night, walking across the desert.' Hamid went back to the camel and returned with a military-style water bottle and knapsack. 'He carried these.'

There was some bread in the knapsack and slabs of army rations. The labels were in Russian.

Salim held one down for Villiers to see, then said to the man in Arabic, 'You are Russian?'

The man was old with white hair, obviously exhausted, his khaki shirt soaked with sweat. He shook his head and his lips were swollen to twice their size. Salim held out the ladle filled with water. The man drank.

Villiers spoke fair Russian. He said, 'He wants to know who you are. Are you from Fasari?'

'Who are you?' the old man croaked.

'I'm a British officer. I was working for the Sultan's forces in Dhofar. Their people ambushed my patrol, killed my men and took me prisoner.'

'Does he speak English?'

'About three words. Presumably you have no Arabic?'

'No, but I think my English is probably better than your Russian. My name is Viktor Levin. I'm from Fasari. I was trying to get to Dhofar.'

'To defect?' Villiers asked.

'Something like that.'

Salim said in Arabic. 'So, he speaks English to you. Is he not Russian, then?'

Villiers said quietly to Levin, 'No point in lying about you. Your people are turning up here today to pick me up.' He turned to Salim. 'Yes, Russian, from Fasari.'

'And what was he doing in Rashid country?'

'He was trying to reach Dhofar.'

Salim stared at him, eyes narrow. 'To escape from his own people?' He laughed out loud and slapped his thigh. 'Excellent. They should pay well for him, also. A bonus, my friend. Allah is good to me.' He nodded to Hamid. 'Put them inside and see that they are fed, then come to me,' and he walked away.

Levin was placed in a similar wooden halter to Villiers. They sat side-by-side against the wall in the cell. After a while, a woman in a black mask entered, squatted, and fed them in turn from a large wooden bowl containing goatmeat stew. It was impossible to see whether she was young or old. She wiped their mouths carefully, then left, closing the door.

Levin said, 'Why the masks? I don't understand that?'

'A symbol of the fact that they belong to their husbands. No other man may look.'

'A strange country,' Levin closed his eyes. 'Too hot.'

'How old are you?' Villiers asked.

'Sixty-eight.'

'Isn't that a little old for the defecting business? I should have thought you'd left it rather late.'

Levin opened his eyes and smiled gently. 'It's quite simple. My wife died last week in Leningrad. I've no children, so no one they can blackmail me with when I reach freedom.'

'What do you do?'

'I'm Professor of Structural Engineering at the University of Leningrad. I've a particular interest in aircraft design. The Soviet Airforce has five MIG 23s at Fasari, ostensibly in a training role, so it's the training version of the plane they are using.'

'With modifications?' Villiers suggested.

'Exactly, so that it can be used in a ground attack role in mountainous country. The changes were made in Russia, but there have been problems which I was brought in to solve.'

'So, you've finally had enough? What were you hoping to do, go to Israel?'

'Not particularly. I'm not a convinced Zionist for one thing. No, England would be a much more attractive proposition. I was over there with a trade delegation in nineteen thirty-nine, just before the war started. The best two months of my life.'

'I see.'

'I was hoping to get out in nineteen fifty-nine. Corresponded secretly with relatives in Israel who were going to help, then I was betrayed by someone I had thought a true friend. An old story, I was sentenced to five years.'

'In the Gulag.'

'No, somewhere much more interesting. Would you believe, a little Ulster town called Drumore?'

Villiers turned, surprise on his face. 'I don't understand?'

'A little Ulster town called Drumore in the middle of the Ukraine.' The old man smiled at the look of astonishment on Villiers' face. 'I think I'd better explain.'

When he was finished, Villiers sat there thinking about it. Subversion techniques and counter-terrorism had been very much his business for several years now, particularly in Ireland, so Levin's story was fascinating to say the least. 'I knew about Gaczyna, where the KGB train operatives to work in English and so on, but this other stuff is new to me.'

'And probably to your intelligence people, I think!'

'In Rome in the old days,' Villiers said, 'slaves and prisoners of war were trained as gladiators, to fight in the arena.'

'To the death,' Levin said.

'With a chance to survive if you were better than the other man. Just like those dissidents at Drumore playing policemen.'

'They didn't stand much chance against Kelly,' Levin said.

'No, he sounds as if he was a very special item.'

The old man closed his eyes. His breathing was hoarse and troubled but he was obviously asleep within a few moments. Villiers leaned back in the corner, wretchedly uncomfortable. He kept thinking about Levin's strange story. He'd known a lot of Ulster market towns himself, Crossmaglen for example.

A bad place to be. So dangerous that troops had to be taken in and out by helicopter. But Drumore in the Ukraine – that was something else. After a while, his chin dropped on to his chest and he too drifted into sleep.

He came awake to find himself being shaken vigorously by one of the Rashid tribesmen. Another was waking Levin. The man pulled Villiers to his feet and sent him stumbling through the door. It was afternoon now, he knew that from the position of the sun. Much more interesting was the half-track armoured personnel carrier. A converted BTR. What the Russians called a Sandcruiser, painted in desert camouflage. Half a dozen soldiers stood beside it wearing khaki drill uniforms, each man holding an AK assault rifle at the ready. Two more stood inside the Sandcruiser, manning a 12.7mm heavy machine gun with which they covered the dozen or so Rashid who stood watching, rifles cradled in their arms.

Salim turned as Levin was brought out behind Villiers. 'So, Villiers Sahib, we must part. What a pity. I've enjoyed our conversations.'

The Russian officer who approached, a sergeant at his shoulder, wore drill uniform like his men and a peaked cap and desert goggles that gave him an uncanny resemblance to one of Rommel's Afrika Corps officers. He stood looking at them for a while, then pushed up the goggles. He was younger than Villiers would have thought, with a smooth unlined face and very blue eyes. 'Professor Levin,' he said in Russian, 'I'd like to think you lost your way while out walking, but I'm afraid our friends of the KGB will take a rather different point of view.'

'They usually do,' Levin told him.

The officer turned to Villiers and said calmly, 'Yuri Kirov, Captain, 21st Specialist Parachute Brigade.' His English was excellent. 'And you are Major Anthony Villiers, Grenadier Guards, but rather more importantly, of the 22nd Special Air Service Regiment.'

'You're very well informed,' Villiers said. 'And allow me to compliment you on your English.'

'Thank you,' Kirov said. 'We're using exactly the same language laboratory techniques as those pioneered by the SAS at Bradbury Line Barracks in Hereford. You, also, the KGB will take a special interest in.'

'I'm sure they will,' Villiers said amiably.

'So.' Kirov turned to Salim. 'To business.' His Arabic was not as good as his English, but serviceable enough.

He snapped a finger and the sergeant stepped forward and handed the Arab a canvas pouch. Salim opened it, took out a handful of coins and gold glinted in the sun. He smiled and handed the pouch to Hamid who stood behind him.

'And now,' Kirov said, 'if you will be good enough to unpadlock these two, we'll get moving.'

'Ah, but Kirov Sahib is forgetting,' Salim smiled. 'I was also promised a machine gun and twenty thousand rounds of ammunition.'

'Yes, well my superiors feel that would be putting far too much temptation in the way of the Rashid,' Kirov said.

Salim stopped smiling. 'This was a firm promise.'

Most of his men, sensing trouble, raised their rifles. Kirov snapped fingers and thumb on his right hand, there was a sudden burst of fire from the heavy machine gun, raking the wall above Salim's head. As the echoes died away, Kirov said patiently, 'Take the gold, I would earnestly advise it.'

Salim smiled and flung his arms wide. 'But of course. Friendship is everything. Certainly not worth losing for the sake of a trifling misunderstanding.'

He produced a key from a pouch at his belt and unlocked the padlock, first on the wooden halter which held Levin. Then he moved to Villiers. 'Sometimes Allah looks down through the clouds and punishes the deceiver,' he murmured.

'Is that in the Koran?' Villiers asked, as Hamid removed the halter and he stretched his aching arms.

Salim shrugged and there was something in his eyes. 'If not, then it should be.'

Two soldiers doubled forward on the sergeant's command and ranged themselves on either side of Levin and Villiers. They walked to the Sandcruiser. Villiers and Levin climbed inside. The soldiers followed,

Kirov bringing up the rear. Villiers and Levin sat down, flanked by armed guards, and Kirov turned and saluted as the engine rumbled into life.

'Nice to do business with you,' he called to Salim.

'And you, Kirov Sahib!'

The Sandcruiser moved away in a cloud of dust. As they went up over the edge of the first sand dune, Villiers looked back and saw that the old Rashid was still standing there, watching them go, only now his men had moved in behind him. There was a curious stillness about them, a kind of threat, and then the Sandcruiser went over the ridge and Bir al Gafani disappeared from view.

The concrete cell on the end of the administrative block at Fasari was a distinct improvement on their previous quarters, with whitewashed walls and chemical toilet and two narrow iron cots, each supplied with a mattress and blankets. It was one of half a dozen such cells, Villiers had noticed that on the way in, each with a heavy steel door complete with spyhole, and there seemed to be three armed guards constantly on duty.

Through the bars of the window, Villiers looked out at the airstrip. It was not as large as he had expected: three prefabricated hangars with a single tarmacadam runway. The five MIG 23s stood wingtip to wingtip in a line in front of the hangars, looking, in the evening light just before dark, like strange primeval creatures, still, brooding. There were two Mi-8 troop-carrying helicopters on the far side of them and trucks and motor vehicles of various kinds.

'Security seems virtually non-existent,' he murmured.

Beside him, Levin nodded. 'Little need for it. They are, after all, in friendly territory entirely surrounded by open desert. Even your SAS people would have difficulty with such a target, I suppose.'

Behind them, the bolts rattled in the door. It opened and a young corporal stepped in, followed by an Arab carrying a pail and two enamel bowls. 'Coffee,' the corporal said.

'When do we eat?' Villiers demanded.

'Nine o'clock.'

He ushered the Arab out and closed the door. The coffee was surprisingly good and very hot. Villiers said, 'So they use some Arab personnel?'

'In the kitchens and for sanitary duties and that sort of thing. Not from the desert tribes. They bring them from Hauf, I believe.'

'What do you think will happen now?'

'Well, tomorrow is Thursday and there's a supply plane in. It will probably take us back with it to Aden.'

'Moscow next stop?'

There was no answer to that, of course, just as there was no answer to concrete walls, steel doors and bars. Villiers lay on one bed, Levin on the other.

The old Russian said, 'Life is a constant disappointment

to me. When I visited England, they took me to Oxford. So beautiful.' He sighed. 'It was a fantasy of mine to return one day.'

'Dreaming spires,' Villiers observed. 'Yes, it's quite a place.'

'You know it then?'

'My wife was at university there. St Hugh's College. She went there after the Sorbonne. She's half-French.'

Levin raised himself on one elbow. 'You surprise me. If you'll forgive me saying so, you don't have the look of a married man.'

'I'm not,' Villiers told him. 'We got divorced a few months ago.'

'I'm sorry.'

'Don't be. As you said, life is a constant disappointment. We all want something different, that's the trouble with human beings, particularly men and women. In spite of what the feminists say, they are different.'

'You still love her, I think?'

'Oh, yes,' Villiers said. 'Loving is easy. It's the living together that's so damned hard.'

'So what was the problem?'

'To put it simply, my work. Borneo, the Oman, Ireland. I was even in Vietnam when we very definitely weren't supposed to be. As she once told me, I'm truly good at only one thing, killing people, and there came a time when she couldn't take that any more.'

Levin lay back without a word and Tony Villiers stared up at the ceiling, head pillowed in his hands,

thinking of things that would not go away as darkness
fell.

He came awake with a start, aware of footsteps in the
passageway outside, the murmur of voices. The light in
the ceiling must have been turned on whilst he slept.
They hadn't taken his Rolex from him and he glanced
at it quickly, aware of Levin stirring on the other bed.

'What is it?' the old Russian asked.

'Nine-fifteen. Must be supper.'

Villiers got up and moved to the window. There was
a half-moon in a sky alive with stars and the desert was
luminous, starkly beautiful, the MIG 23s like black
cutouts. *God*, he thought. *There must be a way*. He
turned, his stomach tightening.

'What is it?' Levin whispered as the first bolt was
drawn.

'I was just thinking,' Villiers said, 'that to make a
run for it at some point, even if it means a bullet in the
back, would be infinitely preferable to Moscow and the
Lubianka.'

The door was flung open and the corporal stepped
in, followed by an Arab holding a large wooden tray
containing two bowls of stew, black bread and coffee.
His head was down and yet there was something familiar
about him.

'Come on, hurry up!' the corporal said in bad Arabic.

The Arab placed the tray on the small wooden table

at the foot of Levin's bed and glanced up, and in the moment that Villiers and Levin realized that he was Salim bin al Kaman, the corporal turned to the door. Salim took a knife from his left sleeve, his hand went around the man's mouth, a knee up pulling him off balance, the knife slipped under his ribs. He eased the corporal down on the bed and wiped the knife on his uniform.

He smiled. 'I kept thinking about what you said, Villiers Sahib. That your people in the Dhofar would pay a great deal to have you back.'

'So, you get paid twice – once by both sides. Sound business sense,' Villiers told him.

'Of course, but in any case, the Russians were not honest with me. I have my honour to think of.'

'What about the other guards?'

'Gone to supper. All this I discovered from friends in the kitchens. The one whose place I took has suffered a severe bump on the head on the way here, by arrangement, of course. But come, Hamid awaits on the edge of the base with camels.'

They went out. He bolted the door and they followed him along the passageway quickly and moved outside. The Fasari airbase was very quiet, everything still in the moonlight.

'Look at it,' Salim said. 'No one cares. Even the sentries are at supper. Peasants in uniform.' He reached behind a steel drum which stood against the wall and produced a bundle. 'Put these on and follow me.'

They were two woollen cloaks of the kind worn by the Bedouin at night in the intense cold of the desert, each with a pointed hood to pull up. They put them on and followed him across to the hangars.

'No fence around this place, no wall,' Villiers whispered.

'The desert is the only wall they need,' Levin said.

Beyond the hangars, the sand dunes lifted on either side of what looked like the mouth of a ravine. Salim said, 'The Wadi al Hara. It empties into the plain a quarter of a mile from here where Hamid waits.'

Villiers said, 'Had it occurred to you that Kirov may well put two and two together and come up with Salim bin al Kaman?'

'But of course. My people are already half-way to the Dhofar border by now.'

'Good,' Villiers said. 'That's all I wanted to know. I'm going to show you something very interesting.'

He turned towards the Sandcruiser standing nearby and pulled himself over the side while Salim protested in a hoarse whisper. 'Villiers Sahib, this is madness.'

As Villiers dropped behind the driving wheel, the Rashid clambered up into the vehicle, followed by Levin. 'I've a dreadful feeling that all this is somehow my fault,' the old Russian said. 'We are, I presume, to see the SAS in action?'

'During the Second World War, the SAS under David Stirling destroyed more Luftwaffe planes on the ground in North Africa than the RAF and Yanks managed in aerial combat. I'll show you the technique,' Villiers told him.

'Possibly another version of that bullet in the back you were talking about.'

Villiers switched on and as the engine rumbled into life, said to Salim in Arabic, 'Can you manage the machine gun?'

Salim grabbed the handles of the Degtyarev. 'Allah, be merciful. There is fire in his brain. He is not as other men.'

'Is that in the Koran, too?' Villiers demanded, and the roaring of the 110 horsepower engine as he put his foot down hard drowned the Arab's reply.

The Sandcruiser thundered across the tarmac. Villiers swung hard and it spun round on its half tracks and smashed the tailplane of the first MIG, continuing right down the line as he increased speed. The tailplanes of the two helicopters were too high, so he concentrated on the cockpit areas at the front, the Sandcruiser's eight tons of armoured steel crumpling the perspex with ease.

He swung round in a wide loop and called to Salim. 'The helicopters. Try for the fuel tanks.'

There was the sound of an alarm klaxon from the main administration block now, voices crying in the night and shooting started. Salim raked the two helicopters with a continuous burst and the fuel tank on the one on the left exploded, a ball of fire mushrooming into the night, burning debris cascading everywhere.

A moment later, the second helicopter exploded against the MIG next to it and that also started to burn.

'That's it!' Villiers said. 'They'll all go now. Let's get out of here.'

As he spun the wheel, Salim swung the machine gun, driving back the soldiers running towards them. Villiers was aware of Kirov standing as the men went down on the other side of the tarmac, firing his pistol deliberately in a gallant, but futile gesture. And then they were climbing up the slope of the dunes, tracks churning sand and entering the mouth of the *wadi*. The dried bed of the old stream was rough with boulders here and there, but visibility in the moonlight was good. Villiers kept his foot down and drove fast.

He called to Levin. 'You okay?'

'I think so,' the old Russian told him. 'I'll keep checking.'

Salim patted the Degtyarev machine gun. 'What a darling. Better than any woman. This, I keep, Villiers Sahib.'

'You've earned it,' Villiers told him. 'Now all we have to do is pick up Hamid and drive like hell for the border.'

'No helicopters to chase us,' Levin shouted.

'Exactly.'

Salim said, 'You deserve to be Rashid, Villiers Sahib. I have not enjoyed myself so much in many years.' He raised an arm. 'I have held them in the hollow of my hand and they are as dust.'

'The Koran again?' Villiers asked.

'No, my friend,' Salim bin al Kaman told him. 'It is from your own Bible this time. The Old Testament,' and he laughed out loud exultantly as they emerged from the *wadi* and started down to the plain below where Hamid waited.

2

D15, that branch of the British Secret Intelligence Service which concerns itself with counter-espionage and the activities of secret agents and subversion within the United Kingdom, does not officially exist, although its offices are to be found in a large white and red brick building not far from the Hilton Hotel in London. D15 can only carry out an investigation and has no powers of arrest. It is the officers of the Special Branch at Scotland Yard who handle that end of things.

But the growth of international terrorism and its effects in Britain, particularly because of the Irish problem, were more than even Scotland Yard could handle and in 1972, the Director General of D15, with the support of 10 Downing Street, created a section known as Group Four with powers held directly from the Prime Minister of the day to co-ordinate the handling of all cases of terrorism and subversion.

After ten years, Brigadier Charles Ferguson was still in charge. A large, deceptively kindly-looking man, the Guards tie was the only hint of a military background. The crumpled grey suits he favoured, and half-moon reading glasses, combined with untidy grey hair to give him the look of some minor academic in a provincial university.

Although he had an office at the Directorate General, he preferred to work from his flat in Cavendish Square. His second daughter, Ellie, who was in interior design, had done the place over for him. The Adam fireplace was real and so was the fire. Ferguson was a fire person. The rest of the room was also Georgian and everything matched to perfection, including the heavy curtains.

The door opened and his manservant, an ex-Gurkha *naik* named Kim, came in with a silver tray which he placed by the fire. 'Ah, tea,' Ferguson said. 'Tell Captain Fox to join me.'

He poured tea into one of the china cups and picked up *The Times*. The news from the Falklands was not bad. British forces had landed on Pebble Island and destroyed eleven Argentine aircraft plus an ammo dump. Two Sea Harriers had bombed merchant shipping in Falkland Sound.

The green baize door leading to the study opened and Fox came in. He was an elegant man in a blue flannel suit by Huntsman of Savile Row. He also wore a Guards tie, for he had once been an acting captain in the Blues and Royals until an unfortunate incident with a bomb in Belfast during his third tour of duty had deprived him of his left hand. He now wore a rather clever replica which, thanks to the miracle of the microchip, served him almost as well as the original. The neat leather glove made it difficult to tell the difference.

'Tea, Harry?'

'Thank you, sir. I see they've got the Pebble Island story.'

'Yes, all very colourful and dashing,' Ferguson said as he filled a cup for him. 'But frankly, as no one knows better than you, we've got enough on our plate without the Falklands. I mean, Ireland's not going to go away and then there's the Pope's visit. Due on the twenty-eighth. That only gives us eleven days. And he makes such a target of himself. You'd think he'd be more careful after the Rome attempt on his life.'

'Not that kind of man, is he, sir?' Fox sipped some of his tea. 'On the other hand, the way things are going, perhaps he won't come at all. The South American connection is of primary importance to the Catholic Church and they see us as the villain of the piece in this Falklands business. They don't want him to come and the speech he made in Rome yesterday seemed to hint that he wouldn't.'

'I'll be perfectly happy with that,' Ferguson said. 'It would relieve me of the responsibility of making sure some madman or other doesn't try to shoot him while he's in England. On the other hand, several million British Catholics would be bitterly disappointed.'

'I understand the Archbishops of Liverpool and Glasgow

have flown off to the Vatican today to try to persuade him to change his mind,' Fox said.

'Yes, well let's hope they fail miserably.'

The bleeper sounded on the red telephone on Ferguson's desk, the phone reserved for top security rated traffic only.

'See what that is, Harry.'

Fox lifted the receiver. 'Fox here.' He listened for a moment then turned, face grave and held out the phone. 'Ulster, sir. Army headquarters Lisburn and it isn't good!'

It had started that morning just before seven o'clock outside the village of Kilgannon some ten miles from Londonderry. Patrick Leary had delivered the post in the area for fifteen years now and his Royal Mail van was a familiar sight.

His routine was always the same. He reported for work at headquarters in Londonderry at five-thirty promptly, picked up the mail for the first delivery of the day, already sorted by the night staff, filled up his petrol tank at the transport pumps then set off for Kilgannon. And always at half past six he would pull into the track in the trees beside Kilgannon Bridge to read the morning paper, eat his breakfast sandwiches and have a cup of coffee from his thermos flask. It was a routine which, unfortunately for Leary, had not gone unnoticed.

Cuchulain watched him for ten minutes, waiting patiently for Leary to finish his sandwiches. Then the man got out, as he always did, and walked a little way into the wood. There was a slight sound behind him of a twig cracking under a foot. As he turned in alarm, Cuchulain slipped out of the trees.

He presented a formidable figure and Leary was immediately terrified. Cuchulain wore a dark anorak and a black balaclava helmet which left only his eyes, nose and mouth exposed. He carried a PPK semi-automatic pistol in his left hand with a Carswell silencer screwed to the end of the barrel.

'Do as you're told and you'll live,' Cuchulain said. His voice was soft with a Southern Irish accent.

'Anything,' Leary croaked. 'I've got a family – please.'

'Take off your cap and the raincoat and lay them down.' Leary did as he was told and Cuchulain held out his right hand so that Leary saw the large white capsule nestling in the centre of the glove. 'Now, swallow that like a good boy.'

'Would you poison me?' Leary was sweating now.

'You'll be out for approximately four hours, that's all,' Cuchulain reassured him. 'Better that way.' He raised the gun. 'Better than this.'

Leary took the capsule, hand shaking, and swallowed it down. His legs seemed to turn to rubber, there was an air of unreality to everything, then a hand was on his shoulder pushing him down. The grass was cool against his face, then there was only the darkness.

*   *   *

Dr Hans Wolfgang Baum was a remarkable man. Born in Berlin in 1950, the son of a prominent industrialist, on his father's death in 1970 he had inherited a fortune equivalent to ten million dollars and wide business interests. Many people in his position would have been content to live a life of pleasure, which Baum did, with the important distinction that he derived his pleasure from work.

He had a doctorate in engineering science from the University of Berlin, a law degree from the London School of Economics, and a master's degree in business administration from Harvard. And he had put them all to good use, expanding and developing his various factories in West Germany, France and the United States, so that his personal fortune was now estimated to be in excess of one hundred million dollars.

And yet the project closest to his heart was the development of the plant to manufacture tractors and general agricultural machinery outside Londonderry near Kilgannon. Baum Industries could have gone elsewhere, indeed the members of the board of management had wanted to. Unfortunately for them and the demands of sound business sense, Baum was a truly good man, a rare commodity in this world, and a committed Christian. A member of the German Lutheran Church, he had done everything possible to make the factory a genuine partnership between Catholic and Protestant. He and his wife were totally committed to the local community, his three children attended local schools.

It was an open secret that he had met the Provisional IRA, some said the legendary Martin McGuiness himself. Whether true or not, the PIRA had left the Kilgannon factory alone to prosper, as it had done, and to provide work for more than a thousand Protestants and Catholics previously unemployed.

Baum liked to keep in shape. Each morning, he awakened at exactly the same time, six o'clock, slid out of bed without disturbing his wife, and pulled on track suit and running shoes. Eileen Docherty, the young maid, was already up and making tea in the kitchen although still in her dressing gown.

'Breakfast at seven, Eileen,' he called. 'My usual. Must get an early start this morning. I've a meeting in Derry at eight-thirty with the Works Committee.'

He let himself out of the kitchen door, ran across the parkland, vaulted a low fence and turned into the woods. He ran rather than jogged at a fast, almost professional pace, following a series of paths, his mind full of the day's planned events.

By six forty-five he had completed his schedule, turned out of the trees and hammered along the grass verge of the main road towards the house. As usual, he met Pat Leary's mail van coming along the road towards him. It pulled in and waited and he could see Leary through the windscreen in uniform cap and coat sorting a bundle of mail.

Baum leaned down to the open window. 'What have you got for me this morning, Patrick?'

The face was the face of a stranger, dark, calm eyes, strong bones, nothing to fear there at all, and yet it was Death come to claim him.

'I'm truly sorry,' Cuchulain said. 'You're a good man,' and the Walther in his left hand extended to touch Baum between the eyes. It coughed once, the German was hurled back to fall on the verge, blood and brains scattering across the grass.

Cuchulain drove away instantly, was back in the track by the bridge where he had left Leary within five minutes. He tore off the cap and coat, dropped them beside the unconscious postman and ran through the trees, clambering over a wooden fence a few minutes later beside a narrow farm track, heavily overgrown with grass. A motorcycle waited there, an old 350cc BSA, stripped down as if for hill climbing with special ribbed tyres. It was a machine much used by hill farmers on both sides of the border to herd sheep. He pulled on a battered old crash helmet with a scratched visor, climbed on and kick-started expertly. The engine roared into life and he rode away, passing only one vehicle, the local milk cart just outside the village.

Back there on the main road it started to rain and it was still falling on the upturned face of Hans Wolfgang Baum thirty minutes later when the local milk cart pulled up beside him. And at that precise moment, fifteen miles away, Cuchulain turned the BSA along a farm track south of Clady and rode across the border into the safety of the Irish Republic.

Ten minutes later, he stopped beside a phone box, dialled the number of the *Belfast Telegraph*, asked for the news desk and claimed responsibility for the shooting of Hans Wolfgang Baum on behalf of the Provisional IRA.

'So,' Ferguson said. 'The motorcyclist the driver of that milk cart saw would seem to be our man.'

'No description, of course,' Fox told him. 'He was wearing a crash helmet.'

'It doesn't make sense,' Ferguson said. 'Baum was well liked by everyone and the local Catholic community was totally behind him. He fought his own board every inch of the way to locate that factory in Kilgannon. They'll probably pull out now, which leaves over a thousand unemployed and Catholics and Protestants at each others' throats again.'

'But isn't that exactly what the Provisionals want, sir?'

'I wouldn't have thought so, Harry. Not this time. This was a dirty one. The callous murder of a thoroughly good man, well respected by the Catholic community. It can do the Provisionals nothing but harm with their own people. That's what I don't understand. It was such a stupid thing to do.' He tapped the file on Baum which Fox had brought in. 'Baum met Martin

McGuiness in secret and McGuiness assured him of the Provisionals' good will, and whatever else you may think of him, McGuiness is a clever man. Too damned clever, actually, but that isn't the point.' He shook his head. 'No, it doesn't add up.'

The red phone bleeped. He picked it up. 'Ferguson here.' He listened for a moment. 'Very well, Minister.' He put the phone down and stood up. 'The Secretary of State for Northern Ireland, Harry. Wants me right away. Get on to Lisburn again. Army Intelligence – anything you can think of. Find out all you can.'

He was back just over an hour later. As he was taking off his coat, Fox came in.

'That didn't take long, sir.'

'Short and sweet. He's not pleased, Harry, and neither is the Prime Minister. She's good and mad and you know what that means.'

'She wants results, sir?'

'Only she wants them yesterday, Harry. All hell's broken loose over there in Ulster. Protestant politicians having a field day. Paisley saying I told you so, as usual. Oh, the West German Chancellor's been on to Downing Street. To be frank, things couldn't be worse.'

'I wouldn't be too sure, sir. According to Army Intelligence at Lisburn the PIRA are more than a little annoyed about this one themselves. They insist they had nothing to do with it.'

'But they claimed responsibility.'

'They run a very tight ship these days, sir, as you know, since the re-organization of their command structure. McGuiness, amongst other things, is still Chief of Northern Command and the word from Dublin is that he categorically denies involvement of any of his people. In fact, he's as angry as anybody else at the news. It seems he thought a great deal of Baum.'

'Do you think it's INLA?'

The Irish National Liberation Front had shown themselves willing to strike in the past more ruthlessly than the Provisionals when they felt the situation warranted it.

'Intelligence says not, sir. They have a good source close to the top where INLA is concerned.'

Ferguson warmed himself at the fire. 'Are you suggesting the other side were responsible? The UVF or the Red Hand of Ulster?'

'Again, Lisburn has good sources in both organizations and the word is definitely no. No Protestant organization was involved.'

'Not officially.'

'It doesn't look as if anyone was involved officially, sir. There are always the cowboys, of course. The madmen who watch too many midnight movies on television and end up willing to kill anybody rather than nobody.'

Ferguson lit a cheroot and sat behind his desk. 'Do you really believe that, Harry?'

'No, sir,' Fox said calmly. 'I was just throwing out all the obvious questions the media crackpots will come up with.'

Ferguson sat there staring at him, frowning. 'You know something, don't you?'

'Not exactly, sir. There could be an answer to this, a totally preposterous one which you aren't going to like one little bit.'

'Tell me.'

'All right, sir. The fact that the *Belfast Telegraph* had a phone call claiming responsibility for the Provisionals is going to make the Provos look very bad indeed.'

'So.'

'Let's assume that was the purpose of the exercise.'

'Which means a Protestant organization did it with that end in view.'

'Not necessarily, as I think you'll see if you let me explain. I got the full report on the affair from Lisburn just after you left. The killer is a professional, no doubt about that. Cold, ruthless and highly organized and yet he doesn't just kill everyone in sight.'

'Yes, that had occurred to me too. He gave the postman, Leary, a capsule. Some sort of knock-out drop.'

'And that stirred my mind, so I put it through the computer.' Fox had a file tucked under his arm and now he opened it. 'The first five killings on the list all involved a witness being forced at gunpoint to take that sort of capsule. First time it occurs is nineteen seventy-five in Omagh.'

Ferguson examined the list and looked up. 'But on two occasions, the victims were Catholics. I accept your argument that the same killer was involved, but it makes a nonsense of your theory that the purpose in killing Baum was to make the PIRA look bad.'

'Stay with it a little longer, sir, please. Description of the killer in each case is identical. Black balaclava and dark anorak. Always uses a Walther PPK. On three occasions was known to escape by motor cycle from the scene of the crime.'

'So?'

'I fed all those details into the computer separately, sir. Any killings where motor cycles were involved. Cross-referencing with use of a Walther, not necessarily the same gun, of course. Also cross-referencing with the description of the individual.'

'And you got a result?'

'I got a result all right, sir.' Fox produced not one sheet, but two. 'At least thirty probable killings since nineteen seventy-five, all linked to the factors I've mentioned. There are another ten possibles.'

Ferguson scanned the lists quickly. 'Dear God!' he whispered. 'Catholic and Protestant alike. I don't understand.'

'You might if you consider the victims, sir. In all cases where the Provisionals claimed responsibility, the target was counter-productive, leaving them looking very bad indeed.'

'And the same where Protestant extremist organizations were involved?'

'True, sir, although the PIRA are more involved than anyone else. Another thing, if you consider the dates when the killings took place, it's usually when things were either quiet or getting better or when some political initiative was taking place. One of the possible cases when our man might have been involved goes back as far as July 1972, when, as you know, a delegation from the IRA met William Whitelaw secretly here in London.'

'That's right,' Ferguson said. 'There was a ceasefire. A genuine chance for peace.'

'Broken because someone started shooting on the Lenadoon estate in Belfast and that's all it took to start the pot boiling again.'

Ferguson sat there, staring down at the lists, his face expressionless. After a while, he said, 'So what you're saying is that somewhere over there is one mad individual dedicated to keeping the whole rotten mess turning over.'

'Exactly, except that I don't think he's mad. It seems to me he's simply following sound Marxist-Leninist principles where urban revolution is concerned. Chaos, disorder, fear. All those factors essential to the breakdown of any kind of orderly government.'

'With the IRA taking the brunt of the smear campaign?'

'Which makes it less and less likely that the Protestants will ever come to a political agreement with them, or our own government, for that matter.'

'And ensures that the struggle continues year after

60

year and a solution always recedes before us.' Ferguson nodded slowly. 'An interesting theory, Harry, and you believe it?'

He looked up enquiringly. Fox shrugged. 'The facts were all there in the computer. We never asked the right questions, that's all. If we had, the pattern would have emerged earlier. It's been there a long time, sir.'

'Yes, I think you could very well be right.' Ferguson sat brooding for a little while longer.

Fox said gently, 'He exists, sir. He is a fact, I'm sure of it. And there's something else. Something that could go a long way to explaining the whole thing.'

'All right, tell me the worst.'

Fox took a further sheet from the file. 'When you were in Washington the other week, Tony Villiers came back from the Oman.'

'Yes, I heard something of his adventures there.'

'In his debriefing, Tony tells an interesting story concerning a Russian Jewish dissident named Viktor Levin whom he brought out with him. A fascinating vignette about a rather unusual KGB training centre in the Ukraine.'

He moved to the fire and lit a cigarette, waiting for Ferguson to finish reading the file. After a while, Ferguson said, 'Tony Villiers is in the Falklands now, did you know that?'

'Yes, sir, serving with the SAS behind enemy lines.'

'And this man, Levin?'

'A highly gifted engineer. We've arranged for one of

the Oxford colleges to give him a job. He's at a safe house in Hampstead at the moment. I've taken the liberty of sending for him, sir.'

'Have you indeed, Harry? What would I do without you?'

'Manage very well, I should say, sir. Ah, and another thing. The psychologist, Paul Cherny, mentioned in that story. He defected in nineteen seventy-five.'

'What, to England?' Ferguson demanded.

'No, sir – Ireland. Went there for an international conference in July of that year and asked for political asylum. He's now Professor of Experimental Psychology at Trinity College, Dublin.'

Viktor Levin looked fit and well, still deeply tanned from his time in the Yemen. He wore a grey tweed suit, soft white shirt and blue tie, and black library spectacles that quite changed his appearance. He talked for some time, answering Ferguson's questions patiently.

During a brief pause he said, 'Do I presume that you gentlemen believe that the man Kelly, or Cuchulain to give him his codename, is actually active in Ireland? I mean, it's been twenty-three years.'

'But that was the whole idea, wasn't it?' Fox said. 'A sleeper to go in deep. To be ready when Ireland exploded. Perhaps he even helped it happen.'

'And you would appear to be the only person outside his own people who has any idea what he looks like, so we'll be asking you to look at some pictures. Lots of pictures,' Ferguson told him.

'As I say, it's been a long time,' Levin said.

'But he did have a distinctive look to him,' Fox suggested.

'That's true enough, God knows. A face like the Devil himself, when he killed, but of course, you're not quite right when you say I'm the only one who remembers him. There's Tanya. Tanya Voroninova.'

'The young girl whose father played the police inspector who Kelly shot, sir,' Fox explained.

'Not so young now. Thirty years old. A lovely girl and you should hear her play the piano,' Levin told them.

'You've seen her since?' Ferguson asked.

'All the time. Let me explain. I made sure they thought I'd seen the error of my ways so I was rehabilitated and sent to work at the University of Moscow. Tanya was adopted by the KGB Colonel, Maslovsky, and his wife who really took to the child.'

'He's a general now, sir,' Fox put in.

'She turned out to have great talent for piano. When she was twenty, she won the Tchaikovsky competition in Moscow.'

'Just a minute,' Ferguson said, for classical music was his special joy. 'Tanya Voroninova, the concert pianist. She did rather well at the Leeds Piano Festival two years ago.'

'That's right. Mrs Maslovsky died a month ago. Tanya tours abroad all the time now. With her foster-father a KGB general, she's looked upon as a good risk.'

'And you've seen her recently?'

'Six months ago.'

'And she spoke of the events you've described as taking place at Drumore?'

'Oh, yes. Let me explain. She's highly intelligent and well balanced, but she's always had a thing about what happened. It's as if she has to keep turning it over in her mind. I asked her why once.'

'And what did she say?'

'That it was Kelly. She could never forget him because he was so kind to her, and in view of what happened, she couldn't understand that. She said she often dreamt of him.'

'Yes, well as she's in Russia, that isn't really much help.' Ferguson got to his feet. 'Would you mind waiting in the next room a moment, Mr Levin?'

Fox opened the green baize door and the Russian passed through. Ferguson said, 'A nice man, I like him.' He walked to the window and looked down into the square below. After a while, he said, 'We've got to root him out, Harry. I don't think anything we've handled has ever been so vital.'

'I agree.'

'A strange thing. It would seem to be just as important to the IRA that Cuchulain is exposed as it is to us.'

'Yes, sir, the thought had occurred to me.'

'Do you think they'd see it that way?'

'Perhaps, sir.' Fox's stomach was hollow with excitement as if he knew what was coming.

'All right,' Ferguson said. 'God knows, you've given

enough to Ireland, Harry. Are you willing to risk the other hand?'

'If you say so, sir.'

'Good. Let's see if they're willing to show some sense for once. I want you to go to Dublin to see the PIRA Army Council or anyone they're willing to delegate to see you. I'll make the right phone calls to set it up. Stay at the Westbourne as usual. And I mean today, Harry. I'll see to Levin.'

'Right, sir,' Fox said calmly. 'Then if you'll excuse me, I'll get started,' and he went out.

Ferguson went back to the window and looked out at the rain. Crazy, of course, the idea that British Intelligence and the IRA could work together and yet it made sense this time. The question was, would the wild men in Dublin see it that way?

Behind him, the study door opened and Levin appeared. He coughed apologetically, 'Brigadier, do you still need me?'

'But of course, my dear chap,' Charles Ferguson said. 'I'll take you along to my headquarters now. Pictures – lots of pictures, I'm afraid.' He picked up his coat and hat and opened the door to usher Levin out. 'But who knows? You might just recognize our man.'

In his heart, he did not believe it for a moment, but he didn't tell Levin that as they went down in the lift.

3

In Dublin, it was raining, driving across the Liffey in a soft grey curtain as the cab from the airport turned into a side street just off George's Quay and deposited Fox at his hotel.

The Westbourne was a small old-fashioned place with only one bar-restaurant. It was a Georgian building and therefore listed against redevelopment. Inside however, it had been refurbished to a quiet elegance exactly in period. The clientele, when one saw them at all, were middle-class and distinctly ageing, the sort who'd been using it for years when up from the country for a few days. Fox had stayed there on numerous occasions, always under the name of Charles Hunt, profession, wine wholesaler, a subject he was sufficiently expert on to make an eminently suitable cover.

The receptionist, a plain young woman in a black suit, greeted him warmly. 'Nice to see you again, Mr Hunt.

I've managed you number three on the first floor. You've stayed there before.'

'Fine,' Fox said. 'Messages?'

'None, sir. How long will you be staying?'

'One night, maybe two. I'll let you know.'

The porter was an old man with the sad, wrinkled face of the truly disillusioned and very white hair. His green uniform was a little too large and Fox, as usual, felt slightly embarrassed when he took the bags.

'How are you, Mr Ryan?' he enquired as they went up in the small lift.

'Fine, sir. Never better. I'm retiring next month. They're putting me out to pasture.'

He led the way along the small corridor and Fox said, 'That's a pity. You'll miss the Westbourne.'

'I will so, sir. Thirty-eight years.' He unlocked the bedroom door and led the way in. 'Still, it comes to us all.'

It was a pleasant room with green damask walls, twin beds, a fake Adam fireplace and Georgian mahogany furniture. Ryan put the bag down on the bed and adjusted the curtains.

'The bathroom's been done since you were last here, sir. Very nice. Would you like some tea?'

'Not right now, Mr Ryan.' Fox took a five pound note from his wallet and passed it over. 'If there's a message, let me know straight away. If I'm not here, I'll be in the bar.'

There was something in the old man's eyes, just for

a moment; then he smiled faintly. 'I'll find you, sir, never fear.'

That was the thing about Dublin these days, Fox told himself as he dropped his coat on the bed and went to the window. You could never be sure of anyone and there were sympathizers everywhere, of course. Not necessarily IRA, but thousands of ordinary, decent people who hated the violence and the bombing, but approved of the political ideal behind it all.

The phone rang and when he answered it, Ferguson was at the other end.

'It's all set. McGuiness is going to see you.'

'When?'

'They'll let you know.'

The line went dead and Fox replaced the receiver. Martin McGuiness, Chief of Northern Command for the PIRA, amongst other things; at least he would be dealing with one of the more intelligent members of the Army Council.

He could see the Liffey at the far end of the street, and rain rattled against the window. He felt unaccountably depressed. Ireland, of course. For a moment, he felt a distinct ache in the left hand again, the hand that was no longer there. All in the mind, he told himself, and went downstairs to the bar.

It was deserted except for a young Italian barman. Fox ordered a Scotch and water and sat in a corner by the window. There was a choice of newspapers on the table and he was working his way through *The Times* when Ryan appeared like a shadow at his shoulder.

'Your cab's here, sir.'

Fox glanced up. 'My cab? Oh, yes, of course.' He frowned, noticing the blue raincoat across Ryan's arm. 'Isn't that mine?'

'I took the liberty of getting it for you from your room, sir. You'll be needing it. This rain's with us for a while yet, I think.'

Again, there was something in the eyes, almost amusement. Fox allowed him to help him on with the coat and followed him outside and down the steps to where a black taxicab waited.

Ryan opened the door for him and said, as Fox got in, 'Have a nice afternoon, sir.'

The cab moved away quickly. The driver was a young man with dark, curly hair. He wore a brown leather jacket and white scarf. He didn't say a word, simply turned into the traffic stream at the end of the street and drove along George's Quay. A man in a cloth cap and reefer coat stood beside a green telephone box. The cab slid into the kerb, the man in the reefer coat opened the rear door and got in beside Fox smoothly.

'On your way, Billy,' he said to the driver and turned to Fox genially. 'Jesus and Mary, but I thought I'd drown out there. Arms up, if you please, Captain. Not too much. Just enough.' He searched Fox thoroughly and professionally and found nothing. He leaned back and lit a cigarette, then he took a pistol from his pocket and held it on his knee. 'Know what this is, Captain?'

'A Ceska, from the look of it,' Fox said. 'Silenced version the Czechs made a few years back.'

'Full marks. Just remember I've got it when you're talking to Mr McGuiness. As they say in the movies, one false move and you're dead.'

They continued to follow the line of the river, the traffic heavy in the rain and finally pulled in at the kerb half-way along Victoria Quay.

'Out!' the man in the reefer coat said and Fox followed him. Rain drove across the river on the wind and he pulled up his collar against it. The man in the reefer coat passed under a tree and nodded towards a small public shelter beside the quay wall. 'He doesn't like to be kept waiting. He's a busy man.'

He lit another cigarette and leaned against the tree and Fox moved along the pavement and went up the steps into the shelter. There was a man sitting on the bench in the corner reading a newspaper. He was well dressed, a fawn raincoat open revealing a well-cut suit of dark blue, white shirt and a blue and red striped tie. He was handsome enough with a mobile, intelligent mouth and blue eyes. Hard to believe that this rather pleasant-looking man had featured on the British Army's most wanted list for almost thirteen years.

'Ah, Captain Fox,' Martin McGuiness said affably. 'Nice to see you again.'

'But we've never met,' Fox said.

'Derry, 1972,' McGuiness told him. 'You were a cornet, isn't that what you call second lieutenants in the Blues and Royals? There was a bomb in a pub in Prior Street. You were on detachment with the Military Police at the time.'

'Good God!' Fox said. 'I remember now.'

'The whole street was ablaze. You ran into a house next to the grocer's shop and brought out a woman and two kids. I was on the flat roof opposite with a man with an Armalite rifle who wanted to put a hole in your head. I wouldn't let him. It didn't seem right in the circumstances.'

For a moment, Fox felt rather cold. 'You were in command in Derry for the IRA at that time.'

McGuiness grinned. 'A funny old life, isn't it? You shouldn't really be here. Now then, what is it that old snake, Ferguson, wants you to discuss with me?'

So Fox told him.

When he was finished McGuiness sat there brooding, hands in the pockets of his raincoat, staring across the Liffey. After a while, he said, 'That's Wolfe Tone Quay over there, did you know that?'

'Wasn't he a Protestant?' Fox asked.

'He was so. Also one of the greatest Irish patriots there ever was.'

He whistled tunelessly between his teeth. Fox said, 'Do you believe me?'

'Oh, yes,' McGuiness said softly. 'A devious bloody lot, the English, but I believe you all right and for one very simple reason. It fits, Captain, dear. All those hits over the years, the shit that's come our way because of it and sometimes internationally. I know the times we've not been responsible and so does the Army Council. The thing is, one always thought it was the idiots, the cowboys, the wild men.' He grinned crookedly. 'Or British Intelligence, of course. It never occurred to any of us that it could have been the work of one man. A deliberate plan.'

'You've got a few Marxists in your own organization, haven't you?' Fox suggested. 'The kind who might see the Soviets as Saviour.'

'You can forget that one.' Anger showed in McGuiness's blue eyes for a moment. 'Ireland free and Ireland for the Irish. We don't want any Marxist pap here.'

'So, what happens now? Will you go to the Army Council?'

'No, I don't think so. I'll talk to the Chief of Staff. See what he thinks. After all, he's the one that sent me. Frankly, the fewer people in on this, the better.'

'True.' Fox stood up. 'Cuchulain could be anyone. Maybe somebody close to the Army Council itself.'

'The thought had occurred to me.' McGuiness waved and the man in the reefer coat moved out from under the tree. 'Murphy will take you back to the Westbourne now. Don't go out. I'll be in touch.'

Fox walked a few paces away, paused and turned. 'By the way, that's a Guards tie you're wearing.'

Martin McGuiness smiled beautifully. 'And didn't I know it? Just trying to make you feel at home, Captain Fox.'

Fox dialled Ferguson from a phone booth in the foyer of the Westbourne so that he didn't have to go through the hotel switchboard. The Brigadier wasn't at the flat, so he tried the private line to his office at the Directorate-General and got through to him at once.

'I've had my preliminary meeting, sir.'

'That was quick. Did they send McGuiness?'

'Yes, sir.'

'Did he buy it?'

'Very much so, sir. He'll be back in touch, maybe later tonight.'

'Good. I'll be at the flat within the hour. No plans to go out. Phone me the moment you have more news.'

Fox showered, then changed and went downstairs to the bar again. He had another small Scotch and water and sat there, thinking about things for a while and of McGuiness in particular. A clever and dangerous man, no doubt about that. Not just a gunman, although he'd done his share of killing, but one of the most import-ant leaders thrown up by the Troubles. The annoying thing was that Fox realized, with a certain sense of ir-ritation, that he had really rather liked the man. That wouldn't do at all, so he went into the restaurant and had an early dinner, sitting in solitary splendour, a copy of the *Irish Press* propped up in front of him.

Afterwards, he had to pass through the bar on the way to the lounge. There were a couple of dozen people in there now, obviously other guests from the look of them, except for the driver of the cab who'd taken him to meet McGuiness earlier. He was seated on a stool at the end of the bar, a glass of lager in front of him, the main difference being that he now wore a rather smart grey suit. He showed no sign of recognition and Fox carried on into the lounge where Ryan approached him.

'If I remember correctly, sir, it's tea you prefer after your dinner and not coffee?'

Fox, who had sat down, said, 'That's right.'

'I've taken the liberty of putting a tray in your room, sir. I thought you might prefer a bit of peace and quiet.'

He turned without a word and led the way to the lift. Fox played along, following him, expecting perhaps a further message, but the old man said nothing and when they reached the first floor, led the way along the corridor and opened the bedroom door for him.

Martin McGuiness was watching the news on television. Murphy stood by the window. Like the man in the bar, he now wore a rather conservative suit, in his case, of navy-blue worsted material.

McGuiness switched off the television. 'Ah, there you are. Did you try the Duck à l'Orange? It's not bad here.'

The tray on the table with the tea things on it carried two cups. 'Shall I pour, Mr McGuiness?' Ryan asked.

'No, we can manage.' McGuiness reached for the teapot and said to Fox as Ryan withdrew, 'Old Patrick, as you can see, is one of our own. You can wait outside, Michael,' he added.

Murphy went out without a word. 'They tell me no gentleman would pour his milk in first, but then I suppose no real gentleman would bother about rubbish like that. Isn't that what they teach you at Eton?'

'Something like that.' Fox took the proffered cup. 'I didn't expect to see you quite so soon.'

'A lot to do and not much time to do it in.' McGuiness drank some tea and sighed with pleasure. 'That's good. Right, I've seen the Chief of Staff and he believes, with me, that you and your computer have stumbled on something that might very well be worth pursuing.'

'Together?'

'That depends. In the first place, he's decided not to discuss it with the Army Council, certainly not at this stage, so it stays with just me and himself.'

'That seems sensible.'

'Another thing, we don't want the Dublin police in on this, so keep Special Branch out of it and no military intelligence involvement either.'

'I'm sure Brigadier Ferguson will agree.'

'He'll bloody well have to, just as he'll have to accept that there's no way we're going to pass across general information about IRA members, past or present. The kind of stuff you could use in other ways.'

'All right,' Fox said, 'I can see that, but it could be a tricky one. How do we co-operate if we don't pool resources?'

'There is a way.' McGuiness poured himself another cup of tea. 'I've discussed it with the Chief of Staff and he's agreeable if you are. We use a middle-man.'

'A middle-man?' Fox frowned. 'I don't understand?'

'Someone acceptable to both sides. Equally trusted, if you know what I mean.'

Fox laughed. 'There's no such animal.'

'Oh, yes there is,' McGuiness said. 'Liam Devlin, and don't tell me you don't know who *he* is.'

Harry Fox said slowly, 'I know Liam Devlin very well.'

'And why wouldn't you. Didn't you and Faulkner have him kidnapped by the SAS back in seventy-nine to help you break Martin Brosnan out of that French prison to hunt down that mad dog, Frank Barry.'

'You're extremely well informed.'

'Yes, well Liam's here in Dublin now, a professor at Trinity College. He has a cottage in a village called Kilrea, about an hour's drive out of town. You go and see him. If he agrees to help, then we'll discuss it further.'

'When?'

'I'll let you know, or maybe I'll just turn up unexpected, like. The one way I kept ahead of the British Army all those years up north.' He stood up. 'There's a lad at the bar downstairs. Maybe you noticed?'

'The cab driver.'

'Billy White. Left or right hand, he can still shoot a fly off the wall. He's yours while you're here.'

'Not necessary.'

'Oh, but it is.' McGuiness got up and pulled on his coat. 'Number one, I wouldn't like anything to happen to you, and number two, it's a convenience to know where you are.' He opened the door, and beyond him, Fox saw Murphy waiting. 'I'll be in touch, Captain.' McGuiness saluted mockingly, the door closed behind him.

Ferguson said, 'It makes sense, I suppose, but I'm not sure Devlin will work for us again, not after that Frank Barry affair. He felt we'd used him and Brosnan rather badly.'

'As I recall, we did, sir,' Fox said. 'Very badly indeed.'

'All right, Harry, no need to make a meal of it. Phone and see if he's at home. If he is, go and see him.'

'Now, sir?'

'Why not? It's only nine-thirty. If he is in, let me know and I'll speak to him myself. Here's his phone number, by the way. Take it down.'

Fox went along to the bar and changed a five pound note for 50p coins. Billy White was still sitting there, reading the evening paper. The glass of lager looked untouched.

'Can I buy you a drink, Mr White?' Fox asked.

'Never touch the stuff, Captain.' White smiled cheerfully and emptied the glass in one long swallow. 'A Bushmills would chase that down fine.'

78

Fox ordered him one. 'I may want to go out to a village called Kilrea. Do you know it?'

'No problem,' White told him. 'I know it well.'

Fox went back to the phone booth and closed the door. He sat there for a while thinking about it, then dialled the number Ferguson had given him. The voice, when it answered, was instantly recognizable. The voice of perhaps the most remarkable man he had ever met.

'Devlin here.'

'Liam? This is Harry Fox.'

'Mother of God!' Liam Devlin said. 'Where are you?'

'Dublin – the Westbourne Hotel. I'd like to come and see you.'

'You mean right now?'

'Sorry if it's inconvenient.'

Devlin laughed. 'As a matter of fact, at this precise moment in time I'm losing at chess, son, which is something I don't like to do. Your intervention could be looked upon as timely. Is this what you might term a business call?'

'Yes, I'm to ring Ferguson and tell him you're in. He wants to talk to you himself.'

'So the old bastard is still going strong? Ah, well, you know where to come?'

'Yes.'

'I'll see you in an hour then. Kilrea Cottage, Kilrea. You can't miss it. Next to the convent.'

When Fox came out of the booth after phoning Ferguson,

White was waiting for him. 'Are we going out then, Captain?'

'Yes,' Fox said. 'Kilrea Cottage, Kilrea. Next to a convent apparently. I'll just get my coat.'

White waited until he'd entered the lift, then ducked into the booth and dialled a number. The receiver at the other end was lifted instantly. He said, 'We're leaving for Kilrea now. Looks like he's seeing Devlin tonight.'

As they drove through the rain-swept streets, White said casually, 'Just so we know where we stand, Captain, I was a lieutenant in the North Tyrone Brigade of the Provisional IRA the year you lost that hand.'

'You must have been young.'

'Born old, that's me, thanks to the B Specials when I was a wee boy and the sodding RUC.' He lit a cigarette with one hand. 'You know Liam Devlin well, do you?'

'Why do you ask?' Fox demanded warily.

'That's who we're going to see, isn't it? Jesus, Captain, and who wouldn't be knowing Liam Devlin's address?'

'Something of a legend to you, I suppose?'

'A legend, is it? That man wrote the book. Mind you, he won't have any truck with the movement these days. He's what you might call a moralist. Can't stand the bombing and that kind of stuff.'

'And can you?'

'We're at war, aren't we? You bombed the hell out

of the Third Reich. We'll bomb the hell out of you if that's what it takes.'

Logical but depressing, Fox thought, for where did it end? A charnelhouse with only corpses to walk on. He shivered, face bleak.

'About Devlin,' White said as they started to leave the city. 'There's a tale I heard about him once. Would you know if it's true, I wonder?'

'Ask me.'

'The word is, he went to Spain in the thirties, served against Franco and was taken prisoner. Then the Germans got hold of him and used him as an agent here during the big war.'

'That's right.'

'The way I heard it, after that, they sent him to England. Something to do with an attempt by German paratroopers to kidnap Churchill in nineteen forty-three. Is there any truth in that?'

'Sounds straight out of a paperback novel to me,' Fox said.

White sighed and there was regret in his voice. 'That's what I thought. Still, one hell of a man for all that,' and he sat back and concentrated on his driving.

An understatement as a description of Liam Devlin, Fox thought, sitting there in the darkness: a brilliant student who had entered Trinity College, Dublin, at the age of sixteen and had taken a first class honours degree at nineteen, scholar, writer, poet and highly dangerous gunman for the IRA in the thirties, even when still a student.

Most of what White had said was true. He had gone to Spain to fight for the anti-fascists, he had worked for the Abwehr in Ireland. As to the Churchill affair? A story whispered around often enough, but as to the truth of it? Well, it would be years before those classified files were opened.

During the post-war period, Devlin had been a Professor at a Catholic seminary called All Souls just outside Boston. He'd been involved with the abortive IRA campaign of the late fifties and had returned to Ulster in 1969 as the present troubles had begun. One of the original architects of the Provisional IRA, he had become increasingly disillusioned by the bombing campaign and had withdrawn active support to the movement. Since 1976, he had held a position in the English Faculty at Trinity.

Fox had not seen him since 1979 when he had been coerced, indeed, blackmailed, by Ferguson into giving his active assistance in the hunting down of Frank Barry, ex-IRA activist turned international terrorist for hire. There had been various reasons why Devlin had gone along with that business, mostly because he had believed Ferguson's lies. So, how would he react now?

They had entered a long village street. Fox pulled himself together with a start as White said, 'Here we are – Kilrea, and there's the convent and that's Devlin's cottage, set back from the road behind the wall.'

He turned the car into a gravel driveway and cut the engine. 'I'll wait for you, Captain, shall I?'

Fox got out and walked up a stone flagged path between rose bushes to the green painted porch. The cottage was pleasantly Victorian with most of the original woodwork and gable ends. A light glowed behind drawn curtains at a bow window. He pressed the bell-push. There were voices inside, footsteps and then the door opened and Liam Devlin stood looking out at him.

4

Devlin wore a dark blue flannel shirt open at the neck, grey slacks and a pair of highly expensive-looking Italian brogues in brown leather. He was a small man, no more than five foot five or six, and at sixty-four his dark, wavy hair showed only a light silvering. There was a faded scar on the right side of his forehead, an old bullet wound, the face pale, the eyes extraordinarily vivid blue. A slight ironic smile seemed permanently to lift the corner of his mouth – the look of a man who had found life a bad joke and had decided that the only thing to do was laugh about it.

The smile was charming and totally sincere. 'Good to see you, Harry.' His arms went around Fox in a light embrace.

'And you, Liam.'

Devlin looked beyond him at the car and Billy White behind the wheel. 'You've got someone with you?'

'Just my driver.'

Devlin moved past him, went along the path and leaned down to the window.

'Mr Devlin,' Billy said.

Devlin turned without a word and came back to Fox. 'Driver, is it, Harry? The only place that one will drive you to is straight to Hell.'

'Have you heard from Ferguson?'

'Yes, but leave it for the moment. Come along in.'

The interior of the house was a time capsule of Victoriana: mahogany panelling and William Morris wallpaper in the hall with several night scenes by the Victorian painter, Atkinson Grimshaw, on the walls. Fox examined them with admiration as he took off his coat and gave it to Devlin. 'Strange to see these here, Liam. Grimshaw was a very Yorkshire Englishman.'

'Not his fault, Harry, and he painted like an angel.'

'Worth a bob or two,' Fox said, well aware that ten thousand pounds at auction was not at all out of the way for even quite a small Grimshaw.

'Do you tell me?' Devlin said lightly. He opened one half of a double mahogany door and led the way into the sitting room. Like the hall, it was period Victorian: green flock wallpaper stamped with gold, more Grimshaws on the walls, mahogany furniture and a fire burning brightly in a fireplace that looked as if it was a William Langley original.

The man who stood before it was a priest in dark cassock and he turned from the fire to greet them.

He was about Devlin's height with iron-grey hair swept back over his ears. A handsome man, particularly at this moment as he smiled a welcome; there was an eagerness to him, an energy that touched something in Fox. It was not often that one liked another human being so completely and instinctively.

'With apologies to Shakespeare, two little touches of Harry in the night,' Devlin said. 'Captain Harry Fox, meet Father Harry Cussane.'

Cussane shook hands warmly. 'A great pleasure, Captain Fox. Liam was telling me something about you after you rang earlier.'

Devlin indicated the chess table beside the sofa. 'Any excuse to get away from that. He was beating the pants off me.'

'A gross exaggeration as usual,' Cussane said. 'But I must get going. Leave you two to your business.' His voice was pleasant and rather deep. Irish, yet more than a hint of American there.

'Would you listen to the man?' Devlin had brought three glasses and a bottle of Bushmills from the cabinet in the corner. 'Sit down, Harry. Another little snifter before bed won't kill you.' He said to Fox, 'I've never known anyone so much on the go as this one.'

'All right, Liam, I surrender,' Cussane said. 'Fifteen minutes, that's all, then I must go. I like to make a late round at the hospice as you know and then there's Danny Malone. Living is a day-to-day business with him right now.'

Devlin said, 'I'll drink to him. It comes to us all.'

'You said hospice?' Fox enquired.

'There's a convent next door, the Sacred Heart, run by the Little Sisters of Pity. They started a hospice for terminal patients some years ago.'

'Do you work there?'

'Yes, as a sort of administrator cum priest. Nuns aren't supposed to be worldly enough to do the accounts. Absolute rubbish. Sister Anne Marie, who's in charge over there, knows to every last penny. And this is a small parish so the local priest doesn't have a curate. I give him a hand.'

'In between spending three days a week in charge of the press office at the Catholic Secretariat in Dublin,' Devlin said. 'Not to mention flogging the local youth club through a very average five performances of *South Pacific*, complete with a star cast of ninety-three local school kids.'

Cussane smiled. 'Guess who was stage manager? We're trying *West Side Story* next. Liam thinks it too ambitious, but I believe it better to rise to a challenge than go for the easy choice.'

He swallowed a little of his Bushmills. Fox said, 'Forgive me for asking, Father, but are you American or Irish? I can't quite tell.'

'Most days, neither can he,' Devlin laughed.

'My mother was an Irish-American who came back to Connacht in 1938 after her parents died, to seek her roots. All she found was me.'

'And your father?'

'I never knew him. Cussane was her name. She was a Protestant, by the way. There are still a few in Connacht, descendants of Cromwell's butchers. Cussane is often called Patterson in that part of the country by pseudo-translation from Casan, which in Irish means path.'

'Which means he's not quite certain who he is,' Devlin put in.

'Only some of the time.' Cussane smiled. 'My mother returned to America in 1946 after the war. She died of influenza a year later and I was taken in by her only relative, an old great-uncle who ran a farm in the Ontario wheat belt. He was a fine man and a good Catholic. It was under his influence that I decided to enter the Church.'

'Enter the Devil, stage left.' Devlin raised his glass.

Fox looked puzzled and Cussane explained. 'The seminary that accepted me was All Souls at Vine Landing outside Boston. Liam was English professor there.'

'He was a great trial to me,' Devlin said. 'Mind like a steel trap. Constantly catching me out misquoting Eliot in class.'

'I served in a couple of Boston parishes and another in New York,' Cussane said, 'but I always hoped to get back to Ireland. Finally, I got a move to Belfast in 1968. A church on the Falls Road.'

'Where he promptly got burned out by an Orange mob the following year.'

'I tried to keep the parish together using a school hall,' Cussane said.

Fox glanced at Devlin, 'While you ran around Belfast adding fuel to the flames?'

'God might forgive you for that,' Devlin said piously, 'for I cannot.'

Cussane emptied his glass. 'I'll be off then. Nice to meet you, Harry Fox.'

He held out his hand. Fox shook it and Cussane moved to the French windows and opened them. Fox saw the convent looming up into the night on the other side of the garden wall. Cussane walked across the lawn, opened a gate and passed through.

'Quite a man,' he said, as Devlin closed the windows.

'And then some.' Devlin turned, no longer smiling. 'All right, Harry. Ferguson being his usual mysterious self, it looks as if it's up to you to tell me what this is about.'

In the hospice, all was quiet. It was as unlike the conventional idea of a hospital as it was possible to be and the architect had designed the ward area in a way that gave each occupant of a bed a choice of privacy or intimacy with other patients. The night sister sat at her desk, the only light a shaded lamp. She didn't hear Cussane approach, yet suddenly he was there, looming out of the darkness.

'How's Malone?'

'The same, Father. Very little pain. We have the drug in-put just about in balance.'

'Is he lucid?'

'Some of the time.'

'I'll go and see him.'

Danny Malone's bed, divided from the others by bookshelves and cupboards, was angled towards a glass window that gave a view of grounds and the night sky. The night light beside the bed brought his face into relief. He was not old, no more than forty, his hair prematurely white, the face like a skull under taut skin, etched in pain caused by the cancer that was slowly and relentlessly taking him from this life to the next.

As Cussane sat down, Malone opened his eyes. He gazed blankly at Cussane, then recognition dawned. 'Father, I thought you weren't coming.'

'I promised, didn't I? I was having a nightcap with Liam Devlin, is all.'

'Jesus, Father, you're lucky you got away with just the one with him, but big for the cause, Liam, I'll give him that. There's no man living done, more for Ireland.'

'What about yourself?' Cussane sat down beside the bed. 'No stronger fighter for the movement than you, Danny.'

'But how many did I kill, Father, there's the rub, and for what?' Malone asked him. 'Daniel O'Connel once said in a speech that, although the ideal of Irish freedom was just, it was not worth a single human life. When I was young, I disputed that. Now I'm dying, I think I know what he meant.' He winced in pain and turned to look at Cussane. 'Can we talk some more, Father? It helps get it straight in my own mind.'

'Just for a while, then you must get some sleep,' Cussane smiled. 'One thing a priest is good at is listening, Danny.'

Malone smiled contentedly. 'Right, where were we? I was telling you about the preparation for the bombing campaign on the English Midlands and London in seventy-two.'

'You were saying the papers nicknamed you the Fox,' Cussane said, 'because you seemed to go backwards and forwards between England and Ireland at will. All your friends were caught, Danny, but not you. How was that?'

'Simple, Father. The greatest curse on this country of ours is the informer and the second greatest curse is the inefficiency of the IRA. People full of ideology and revolution blow a lot of wind and are often singularly lacking in good sense. That's why I preferred to go to the professionals.'

'Professionals?'

'What you would call the criminal element. For example, there wasn't an IRA safe house in England during the seventies that wasn't on the Special Branch's list at Scotland Yard sooner or later. That's how so many got caught.'

'And you?'

'Criminals on the run or needing a rest when things

get too hot have places they can go, Father. Expensive places, I admit, but safe and that's what I used. There was one in Scotland south from Glasgow in Galloway run by a couple of brothers called Mungo. What you might call a country retreat. Absolute bastards, mind you.'

The pain was suddenly so bad that he had to fight for breath. 'I'll get sister,' Cussane told him in alarm.

Malone grabbed him by the front of his cassock. 'No, you damn well won't. No more painkillers, Father. They mean well, the sisters, but enough is enough. Let's just keep talking.'

'All right,' Harry Cussane said. Malone lay back, closed his eyes for a moment, then opened them again. 'Anyway, as I was saying, these Mungo brothers, Hector and Angus, were the great original bastards.'

Devlin paced up and down the room restlessly. 'Do you believe it?' Fox asked.

'It makes sense and it would explain a great deal,' Devlin said. 'So let's just say I accept it in principle.'

'So, what do we do about it?'

'What do *we* do about it?' Devlin glared at him. 'The effrontery of the man. Let me remind you, Harry, that the last time I did a job for Ferguson, the bastard conned me. Lied in his teeth. Used me.'

'That was then, this is now, Liam.'

'And what is that pearl of wisdom supposed to mean?'

There was a soft tapping at the French window. Devlin opened the desk drawer, took out an old-fashioned Mauser pistol, with an SS bulbous silencer on the end and cocked it. He nodded to Fox, then Devlin pulled the curtain. Martin McGuiness peered in at them, Murphy at his shoulder.

'Dear God!' Devlin groaned.

He opened the French window and McGuiness smiled as he stepped in. 'God bless all here!' he said mockingly and added to Murphy, 'Watch the window, Michael.' He closed it and walked over to the fire, holding his hands to the warmth. 'Colder as the nights draw in.'

'What do you want?' Devlin demanded.

'Has the Captain here explained the situation to you yet?'

'He has.'

'And what do you think?'

'I don't think at all,' Devlin told him. 'Especially where you lot are concerned.'

'The purpose of terrorism is to terrorize, that's what Mick Collins used to say,' McGuiness told him. 'I fight for my country, Liam, with anything that comes to hand. We're at war.' He was angry now. 'I've got nothing to apologize for.'

'If I could say something,' Fox put in. 'Let's accept that Cuchulain exists, then it isn't a question of taking sides. It's accepting that what he's doing has needlessly protracted the tragic events of the past thirteen years.'

McGuiness helped himself to a whiskey. 'He has a point. When I was O.C. Derry in nineteen seventy-two, I was flown to London with Daithi O'Connell, Seamus Twomey, Ivor Bell and others to meet Willie Whitelaw to discuss peace.'

'And the Lenadoon shooting broke the cease-fire,' Fox said and turned to Devlin. 'It doesn't seem to me to be a question of taking sides any more. Cuchulain has worked deliberately to keep the whole rotten mess going. I would have thought anything that might have helped stop that would be worth it.'

'Morality is it?' Devlin raised a hand and smiled wickedly.

'Good then, let's get down to brass tacks. This fella, Levin, who actually saw Kelly or Cuchulain or whatever his name is, all those years ago. I presume Ferguson is showing him pictures of every known KGB operative.'

'And all known adherents of the IRA, UDA, UVF. Anything and everything,' Fox said. 'That will include looking at what Special Branch in Dublin have because we swop information.'

'The bastards would,' McGuiness said bitterly. 'Still, I think we've got a few that neither the police in Dublin nor your people in London have ever seen.'

'And how do we handle that?' Fox demanded.

'You get Levin over here and he and Devlin look at what we've got – no one else. Is it agreed?'

Fox glanced at Devlin who nodded. 'Okay,' Fox said. 'I'll ring the Brigadier tonight.'

'Fine.' McGuiness turned to Devlin. 'You're sure your phone's not tapped or anything like that. I'm thinking of those Special Branch bastards.'

Devlin opened a drawer in the desk and produced a black metal box which he switched on so that a red light appeared. He approached the telephone and held the box over it. There was no reaction.

'Oh, the wonders of the electronic age,' he said and put the box away.

'Fine,' McGuiness said. 'The only people who know about this are Ferguson, you, Captain, Liam, the Chief of Staff and myself.'

'And Professor Paul Cherny,' Fox said.

McGuiness nodded. 'That's right. We've got to do something about him.' He turned to Devlin. 'Do you know him?'

'I've seen him at drinks parties at the university. Exchanged a civil word, no more than that. He's well liked. A widower. His wife died before he defected. There's a chance he isn't involved in this, of course.'

'And pigs might fly,' McGuiness said crisply. 'The fact that it was Ireland he defected to is too much of a coincidence for me. A pound to a penny he knows our man, so why don't we pull him in and squeeze it out of him?'

'Simple,' Fox told him. 'Some men don't squeeze.'

'He's right,' Devlin said. 'Better to try the softly-softly approach first.'

'All right,' McGuiness said. 'I'll have him watched twenty-four hours a day. Put Michael Murphy in charge.

He won't be able to go to the bathroom without we know it.'

Devlin glanced at Fox. 'Okay by you?'

'Fine,' Fox told him.

'Good.' McGuiness buttoned his raincoat. 'I'll get off then. I'll leave Billy to look after you, Captain.' He opened the French window. 'Mind your back, Liam.' And then he was gone.

Ferguson was in bed when Fox phoned, sitting up against the pillows, working his way through a mass of papers, preparing himself for a Defence committee meeting the following day. He listened patiently to everything Fox had to say. 'So far, so good, Harry, as far as I can see. Levin spent the entire day working through everything we had at the Directorate. Didn't come up with a thing.'

'It's been a long time, sir. Cuchulain could have changed a lot and not just because he's older. I mean, he could have a beard, for example.'

'Negative thinking, Harry. I'll put Levin on the morning flight to Dublin, but Devlin will have to handle him. I need you back here.'

'Any particular reason, sir?'

'Lots to do with the Vatican. It really is beginning to look as if the Pope won't come. However, he's invited the cardinals of Argentina and Britain to confer with him.'

'So the visit could still be on?'

'Perhaps, but more important from our point of view, the war is still on and there's talk of the Argentinians trying to get hold of this damned Exocet missile on the European black market. I need you, Harry. Catch the first flight out. By the way, an interesting development. Tanya Voroninova, remember her?'

'Of course, sir.'

'She's in Paris to give a series of concerts. Fascinating that she should surface at this particular moment.'

'What Jung would call synchronicity, sir?'

'Young, Harry? What on earth are you babbling about?'

'Carl Jung, sir. Famous psychologist. Synchronicity is a word he coined for events having a coincidence in time and, because of this, the feeling that some deeper motivation is involved.'

'The fact that you're in Ireland is no excuse for acting as if you've gone soft in the head, Harry,' Ferguson said testily.

He put down the phone, sat there thinking, then got up, pulled on his robe and went out. He knocked on the door of the guest room and went in. Levin was sitting up in bed wearing a pair of Ferguson's pyjamas and reading a book.

Ferguson sat on the edge of the bed. 'I thought you'd be tired after going through so many photos.'

Levin smiled. 'When you reach my age, Brigadier, sleep eludes you, memory crowds in. You wonder what it has all been about.'

Ferguson warmed to the man. 'Don't we all, my dear chap? Anyway, how would you feel about running over to Dublin on the morning plane?'

'To see Captain Fox?'

'No, he'll be returning here, but a friend of mine, Professor Liam Devlin of Trinity College, will take care of you. He'll probably be showing you a few more photos, courtesy of our friends in the IRA. They'd never let me have them for obvious reasons.'

The old Russian shook his head. 'Tell me, Brigadier, did the war to end all wars finish in nineteen forty-five or am I mistaken?'

'You and a great many other people, my friend.' Ferguson got up and went to the door. 'I'd get some sleep if I were you. You'll need to be up at six to catch the early morning flight from Heathrow. I'll have Kim serve you breakfast in bed.'

He closed the door. Levin sat there for a while, an expression of sadness on his face, then he sighed, closed the book, turned out the light and went to sleep.

At Kilrea Cottage, Fox put down the phone and turned to Devlin. 'All fixed. He'll come in on the breakfast plane. Unfortunately, my flight leaves just before. He'll report to the information desk in the main concourse. You can pick him up there.'

'No need,' Devlin said. 'This minder of yours, young White. He'll be dropping you so he can pick Levin up at the same time and bring him straight here. It's best we do it that way. McGuiness might be in touch early about where I'm supposed to take him.'

'Fine,' Fox said. 'I'd better get moving.'

'Good lad.'

Devlin got his coat for him and took him out to the car where Billy White waited patiently.

'Back to the Westbourne, Billy,' Fox said.

Devlin leaned down at the window. 'Book yourself in there for the night, son, and in the morning, do exactly what the Captain tells you to. Let him down by a single inch and I'll have your balls and Martin McGuiness will probably walk all over the rest of you.'

Billy White grinned affably. 'Sure and on a good day, they tell me I can almost shoot as well as you, Mr Devlin.'

'Go on, be off with you.'

The car moved away. Devlin watched it go, then turned and went inside. There was a stirring in the shrubbery, a footfall, the faintest of sounds only as someone moved away.

The eavesdropping equipment which the KGB had supplied to Cuchulain was the most advanced in the world, developed originally by a Japanese company, the details, as a result of industrial espionage, having reached Moscow four years previously. The directional microphone trained on Kilrea Cottage could pick up every word uttered inside at several hundred yards. Its ultra-frequency secondary function was to catch even the faintest telephone conversation. All this was allied to a sophisticated recording apparatus.

The whole was situated in a small attic concealed behind the loft watertanks just beneath the pantile roof of the house. Cuchulain had listened in on Liam Devlin in this way for a long time now, although it had been some time since anything so interesting had come up. He sat in the attic, smoking a cigarette, running the tape at top speed through the blank spots and the unimportant bits, paying careful attention to the phone conversation with Ferguson.

Afterwards, he sat there thinking about it for a while, then he reset the tape, went downstairs and let himself out. He went into the phone box at the end of the village street by the pub and dialled a Dublin number. The phone was picked up almost immediately. He could hear voices, a sudden laugh, Mozart playing softly.

'Cherny here.'

'It's me. You're not alone?'

Cherny laughed lightly. 'Dinner party for a few faculty friends.'

'I must see you.'

'All right,' Cherny said. 'Usual time and place tomorrow afternoon.'

Cuchulain replaced the receiver, left the booth and went back up the village street, whistling softly, an old Connemara folk song that had all the despair, all the sadness of life in it.

5

Fox had a thoroughly bad night and slept little so that he was restless and ill-at-ease as Billy White took the car expertly through the early morning traffic towards the airport. The young Irishman was cheerful enough as he tapped his fingers on the steering wheel in time to the music from the radio.

'Will you be back, Captain?'

'I don't know. Perhaps.'

'Ah, well, I don't expect you to be over fond of the ould country.' White nodded towards Fox's gloved hand. 'Not after what it's cost you.'

'Is that so?' Fox said.

Billy lit a cigarette. 'The trouble with you Brits is that you never face up to the fact that Ireland's a foreign country. Just because we speak English . . .'

'As a matter of interest, my mother's name was Fitzgerald and she came from County Mayo,' Fox told him. 'She worked for the Gaelic League, was a lifelong friend of de Valera and spoke excellent Irish, a rather difficult language I found when she insisted on teaching it to me when I was a boy. Do you speak Irish, Billy?'

'God save us, but I don't, Captain,' White said in astonishment.

'Well, then I suggest you kindly stop prattling on about the English being unable to understand the Irish.'

He glanced out at the traffic morosely. A police motorcyclist took up station on the left of them, a sinister figure in goggles and crash helmet with a heavy caped raincoat against the early morning downpour. He glanced sideways at Fox once, anonymous in the dark goggles, and dropped back as they turned into the slip road leading to the airport.

Billy left the car in the short stay park. As they entered the concourse, they were already calling Fox's plane. Cuchulain, who had been with them all the way from the hotel, stood at the door by which they had entered and watched Fox book in.

Fox and Billy walked towards the departure gate and Fox said, 'An hour till the British Airways flight lands.'

'Time for a big breakfast,' Billy grinned. 'The fine time we had, Captain.'

'I'll be seeing you, Billy.'

Fox put out his good hand and Billy White took it with a certain reluctance. 'Try to make sure it isn't at the wrong end of some street in Belfast. I'd hate to have you in my sights, Captain.'

Fox went through the gate and Billy made his way across the concourse to stairs leading up to the café terrace. Cuchulain watched him go, then went out, back across the road to the carpark and waited.

An hour later, he was back inside, consulting the nearest arrival screen. The British Airways shuttle from London was just landing and he saw White approach the central information desk and speak to one of the attendants. There was a pause and then an announcement over the tannoy system.

'Will Mr Viktor Levin, a passenger on the London shuttle, please report to the information desk.'

A few moments later, the squat figure of the Russian appeared from the crowd. He carried a small case and wore a rather large brown raincoat and black trilby hat. Cuchulain sensed that it was his quarry even before he spoke to one of the attendants who indicated White. They shook hands. Cuchulain watched them for a moment longer as White started to speak, then turned and left.

'So this is Ireland?' Levin said as they drove down towards the city.

'Your first visit?' White asked.

'Oh, yes. I am from Russia. I have not travelled abroad very much.'

'Russia?' Billy said. 'Jesus, but you'll find it different here.'

'And this is Dublin?' Levin enquired as they followed the traffic down into the city.

'Yes. Kilrea, where we're going, is on the other side.'

'A city of significant history, I think,' Levin observed.

'And that's the understatement of the age,' White told him. 'I'll take you through Parnell Square, it's on our way. A great patriot in spite of being a Prod. And then O'Connell Street and the General Post Office where the boys held out against the whole bloody British Army back in 1916.'

'Good. This I would like very much.' Levin leaned back in his seat and looked out on the passing scene with interest.

At Kilrea, Liam Devlin walked across the back lawn of his cottage, let himself through the gate in the wall and ran for the rear entrance of the hospice as the rain increased into a sudden downpour. Sister Anne-Marie was crossing the hall, accompanied by two young white-coated interns on loan from University College, Dublin.

She was a small, sparse little woman, very fit for her seventy years, and wore a white smock over her nun's robe. She had a doctorate in medicine from the University of London and was a Fellow of the Royal College of Physicians. A lady to be reckoned with. She and Devlin were old adversaries. She had once been French, but that was a long time ago as he was fond of reminding her.

'And what can we do for you, Professor?' she demanded.

'You say that as if to the Devil coming through the door,' Devlin told her.

'An observation of stunning accuracy.'

They started up the stairs and Devlin said, 'Danny Malone – how is he?'

'Dying,' she said calmly. 'Peacefully, I hope. He is one of those patients who responds well to our drug programme which means that pain is only intermittent.'

They reached the first of the open plan wards. Devlin said, 'When?'

'This afternoon, tomorrow – next week.' She shrugged. 'He is a fighter, that one.'

'That's true,' Devlin said. 'Big for the cause all his life, Danny.'

'Father Cussane comes in every night,' she said, 'and sits and lets him talk through this violent past of his. I think it troubles him now that he nears his end. The IRA, the killing.'

'Is it all right if I sit with him for a while?'

'Half-an-hour,' she said firmly and moved away followed by the interns.

Malone seemed to sleep, eyes closed, the skin tight on the facial bones, yellow as parchment. His fingers gripped the edge of a sheet tightly.

Devlin sat down. 'Are you there, Danny?'

'Ah, there you are, Father.' Malone opened his eyes, focused weakly and frowned. 'Liam, is that you?'

'None other.'

'I thought it was Father Cussane. We were just talking.'

'Last night, Danny. You must have fallen asleep. Sure and you know he works in Dublin at the Secretariat during the day.'

Malone licked dry lips. 'God, but I could do with a cup of tea.'

'Let's see if I can get you one,' Devlin got up.

As he did so, there was a sudden commotion on the lower level, voices shouting, drifting up. He frowned and hurried forward to the head of the stairs.

Billy White turned off the main highway on to the narrow road, flanked by fir plantations on either side, that led to Kilrea. 'Not long now.' He half-turned to speak to Levin behind him and noticed, through the rear window, a *Gardai* motorcyclist turn off the main road behind them.

He started to slow and Levin said, 'What is it?'

'Gardai,' Billy told him. 'Police to you. One mile over the limit and they'll book you, those sods.'

The police motorcyclist pulled up alongside and waved them down. With his dark goggles and helmet, White could see nothing of him at all. He pulled in at the side of the road angrily. 'And what in hell does this fella want? I wasn't doing an inch over thirty miles an hour.'

The animal instinct which had protected his life for

many years of violence made him wary enough to have his hand on the butt of the revolver in the left pocket of his raincoat as he got out of the car. The policeman pushed the motorcycle up on to its stand. He took off his gloves and turned, his raincoat very wet.

'And what can we do you for, officer, on this fine morning?' Billy asked insolently.

The policeman's hand came out of the right pocket of his raincoat holding a Walther, a Carswell silencer screwed on the end of the barrel. White recognized all this in the last moment of his violent life as he frantically attempted to draw his revolver. The bullet ripped into his heart, knocking him back against the car. He bounced off and fell on his face in the road.

In the rear seat, Levin was paralysed with horror, yet he was not afraid for there was an inevitability to all this as if it was somehow ordained. The policeman opened the door and looked in. He paused, then pushed up the goggles.

Levin gazed at him in astonishment. 'Dear God in heaven,' he whispered in Russian. 'It's you.'

'Yes,' Cuchulain answered in the same language. 'I'm afraid it is,' and he shot him in the head, the Walther making no more than an angry cough.

He pocketed the weapon, walked back to the bike, pulled it off its stand and rode away. It was no more than five minutes later that a van making morning deliveries of bread to the village came across the carnage. The driver and his assistant got out of their van and approached the scene with trepidation. The driver leaned down to look at White. There was a slight groan from the rear of the car and he glanced inside quickly.

'My God!' he cried. 'There's another in here and he's still alive. Take the van and get down to the village quick as you like and fetch the ambulance from the hospice.'

When Devlin reached the foyer, they were pushing Viktor Levin on a trolley into the receiving room.

'Sister Anne-Marie's on Ward Three. She'll be right down,' he heard one of the ambulancemen tell the young sister in charge. The driver of the bread van stood there helplessly, blood on one sleeve of his overall coat. He was shaking badly. Devlin lit a cigarette and handed it to him. 'What happened?'

'God knows. We found this car a couple of miles up the road. One was dead beside it and him in the back. They're bringing the other in now.'

As Devlin, filled with a terrible premonition, turned towards the door, the ambulancemen hurried in with Billy White's body, his face plain to see. The young sister came out of the receiving room and went next door to check White. Devlin stepped in quickly and approached the trolley on which Levin still lay, moaning softly, blood congealing in a terrible head wound.

Devlin leaned down. 'Professor Levin, can you hear me?' Levin opened his eyes. 'I am Liam Devlin. What happened?'

Levin tried to speak, reached out one hand and got

110

hold of the lapel of Devlin's jacket. 'I recognized him. He's here.'

His eyes rolled, there was a rattle in his throat and as his grip slackened, Sister Anne-Marie hurried in. She pushed Devlin to one side and leaned over Levin, searching for a pulse. After a while, she stepped back. 'You know this man?'

'No,' Devlin told her, which was true in a sense.

'Not that it would matter if you did,' she said. 'He's dead. A miracle he didn't die instantly with a head wound like that.'

She brushed past him and went next door where they had taken White. Devlin stood looking down at Levin, thinking of what Fox had told him of the old man, of the years of waiting to get out. And this was how it had ended. He felt angry, then, at the brutal black humour of life that could allow such a thing to happen.

Harry Fox had only just arrived back at Cavendish Square, had hardly got his coat off, when the phone rang. Ferguson listened, face grave, then placed a hand over the mouthpiece. 'Liam Devlin. It seems the car with your man, Billy White, and Levin was ambushed just outside Kilrea. White was killed instantly, Levin died later in the hospice at Kilrea.'

Fox said, 'Did Liam get to see him?'

'Yes. Levin told him it was Cuchulain. That he recognized him.'

Fox threw his coat on the nearest chair. 'But I don't understand, sir.'

'Neither do I, Harry.' Ferguson spoke into the mouth-piece, 'I'll get back to you, Devlin.'

He put the receiver down and turned, hands out to the fire. Fox said, 'I doesn't make sense. How would he have known?'

'Some sort of leak, Harry, at the IRA end of things. They never keep their mouths shut.'

'The thing is, sir, what do we do about it?'

'More important, what do we do about Cuchulain?' Ferguson said. 'That gentleman is really beginning to annoy me.'

'But there isn't much we can do now, not with Levin gone. After all, he was the only person who had any idea what the bastard looked like.'

'Actually, that isn't quite true,' Ferguson said. 'You're forgetting Tanya Voraninova, who at this precise moment is in Paris. Ten days, four concerts, and that opens up a very interesting possibility.'

About the same time, Harry Cussane was at his desk in the press office of the Catholic Secretariat in Dublin talking to Monsignor Halloran who was responsible for public relations.

From his comfortable chair, Halloran said, 'It's a terrible thing that such a significantly historical event as the Holy Father's visit to England should be put in such jeopardy. Just think of it, Harry, His Holiness at Canterbury Cathedral. The first Pope in history to visit it. And now . . .'

'You think it won't come off?' Cussane asked.

'Well, they're still talking away in Rome, but that's how it looks to me. Why, do you know something I don't?'

'No,' Cussane told him. He picked up a typed sheet. 'I've had this from London. His planned itinerary, so they are still acting as if he's coming.' He ran an eye over it. 'Arrives on the morning of 28th May at Gatwick Airport. Mass at Westminster Cathedral in London. Meets the Queen at Buckingham Palace in the afternoon.'

'And Canterbury?'

'That's the following day – Saturday. He starts early with a meeting with religious at a London college. Mainly monks and nuns from enclosed orders. Then by helicopter to Canterbury, stopping at Stokely Hall on the way. That's unofficial, by the way.'

'For what reason?'

'The Stokelys were one of the great Catholic families that managed to survive Henry VIII and hung on to their faith over the centuries. The National Trust own the house now, but it contains a unique feature: the family's private chapel. The oldest Catholic church of any description in England. His Holiness wishes to pray there. Afterwards, Canterbury.'

'All of which, at the moment, is on paper only,' Halloran said.

The phone rang. Cussane picked it up. 'Press office.

Cussane here.' His face grew grave. He said, 'Is there anything I can do?' A pause. 'I'll see you later then.'

Halloran said, 'Problems?'

Cussane replaced the receiver. 'A friend from Kilrea. Liam Devlin of Trinity College. It seems there's been a shooting incident outside the village. Two men taken to the hospice. Both dead.'

Halloran crossed himself. 'Political, is it?'

'One of them was a known member of the IRA.'

'Will you be needed? Go if you must.'

'Not necessary.' Cussane smiled bleakly. 'They need a coroner now, Monsignor, not a priest. I've plenty to do here anyway.'

'Yes, of course. Well, I'll leave you to it.'

Halloran went out and Cussane lit a cigarette and went and stood at the window looking down into the street. Finally, he turned, sat at his desk and got on with some work.

Paul Cherny had rooms at Trinity College which being, as so many people considered, at the centre of Dublin, suited him very well indeed. But then, everything about that extraordinary city commended itself to him.

His defection had been at Maslovsky's express orders. A KGB general was not to be argued with. He was to defect in Ireland, that had been the plan. One of the universities was certain to offer him a post, his international reputation would assure that. He would then be in a perfect position to act as Cuchulain's control. Difficult in the early days with no Soviet Embassy in Dublin and the necessity always to work through London, but now that had been taken care of and his KGB contacts at the Dublin embassy gave him a direct link with Moscow.

Yes, the years had been good and Dublin was the kind of paradise he'd always dreamed of. Intellectual freedom, stimulating company and the city – the city he had grown to love. He was thinking these things as he left Trinity that afternoon, walked through College Green, and made towards the river.

Michael Murphy followed at a discreet distance and Cherny, unaware that he was being tailed, walked briskly along beside the Liffey until he reached Usher's Quay. There was a rather ugly Victorian church in red brick and he moved up the steps and went inside. Murphy paused to examine the board with the peeling gold paint. It said Our Lady, Queen of the Universe. Underneath were the times of Mass. Confessions were heard at one o'clock and five on weekdays. Murphy pushed open the door and entered.

It was the sort of place that merchant money had been poured into back in the prosperous days of the Quays during the nineteenth century. There was lots of Victorian stained glass and fake gargoyles and the usual smell of candles and incense. Half-a-dozen people waited by a couple of confessional boxes and Paul Cherny joined them, seating himself on the end of the bench.

'Jesus!' Murphy muttered in surprise. 'The bugger must have seen the light.' He positioned himself behind a pillar and waited.

It was fifteen or twenty minutes before Cherny's turn came. He slipped into the oaken confessional box, closed the door and sat down, his head close to the grill.

'Bless me, Father, for I have sinned,' he said in Russian.

'Very funny, Paul,' the reply came from the other side of the grill in the same language. 'Now let's see if you can still smile when you've heard what I've got to say.'

When Cuchulain was finished, Cherny said, 'What are we going to do?'

'No need to panic. They don't know who I am and they aren't likely to find out now that I've disposed of Levin.'

'But me?' Cherny said. 'If Levin told them about Drumore all those years ago, he must have told them of my part in it.'

'Of course. You're under surveillance now. IRA variety, not British Intelligence, so I wouldn't worry just yet. Get in touch with Moscow. Maslovsky should know about this. He might want to pull us out. I'll phone you again tonight. And don't start worrying about your tail. I'll take care of it.'

Cherny went out and Cuchulain watched through a crack in the door as Michael Murphy slipped from behind the pillar and followed him. There was a bang as the sacristy door opened and shut and an old cleaning woman came down the aisle as the priest in alb and black cassock, a violet stole around his shoulders, came out of the confessional box.

'Are you finished, Father?'

'I am so, Ellie.' Harry Cussane turned, a smile of great charm on his face as he slipped off the stole and started folding it.

Murphy, with no reason to think that Cherny was doing anything other than return to college, stayed some distance behind him. Cherny stopped and entered a telephone box. He wasn't in it for long and Murphy, who had paused under a tree as if sheltering from the rain, went after him again.

A car drew into the kerb in front of him and the driver, a priest, got out, went round and looked at the nearside front tyre. He turned and catching sight of Murphy, said, 'Have you got a minute?'

Murphy slowed, protesting, 'I'm sorry, Father, but I've an appointment.'

And then the priest's hand was on his arm and Murphy felt the muzzle of the Walther dig painfully into his side. 'Easy does it, there's a lad. Just keep walking.'

Cussane pushed him to the top of stone steps that went down to a decaying wooden jetty below. They moved along its broken planks, footsteps echoing hollowly. There was a boathouse with a broken roof, holes in the floor. Murphy wasn't afraid, but ready for action, waiting his chance.

'That'll do,' Cussane said.

Murphy stayed, his back towards him, one hand on the butt of the automatic in his raincoat pocket. 'Are you a real priest?' he asked.

'Oh, yes,' Cussane told him. 'Not a very good one, I'm afraid, but real enough.'

Murphy turned slowly. His hand came up out of the raincoat, already too late. The Walther coughed twice, and the bullet caught Murphy in the shoulder spinning him around. The second bullet drove him headfirst into a ragged hole in the floor and he plunged down into the dark water below.

Dimitri Lubov, who was supposedly a commercial attaché at the Soviet Embassy, was, in fact, a captain in the KGB. On receiving Cherny's carefully worded message, he left his office and went to a cinema in the city centre. It was not only relatively dark in there, but reasonably private, for few people went to the cinema in the afternoon. He sat in the back row and waited and Cherny joined him twenty minutes later.

'Is it urgent, Paul?' Lubov said. 'Not often we meet between fixed days.'

'Urgent enough,' Cherny said. 'Cuchulain is blown. Maslovsky must be informed as soon as possible. He may want to pull us out.'

'Of course,' Lubov said, alarmed. 'I'll see to it as soon

as I get back, but hadn't you better fill me in on the details?'

Devlin was working in his study at the cottage, marking a thesis on T.S. Eliot submitted by one of his students, when the phone rang.

Ferguson said, 'It's a fine bloody mess. Someone must have coughed at your end. Your IRA cronies are not exactly the most reliable people in the world.'

'Sticks and stones will get you nowhere,' Devlin told him. 'What do you want?'

'Tanya Voroninova,' Ferguson said. 'Harry told you about her?'

'The little girl from Drumore who was adopted by this Maslovsky character. What about her?'

'She's in Paris at the moment to give a series of piano concerts. The thing is, being foster-daughter to a KGB general gives her a lot of leeway. I mean, she's considered an excellent risk. I thought you might go and see her. There's an evening flight from Dublin direct to Paris. Only two and a half hours, Air France.'

'And what in the hell am I supposed to do? Get her to defect?'

'You never know. When she hears the whole story, she might want to. See her anyway, Liam. It can't do any harm.'

'All right,' Devlin said. 'A little breath of French air might do me good.'

'I knew you'd see it my way,' Ferguson said. 'Report to the Air France desk at Dublin Airport. They've got a reservation. When you arrive at Charles de Gaulle, you'll be met by one of my chaps based in Paris. Fella called Hunter – Tony Hunter. He'll see to everything.'

'I'm sure he will,' Devlin said and rang off.

He packed a bag quickly, feeling unaccountably cheerful and was just pulling on his trenchcoat when the phone went again. It was Martin McGuiness. 'A bad business, Liam. What exactly happened?'

Devlin told him and when he was finished, McGuiness exploded. 'So, he exists, this bastard?'

'It would appear so, but more worrying from your point of view is, how did he know Levin was due in? The one man who might be able to identify him.'

'Why ask me?'

'Because Ferguson thinks there's been a leak at your end.'

'Well, screw Ferguson.'

'I wouldn't advise it, Martin. Listen, I've got to go. I've a flight to Paris to catch.'

'Paris? What's there, for Christ's sake?'

'A girl called Tanya Voroninova who might be able to identify Cuchulain. I'll be in touch.'

He put down the receiver. As he picked up his bag, there was a tap on the French windows. They opened and Harry Cussane entered.

Devlin said, 'Sorry, Harry, I must fly or I'll miss my plane.'

'Where on earth are you going?' Cussane demanded.

'Paris.' Devlin grinned and opened the front door. 'Champagne, loose women, incredible food. Don't you think it's just possible you joined the wrong club, Harry?'

The door banged. Cussane listened to the engine of the car start up, turned and ran out through the French windows, round to his cottage at the back of the hospice. He hurried upstairs to the secret room behind the water tanks in the roof where he had the eavesdropping equipment. Quickly, he ran back the tape and listened to the various conversations Devlin had had that day until he came, in the end, to the important one.

By then, of course, it was too late. He cursed softly, went down to use the phone and rang Paul Cherny's number.

6

In the sacristy of the village church as he robed for evening Mass, Cussane examined himself in the mirror. Like an actor getting ready for a performance. Next thing, he'd be reaching for the make-up. Who am I, he thought? Who am I, really? Cuchulain, mass murderer, or Harry Cussane, priest? Mikhail Kelly didn't seem to enter into it any more. Only an echo of him now like a half-forgotten dream.

For more than twenty years he had lived multiple lives and yet the separate personae had never inhabited his body. They were roles to be played out as the script dictated, then discarded.

He slipped the stole around his neck and whispered to his *alter ego* in the mirror, 'In God's House I am God's priest,' and he turned and went out.

Later, standing at the altar with the candles flickering and the organ playing, there was genuine passion in his voice as he cried, 'I confess to Almighty God and to you, my brothers and sisters, that I have sinned through my own fault.'

And when he struck his breast, asking blessed Mary ever Virgin to pray for him to the Lord our God, there were sudden hot tears in his eyes.

At Charles de Gaulle Airport, Tony Hunter waited beside the exit from customs and immigration. He was a tall man in his mid-thirties with stooped shoulders. The soft brown hair was too long, the tan linen suit creased, and he smoked a Gitane cigarette without once taking it from his mouth as he read *Paris Soir* and kept an eye on the exit. After a while, Devlin appeared. He wore a black Burberry trenchcoat, an old black felt hat slanted over one ear, and carried one bag.

Hunter, who had pulled Devlin's photo and description off the wire, went to meet him. 'Professor Devlin? Tony Hunter. I've got a car waiting.' They walked towards the exit. 'Was it a good flight?'

'There's no such thing,' Devlin told him. 'About a thousand years ago, I flew from Germany to Ireland in a Dornier bomber on behalf of England's enemies and jumped by parachute from six thousand feet. I've never got over it.'

They reached Hunter's Peugeot in the car park and as they drove away, Hunter said, 'You can stay the night with me. I've got an apartment on the Avenue Foch.'

'Doing well for yourself, son, if you're living there. I didn't know Ferguson handed out bags of gold.'

'You know Paris well?'

'You could say that.'

'The apartment's my own, not the Department's. My father died last year. Left me rather well off.'

'What about the girl? Is she staying at the Soviet Embassy?'

'Good God, no. They've got her at the Ritz. She's something of a star, you see. Plays rather well. I heard her do a Mozart concerto the other night. Forgotten which one, but she was excellent.'

'They tell me she's free to come and go?'

'Oh, yes, absolutely. The fact that her foster father is General Maslovsky takes care of that. I followed her all over the place this morning. Luxembourg Gardens, then lunch on one of those boat trips down the Seine. From what I hear, her only commitment tomorrow is a rehearsal at the Conservatoire during the afternoon.'

'Which means the morning is the time to make contact?'

'I should have thought so.' They were well into Paris by now, just passing the Gare du Nord. Hunter added, 'There's a bagman due in from London on the breakfast shuttle with documentation Ferguson's having rushed through. Forged passport. Stuff like that.'

Devlin laughed out loud. 'Does he think all I have to do is ask and she'll come?' He shook his head. 'Mad, that one.'

'All in how it's put to her,' Hunter suggested.

'True,' Devlin told him. 'On the other hand, it would probably be a damned sight easier to slip something in her tea.'

It was Hunter's turn to laugh now. 'You know, I like you, Professor, and I'd started off by not wanting to.'

'And why could that be?' Devlin wondered, interested.

'I was a captain in the Rifle Brigade. Belfast, Derry, South Armagh.'

'Ah, I see what you mean.'

'Four tours between nineteen seventy-two and seventy-eight.'

'And that was four tours too many.'

'Exactly. Frankly, as far as I'm concerned, they can give Ulster back to the Indians.'

'The best idea I've heard tonight,' Liam Devlin told him cheerfully and he lit a cigarette and sprawled back in the passenger seat, felt hat tilted over his eyes.

At that moment in his office at KGB Headquarters in Dzerhinsky Square, Lieutenant-General Ivan Maslovsky was seated at his desk, thinking about the Cuchulain affair. Cherny's message passed on by Lubov, had reached Moscow only a couple of hours earlier. For some reason it made him think back all those years to Drumore in the Ukraine and Kelly in the rain with a gun in his hand, the man who wouldn't do as he was told.

The door opened and his aide, Captain Igor Kurbsky, came in with a cup of coffee for him. Maslovsky drank it slowly. 'Well, Igor, what do you think?'

'I think Cuchulain has done a magnificent job, Comrade General, for so very many years. But now . . .'

'I know what you mean,' Maslovsky said. 'Now that British Intelligence knows he exists it's only a matter of time until they run him down.'

'And Cherny they could pull in at any time.'

There was a knock at the door and an orderly appeared with a signal message. Kurbsky took it and dismissed him. 'It's for you, sir. From Lubov in Dublin.'

'Read it!' Maslovsky ordered.

The gist of the message was that Devlin was proceeding to Paris with the intention of meeting with Tanya Voroninova. At the mention of his foster-daughter's name, Maslovsky stood up and snatched the signal from Kurbsky's hands. It was no secret, the enormous affection the General felt for his foster-daughter, especially since the death of his wife. In some quarters he was known as a butcher, but Tanya Voroninova he truly loved.

'Right,' he said to Kurbsky. 'Who's our best man at the Paris Embassy? Belov, isn't it?'

'Yes, Comrade.'

'Send a message tonight. Tanya's concert tour is cancelled. No arguments. Full security as regards her person until she can be returned safely to Moscow.'

'And Cuchulain?'

127

'Has served his purpose. A great pity.'

'Do we pull him in?'

'No, not enough time. This one needs instant action. Signal Lubov at once in Dublin. I want Cuchulain eliminated. Cherny also, and the sooner the better.'

'If I might point out, I don't think Lubov has had much experience on the wet side of things.'

'He's had the usual training, hasn't he? In any case, they won't be expecting it which should make the whole thing rather easier.'

In Paris, the coding machine in the intelligence section of the Soviet Embassy started whirring. The operator waited until the message had passed line-by-line across the screen. She carefully unloaded the magnetic tape which had recorded the message and took it to the night supervisor.

'This is an Eyes Only signal from KGB, Moscow, for Colonel Belov.'

'He's out of town,' the supervisor said. 'Lyons, I think. Due back tomorrow afternoon. You'll have to hold it anyway. It requires his personal key to decode it.'

The operator logged the tape, placed it in her data drawer and went back to work.

In Dublin, Dimitri Lubov had been enjoying an evening at the Abbey Theatre, an excellent performance of

Brendan Behan's *The Hostage*. Supper afterwards at a well known fish restaurant on the Quays meant that it was past midnight when he returned to the Embassy and found the signal from Moscow.

Even when he'd read it for the third time, he still couldn't believe it. He was to dispose not only of Cherny, but Cussane, and within the next twenty-four hours. His hands were sweating, trembling slightly, which was hardly surprising for in spite of his years in the KGB and all that dedicated training, the plain fact was that Dimitri Lubov had never killed anyone in his life.

Tanya Voroninova came out of the bathroom of her suite at the Ritz as the room waiter brought her breakfast tray in; tea, toast and honey, which was exactly what she'd asked for. She wore a khaki-green jumpsuit and brown boots of soft leather and the combination gave her a vaguely military appearance. She was a small, dark, intense girl with untidy black hair which she constantly had to push back from her eyes. She regarded it with disfavour in the gilt mirror above the fireplace and twisted it into a bun at the nape of her neck, then she sat down and started on breakfast.

There was a knock on the door and her tour secretary, Natasha Rubenova came in. She was a pleasant, grey-haired woman in her mid-forties. 'How are you feeling this morning?'

'Fine. I slept very well.'

'Good. You're wanted at the Conservatoire at two-thirty. Complete run-through.'

'No problem,' Tanya said.

'Are you going out this morning?'

'Yes, I'd like to spend some time at the Louvre. We've been so busy during this visit that it might be my last opportunity.'

'Do you want me to come with you?'

'No thanks. I'll be fine. I'll see you back here for lunch at one o'clock.'

It was a fine soft morning when she left the hotel and went down the steps at the front entrance. Devlin and Hunter were waiting in the Peugeot on the far side of the boulevard.

'Looks as if she's walking,' Hunter said.

Devlin nodded. 'Follow her for a while then we'll see.'

Tanya carried a canvas bag slung from her left shoulder and she walked at quite a fast pace, enjoying the exercise. She was playing Rachmaninov's Fourth Piano Concerto that night. The piece was a particular favourite so that she had none of the usual nervous tension that she sometimes experienced, like most artists, before a big concert.

But then, she was something of an old hand at the game now. Since her successes in both the Leeds and Tchaikovsky festivals she had steadily established an international reputation. There had been little time for anything else. On the one occasion she had fallen in love, she'd been foolish enough to choose a young military doctor on attachment to an airborne brigade. He'd been killed in action in Afghanistan the year before.

The experience, though harrowing, had not broken her. She had given one of her greatest performances on the night that she had received the news, but she had withdrawn from men, there was no doubt about that. There was too much hurt involved and it would not have needed a particularly bright psychiatrist to find out why. In spite of success and fame and the privileged life her position brought her; in spite of having constantly at her shoulder the powerful presence of Maslovsky, she was still, in many ways, the little girl on her knees in the rain beside the father so cruelly torn away from her.

Along the Champs Elysées and into the Place de la Concorde she went, walking steadily.

'Jesus, but she likes her exercise,' Devlin observed.

She turned into the cool peace of the Jardin des Tuileries and Hunter nodded. 'I thought she would. My hunch is that she's making for the Louvre. You go after her on foot from here. I'll drive round, park the car and wait for you at the main entrance.'

There was a Henry Moore exhibit in the Tuileries Gardens. She browsed around it for a little while and Devlin stayed back, but it was obvious that nothing there had much appeal for her and she moved on through the gardens to the great Palais du Louvre itself.

Tanya Voroninova was certainly selective. She moved from gallery to gallery, choosing only works of acknowledged genius and Devlin followed at a discreet distance. From the Victory of Samothrace at the top of the Daru staircase by the main entrance, she moved on to the Venus de Milo. She spent some time in the Rembrandt Gallery on the first floor, then stopped to look at what is possibly the most famous picture in the world – Leonardo da Vinci's 'Mona Lisa'.

Devlin moved in close. 'Is she smiling, would you say?' he tried in English.

'What do you mean?' she asked in the same language.

'Oh, it's an old superstition in the Louvre that some mornings she doesn't smile.'

She turned to look at him. 'That's absurd.'

'But you're not smiling either,' Devlin said. 'Sweet Jesus, are you worried you'd crack the plate?'

'This is total nonsense,' she said, but smiled all the same.

'When you're on your dignity, your mouth turns down at the corners,' he said. 'It doesn't help.'

'My looks, you mean? A matter of indifference to me.'

He stood there, hands in the pockets of the Burberry trenchcoat, the black felt hat slanted over one ear and the eyes were the most vivid blue she had ever seen. There was an air of insolent good humour to him and a kind of self-mockery that was rather attractive in spite of the fact that he must have been twice her age at least. There was a sudden aching excitement that was difficult to control and she took a deep breath to steady herself.

'Excuse me,' she said and walked away.

Devlin gave her some room and then followed. A darling girl and frightened, for some reason. Interesting to know why that should be.

She made her way to the Grande Galerie, finally stopped before El Greco's 'Christ on the Cross' and stood there for quite some time gazing up at the gaunt mystical figure, showing no acknowledgement of Devlin's presence when he moved beside her.

'And what does it say to you?' he asked gently. 'Is there love there?'

'No,' she said. 'A rage against dying, I think. Why are you following me?'

'Am I?'

'Since the Tuileries Gardens.'

'Really? Well, if I was, I can't be very good at it.'

'Not necessarily. You are someone to look at twice,' she said simply.

Strange how suddenly she felt like crying. Wanted to reach out to the incredible warmth of that voice. He took her arm and said gently, 'All the time in the world, girl dear. You still haven't told me what El Greco says to you.'

'I was not raised a Christian,' she said. 'I see no Saviour on the Cross, but a great human being in torment, destroyed by little people. And you?'

'I love your accent,' Devlin said. 'Reminds me of Garbo in the movies when I was a wee boy, but that was a century or so before your time.'

'Garbo is not unknown to me,' she said, 'and I'm duly flattered. However, you still have not told me what it says for you?'

'A profound question when one considers the day,' Devlin told her. 'At seven o'clock this morning, they celebrated a rather special Mass in St Peter's Basilica in Rome. The Pope together with cardinals from Britain and the Argentine.'

'And will this achieve anything?'

'It hasn't stopped the British Navy proceeding on its merry way or Argentine Skyhawks from attacking it.'

'Which means?'

'That the Almighty, if he exists at all, is having one hell of a joke at our expense.'

Tanya frowned. 'Your accent intrigues me. You are not English, I think?'

'Irish, my love.'

'But I thought the Irish were supposed to be extremely religious?'

'And that's a fact. My old Aunt Hannah had callouses on her knees from praying. She used to take me to Mass three times a week when I was a boy in Drumore.'

Tanya Voroninova went very still. 'Where did you say?'

'Drumore. That's a little market town in Ulster. The church there was Holy Name. The thing I remember

134

most was my uncle and his cronies, straight out from Mass and down the road to Murphy's Select Bar.'

She turned, her face very pale now. 'Who are you?'

'Well, one thing's for sure, girl dear.' He ran a hand lightly over her dark hair. 'I'm not Cuchulain, last of the dark heroes.'

Her eyes widened and there was a kind of anger as she plucked at his coat. 'Who are you?'

'In a manner of speaking, Viktor Levin.'

'Viktor?' She looked bewildered. 'But Viktor is dead. Died somewhere in Arabia a month or so ago. My father told me.'

'General Maslovsky? Well, he would, wouldn't he? No, Viktor escaped. Defected, you might say. Ended up in London and then Dublin.'

'He's well?'

'Dead,' Devlin said brutally. 'Murdered by Mikhail Kelly or Cuchulain or the dark bloody hero or whoever you want to call him. The same man who shot your father dead twenty-three years ago in the Ukraine.'

She sagged against him. His arm went round her in support, strong and confident. 'Lean on me, just put one foot in front of the other and I'll take you outside and get you some air.'

They sat on a bench in the Tuileries Gardens and Devlin took out his old silver case and offered her a cigarette. 'Do you use these things?'

'No.'

'Good for you, they'd stunt your growth and you with your green years ahead of you.'

Somewhere, he'd said those self-same words before, a long, long time ago. Another girl very much like this one. Not beautiful, not in any conventional sense, and yet always there would be the compulsion to turn and take a second look. There was pain in the memory that even time had not managed to erase.

'You're a strange man,' she said, 'for a secret agent. That's what you are, I presume?'

He laughed out loud, the sound so clear that Tony Hunter, seated on a bench on the other side of the Henry Moore exhibit reading a newspaper, glanced up sharply.

'God save the day.' Devlin took out his wallet and extracted a scrap of pasteboard. 'My card. Strictly for formal occasions I assure you.'

She read it out loud. 'Professor Liam Devlin, Trinity College, Dublin.' She looked up. 'Professor of what?'

'English literature. I use the term loosely, as academics do, so it would include Oscar Wilde, Shaw, O'Casey, Brendan Behan, James Joyce, Yeats. A mixed bag there. Catholics and Prods, but all Irish. Could I have the card back, by the way? I'm running short . . .'

He replaced it in his wallet. She said, 'But how would a professor of an ancient and famous university come to be involved in an affair like this?'

'You've heard of the Irish Republican Army?'

'Of course.'

'I've been a member of that organization since I was sixteen years of age. No longer active, as we call it. I've some heavy reservations about the way the Provisionals have been handling some aspects of the present campaign.'

'Don't tell me, let me guess.' She smiled. 'You are a romantic at heart, I think, Professor Devlin?'

'Is that a fact?'

'Only a romantic could wear anything so absurdly wonderful as that black felt hat. But there is more, of course. No bombs in restaurants to blow up women and children. You would shoot a man without hesitation. Welcome the hopeless odds of meeting highly trained soldiers face-to-face.'

Devlin was beginning to feel distinctly uneasy. 'Do you tell me?'

'Oh, I do, Professor Devlin. You see, I think I recognize you now. The true revolutionary, the failed romantic who didn't really want it to stop.'

'And what would *it* be, exactly?'

'Why, the game, Professor. The mad, dangerous, wonderful game that alone makes life worth living for a man like you. Oh, you may like the cloistered life of the lecture room or tell yourself that you do, but at the first chance to sniff powder . . .'

'Can I take time to catch my breath?' Devlin asked.

'And worst of all,' she carried on relentlessly, 'is your need to have it both ways. To have all the fun, but also to have a nice clean revolution where no innocent bystanders get hurt.'

She sat there, arms folded in front of her in an inimitable gesture as if she would hold herself in, and Devlin said, 'Have you missed anything out, would you say?'

She smiled tightly. 'Sometimes I get very wound up like a clock spring and I hold it until the spring goes.'

'And it all bursts out and you're into your imitation of Freud,' he told her. 'I bet that goes down big over the vodka and strawberries after dinner at old Maslovsky's summer *dasha*.'

Her face tightened. 'You will not make jokes about him. He has been very good to me. The only father I have known.'

'Perhaps,' Devlin said. 'But it wasn't always so.'

She gazed at him angrily. 'All right, Professor Devlin, we have fenced enough. Perhaps it is time you told me why you are here.'

He omitted nothing, starting with Viktor Levin and Tony Villiers in the Yemen and ending with the murder of Billy White and Levin outside Kilrea. When he was finished, she sat there for a long moment without saying anything.

'Levin said you remembered Drumore and the events surrounding your father's death,' Devlin said gently.

'Like a nightmare, it drifts to the surface of consciousness now and then. Strange, but it is as if it's happening to someone else and I'm looking down at the little girl on her knees in the rain beside her father's body.'

'And Mikhail Kelly or Cuchulain as they call him? You remember him?'

'Till my dying day,' she said flatly. 'It was such a strange face, the face of a ravaged young saint and he was so kind to me, so gentle, that was the strangest thing of all.'

Devlin took her arm. 'Let's walk for a while.' They started along the path and he asked, 'Has Maslovsky ever discussed those events with you?'

'No.'

Her arm under his hand was going rigid. 'Easy, girl dear,' he said softly. 'And tell me the most important thing of all. Have you ever tried to discuss it with him?'

'No, damn you!' She pulled away, turning, her face full of passion.

'But then, you wouldn't want to do that, would you?' he said. 'That would be opening a can of worms with a vengeance.'

She stood there looking at him, holding herself in again. 'What do you want of me, Professor Devlin? You want me to defect like Viktor? Wade through all those thousands of photos in the hope that I might recognize him?'

'That's a reasonable facsimile of the original mad idea. The IRA people in Dublin would never let the material they're holding out of their own hands, you see.'

'Why should I?' She sat on a nearby bench and pulled him down. 'Let me tell you something. You make a big mistake, you people in the West, when you assume that all Russians are straining at the leash, anxious only for a chance to get out. I love my country. I like it there. It suits me. I'm a respected artist. I can travel wherever I like, even in Paris. No KGB – no men in black overcoats watching my every move. I go where I please.'

'With a foster-father, a lieutenant-general in the KGB in command of Department V amongst other things, I'd be surprised if you didn't. It used to be called Department 13, by the way. Distinctly unlucky for some, and then Maslovsky reorganized it in nineteen sixty-eight. It could best be described as an assassination bureau, but then, no well-run organization should be without one.'

'Just like your IRA?' She leaned forward. 'How many men have you killed for a cause you believed in, Professor?'

He smiled gently and touched her cheek in a strangely intimate gesture. 'Point taken, but I can see I'm wasting your time. You might as well have this, though.'

He took a largish buff envelope from his pocket, the one that had been delivered by Ferguson's bagman that morning and placed it in her lap.

'What is it?' she demanded.

'The people in London, being ever hopeful, have made you a present of a British passport with a brand new identity. Your photo looks smashing. There's cash in there – French francs – and details of alternative ways of getting to London.'

'I don't need it.'

'Well, you've got it now. And this.' He took his card from his wallet and gave it to her. 'I'll fly back to Dublin this afternoon. No point in hanging around.'

Which wasn't strictly true, for the bagman from London had flown in with more than the package containing the false passport. There had also been a message from Ferguson for Devlin personally. McGuiness and the Chief of Staff were hopping mad. As far as they were concerned, the leak was none of their doing. They wanted out and Devlin was to mend fences.

She put the packet and the card into her shoulder bag with some reluctance. 'I'm sorry. You came a long way for nothing.'

'You've got my number,' he said. 'Call any time.' He stood up. 'Who knows, you just might start asking questions.'

'I think not, Professor Devlin.' She held out her hand. 'Goodbye.'

Devlin held it for a moment, then turned and walked back along the gardens to where Hunter was sitting. 'Come on!' he said. 'Let's get moving!'

Hunter scrambled to his feet and trailed after him. 'What happened?'

'Nothing,' Devlin told him as they reached the car. 'Not a bloody thing. She didn't want to know. Now let's go back to your place so that I can get my bag, then you can take me up to Charles de Gaulle. With luck, I might make the afternoon flight to Dublin.'

'You're going back?'

'Yes, I'm going back,' Liam Devlin said, and he sank down in his seat and tipped the rim of his black felt hat over his eyes.

Behind them, Tanya Voroninova watched them go, turning out into the traffic of the Rue de Rivoli. She stood there, thinking about things for a moment, then moved out of the gardens and started to walk along the pavement, considering the extraordinary events of the morning. Liam Devlin was a dangerously attractive man, no doubt about it, but more than that, his story had been terribly disturbing for her and events from a past perhaps best forgotten were trying to call her, as if from a great distance.

She was aware of a car pulling into the kerb ahead of her, a black Mercedes saloon. As she approached it, the rear door opened and Natasha Rubenova looked out. She seemed agitated. No, more than that – afraid.

'Tanya!'

Tanya turned towards her. 'Natasha – what on earth are you doing here? What's happened?'

'Please, Tanya. Get in!'

There was a man sitting beside her, young and with a hard, implacable face. He wore a blue suit, dark blue tie and white shirt. He also wore black leather gloves. The man in the passenger seat next to the chauffeur could have been his twin. They looked as if they might be employed by a high class funeral firm and Tanya felt slightly uneasy.

'What on earth is going on?'

In a second, the young man beside Natasha was out of the car, a hand taking Tanya above the left elbow in a grip, light, but strong. 'My name is Turkin – Peter Turkin, Comrade. My colleague is Lieutenant Ivan Shepilov. We are officers of GRU and you will come with us.'

Soviet Military Intelligence. She was more than uneasy now. She was frightened and tried to pull away.

'Please, Comrade.' His grip tightened. 'You'll only hurt yourself by struggling and you have a concert tonight. We don't want to disappoint your fans.'

There was something in his eyes, a hint of cruelty, of perversity, that was very disturbing. 'Leave me alone!' She tried to strike him and he blocked her blow with ease. 'You'll answer for this. Don't you know who my father is?'

'Lieutenant-General Ivan Maslovsky of the KGB, under whose direct orders I am acting now, so be a good girl and do as you are told.'

She had no will to resist, so great was the shock, and found herself sitting next to Natasha who was close to tears. Turkin got in on the other side.

'Back to the Embassy!' he told the chauffeur.

As the Mercedes pulled away, Tanya held on to Natasha's hand tightly. For the first time since she was a little girl, she felt really and truly afraid.

7

Nikolai Belov was in his fifties, a handsome enough man with the slightly fleshy face of someone who enjoyed the good things of life more than was healthy for him, the kind of good Marxist whose dark suit and overcoat had been tailored in London's Savile Row. The silver hair and decadent good looks gave him the air of an ageing and rather distinguished actor instead of a colonel in the KGB.

This trip to Lyons could hardly have been classified as essential business, but it had been possible to take his secretary, Irana Vronsky, with him. As she had been his mistress for some years now, it meant that they had enjoyed an extremely pleasurable couple of days, the memory of which had faded rather rapidly when he discovered the situation waiting for him on his return to the Soviet Embassy.

He had hardly settled into his office when Irana

came in. 'There's an urgent communication from KGB Moscow for your eyes only.'

'Who's it from?'

'General Maslovsky.'

The name alone was enough to bring Belov to his feet. He went out and she followed him down to the coding office where the operator got the relevant tape. Belov keyed in his personal code, the machine whirred, the operator tore off the print-out sheet and handed it to him. Belov read it and swore softly. He took Irana by the elbow and hurried her out. 'Get me Lieutenant Shepilov and Captain Turkin. Whatever else they're on, they drop.'

Belov was seated at his desk, working his way through papers when the door opened and Irana Vronsky ushered in Tanya, Natasha Rubenova and Shepilov and Turkin. Belov knew Tanya well. His official position at the Embassy for some years had been senior cultural attaché. As part of that cover role he had escorted her to parties on a number of occasions.

He stood up. 'It's good to see you.'

'I demand to know what's going on here,' she told him passionately. 'I'm pulled off the pavement by these bully boys here and . . .'

'I'm sure Captain Turkin was only acting as he saw fit.' Belov nodded to Irana. 'Get the Moscow call now.' He turned to Tanya. 'Calm yourself and sit down.'

She stood there, mutinous, then glanced at Shepilov and Turkin standing against the wall, gloved hands folded in front of them. 'Please,' Belov said.

She sat and he offered her a cigarette. Such was her agitation that she took it and Turkin moved in smoothly and lit it for her. His lighter was not only by Cartier, but gold. She coughed as the smoke caught at the back of her throat.

Belov said, 'Now tell me what you did this morning.'

'I walked to the Tuileries Gardens.' The cigarette was helping, calming her down. She had control now and that meant she could fight.

'And then?'

'I went into the Louvre.'

'And who did you talk to?'

The question was direct and meant to entrap by causing an automatic response. To her own surprise, she found herself replying calmly, 'I was on my own. I didn't go with anyone. Perhaps I didn't make that clear?'

'Yes, I know that,' he said patiently. 'But did you speak to anyone when you got there? Did anyone approach you?'

She managed a smile. 'You mean, did anyone try to pick me up? No such luck. Considering its reputation, Paris can be very disappointing.' She stubbed out the cigarette. 'Look, what's going on, Nikolai? Can't you tell me?'

Belov had no reason to disbelieve her. In fact he very much wanted to. He had, in effect, been absent from duty the night before. If he had not been, he would have received Maslovsky's directive then and Tanya Voroninova would not have been allowed to stir from her suite at the Ritz that morning. Certainly not unaccompanied.

The door opened and Irana entered. 'General Maslovsky on line one.'

Belov picked up the phone and Tanya tried to snatch it. 'Let me speak to him.'

Belov pulled away from her. 'Belov here, General.'

'Ah, Nikolai, she is with you now?'

'Yes, General.' It was a measure of the length of their friendship that Belov missed out the Comrade.

'And she is under guard? She has spoken to no one?'

'Yes to both questions, General.'

'And the man Devlin has not attempted to get in touch with her?'

'It would seem not. We've had the computer pull him out of the files for us. Pictures, everything. If he tries to get close, we'll know.'

'Fine. Now give me Tanya.'

Belov handed her the phone and she almost snatched it from him. 'Papa?'

She had called him so for years and his voice was warm and kindly as always. 'You are well?'

'Bewildered,' she said. 'No one will tell me what is happening.'

'It is sufficient for you to know that for reasons which are unimportant now, you have become involved in a matter of state security. A very serious business indeed. You must be returned to Moscow as soon as may be.'

'But my tour?'

The voice of the man at the other end of the line was suddenly cold, implacable and detached. 'Will be cancelled. You will appear at the Conservatoire tonight and fulfil that obligation. The first direct flight to Moscow is not until tomorrow morning anyway. There will be a suitable press release. The old wrist injury giving problems again. A need for further treatment. That should do nicely.'

All her life, or so it seemed, she had done his bidding, allowed him to shape her career, aware of his genuine concern and love, but this was new territory.

She tried again, 'But Papa!'

'Enough of argument. You will do as you are told and you will obey Colonel Belov in everything. Put him back on.'

She handed the phone to Belov mutely, hand shaking. Never had he spoken to her like this. Was she no longer his daughter? Simply another Soviet citizen to be ordered about at will?

'Belov, General.' He listened for a moment or two then nodded. 'No problem. You can rely on me.'

He put the phone down and opened a file on his desk. The photo he took from it and held up to her was of Liam Devlin, a few years younger perhaps, but Devlin unmistakably.

'This man is Irish. His name is Liam Devlin. He is a

university professor from Dublin with a reputation for a certain Irish charm. It would be a mistake for anyone to take him lightly. He has been a member of the Irish Republican Army for all his adult life. An important leader at one stage. He is also a ruthless and capable gunman who has killed many times. As a young man, he was an official executioner for his people.'

Tanya took a deep breath. 'And what has he to do with me?'

'That need not concern you. It is sufficient for you to know that he would very much like to talk to you and *that* we simply can't allow, can we Captain?'

Turkin showed no emotion. 'No, Colonel.'

'So,' Belov told her, 'you will return to the Ritz now, you and Comrade Rubenova with Lieutenant Shepilov and Captain Turkin in attendance. You will not go out again until tonight's performance when they will escort you to the Conservatoire. I will be there myself because of the reception afterwards. The Ambassador will be there and the President of the Republic Monsieur Mitterand, himself. His presence is the only reason we are not cancelling tonight's concert. Is there anything you don't understand in all this?'

'No,' she said coldly, her face white and strained. 'I understand only too well.'

'Good,' he said. 'Then go back to the hotel now and get some rest.'

She turned, Turkin opened the door for her, a slight, twisted smile on his mouth. She brushed past him, followed by a thoroughly frightened Natasha Rubenova and Shepilov and Turkin moved in behind.

In Kilrea, Devlin had not been long back at the cottage. He didn't have a regular housekeeper, just an old lady who came in twice a week, knocked the place into shape and did the laundry, but he preferred it that way. He put the kettle on in the kitchen, went into the living room and quickly made the fire. He had just put a match to it when there was a rap on the French window and he turned to find McGuiness there.

Devlin unlocked it quickly. 'That was quick. I'm only just back.'

'So I was told within five minutes of you landing at the airport.' McGuiness was angry. 'What's the score, Liam? What's going on?'

'What do you mean?'

'Levin and Billy, and now Mike Murphy's been pulled out of the Liffey with two bullets in him. It must have been Cuchulain. You know it and I know it. The thing is, how did he know?'

'I don't have any fast answer on that one.' Devlin found two glasses and the Bushmills and poured. 'Try this for size and calm down.'

McGuiness swallowed a little. 'A leak is what I think, at the London end. It's a well-known fact that the British security service has been heavily infiltrated by the Soviets for years.'

'A slight exaggeration, but some truth to it,' Devlin said. 'As mentioned earlier, I know that Ferguson thinks the leak is from your people.'

'To hell with that. I say we pull in Cherny and squeeze him dry.'

'Maybe,' Devlin said. 'I'd have to check on that with Ferguson. Let's give it another day.'

'All right,' McGuiness said with obvious reluctance. 'I'll be in touch, Liam. Close touch.' And he went out through the French windows.

Devlin poured another whiskey and sat there savouring it and thinking, then he picked up the phone. He was about to dial, then hesitated. He replaced the receiver, got the black plastic box from the desk and switched it on. There was no positive response from the telephone, nor indeed from anywhere in the room.

'So,' he said softly, 'Ferguson or McGuiness. It's one or other of the buggers that it's down to.'

He dialled the Cavendish Square number and the receiver was picked up at once. 'Fox here.'

'Is he there, Harry?'

'Not at the moment. How was Paris?'

'A nice girl. I liked her. Pretty confused. Nothing more I could do than present the facts. I gave her the material your bagman brought over. She took it, but I wouldn't be too sanguine.'

'I never was,' Fox said. 'Will you be able to smooth things down in Dublin?'

'McGuiness has already been to see me. He wants to move on Cherny. Try some old-fashioned pressure.'

'That might be the best solution.'

'Jesus, Harry, but Belfast left its mark on you. Still, you could be right. I've stalled him for a day. If you want me, I'll be here. I gave the girl my card, by the way. She thought I was a failed romantic, Harry. Have you ever heard the like?'

'You give a convincing imitation, but I've never bought it.'

Fox laughed and rang off. Devlin sat there for a while, a frown on his face, then there was another tap on the French window. It opened and Cussane entered.

'Harry,' Devlin said, 'you're sent from heaven. As I've often told you, you make the best scrambled eggs in the world.'

'Flattery will get you anywhere.' Cussane poured himself a drink. 'How was Paris?'

'Paris?' Devlin said. 'Sure and I was only joking. I've been to Cork. Some university business to do with the film festival. Had to stay over. Just driven back. I'm the original starving man.'

'Right,' Harry Cussane told him. 'You lay the table and I'll scramble the eggs.'

'You're a good friend, Harry,' Devlin said.

Cussane paused in the door. 'And why not, Liam. It's been a long time,' and he smiled and went into the kitchen.

* * *

Tanya had a hot bath, hoping it would relax her. There was a knock at the door and Natasha Rubenova entered. 'Coffee?'

'Thank you.' Tanya lay back in the warm, foamy water and sipped the coffee gratefully.

Natasha pulled a small stool forward and sat down. 'You must be very careful, my love. You understand me?'

'Strange,' Tanya said. 'No one has ever told me to be careful before.'

It occurred to her then that she had always been sheltered from the cold, ever since the nightmare of Drumore that surfaced only in her dreams. Maslovsky and his wife had been good parents. She had wanted for nothing. In a Marxist society that had been envisaged in the great days of Lenin and the revolution as giving power to the people, power had quickly become the prerogative of the few.

Soviet Russia had become an elitist society in which who you were was more important than what you were and she, to all intents and purposes, was Ivan Maslovsky's daughter. The best housing, the superior schools, her talent carefully nurtured. When she drove through Moscow to their country house, it was in a chauffeured limousine, travelling in the traffic-free lane kept open for the use of the important people in the hierarchy. The delicacies that graced their table, the clothes she wore, all bought on a special card at GUM.

All this she had ignored, just as she had ignored the realities of the state trials of the Gulag. Just as she had turned from the even harsher reality of Drumore, her father dead on the street and Maslovsky in charge.

Natasha said, 'You are all right?'

'Of course. Pass me a towel,' Tanya wrapped it around herself. 'Did you notice the lighter that Turkin used when he lit my cigarette?'

'Not particularly.'

'It was by Cartier. Solid gold. What was it Orwell said in that book of his? All animals are equal, but some are more equal than others?'

'Please, darling,' Natasha Rubenova was obviously agitated. 'You mustn't say things like that.'

'You're right.' Tanya smiled. 'I'm angry, that's all. Now I think I would like to sleep. I must be fresh for tonight's concert.' They went into the other room and she got into the bed, the towel around her. 'They're still out there?'

'Yes.'

'I'll sleep now.'

Natasha closed the curtains and went out. Tanya lay there in the darkness thinking about things. The events of the past few hours had been a shock in themselves, but strangely enough, the most significant thing had been the way in which she had been treated. Tanya Voroninova, internationally acclaimed artist, who had received the Medal of Culture from Brezhnev himself, had felt the full weight of the State's hand. The truth was that for most of her life she had been somebody, thanks to Maslovsky. Now it had been made plain that, when the chips were down, she was just another cypher.

It was enough. She switched on the bedside lamp, reached for her handbag and took out the packet which Devlin had given her. The British passport was excellent; issued, according to the date, three years before. There was an American visa. She had entered that country twice, also Germany, Italy, Spain and France one week previously. A nice touch. Her name was Joanna Frank, born in London, professional journalist. The photo, as Devlin had said, was an excellent likeness. There were even one or two personal letters with her London address in Chelsea, an American Express credit card and a British driver's licence. They'd thought of everything.

The alternative routes were clearly outlined. There was the direct plane flight from Paris to London, but that wasn't on. Surprising how cool and calculating she was now. She would have only the slimmest of chances of getting away, if an opportunity presented itself at all, and she would be missed almost at once. They would have the airports covered instantly.

It seemed obvious that the same would be true of the ferry terminals at Calais and Boulogne. But the people in London had indicated another way, one which might possibly be overlooked. There was a train service from Paris to Rennes, changing there for St Malo on the Brittany coast. From there, a hydrofoil service to Jersey

156

in the Channel Islands. And from Jersey, there were several planes a day to London.

She got up quietly, tiptoed into the bathroom and closed the door. Then she lifted the receiver on the wall telephone and called Reception. They were extremely efficient. Yes, there was a night train to Rennes, leaving the Gare du Nord at eleven. In Rennes, there would be a delay, but she could be in St Malo for breakfast. Ample time to catch the hydrofoil.

She flushed the toilet and went back in the bedroom, rather pleased with herself for she hadn't quoted a room number or given her name. The enquiry could have come from any one of hundreds of guests.

'They're turning you into a jungle animal, Tanya,' she told herself softly.

She got her holdall bag from the wardrobe, the one she used to take all her bits and pieces to the concerts. She couldn't secrete much in there. It would show. She thought about it for a while, then took out a pair of soft suede boots and rolled them up so they fitted neatly in the bottom of the bag. She next took a black cotton jumpsuit from its hanger, folded it and laid it in the case. She placed the concerto score and the orchestra parts she had been studying on top.

So, nothing more to be done. She went to the window and peered out. It was raining again and she shivered, suddenly lonely, and remembered Devlin and his strength. For a moment she thought of phoning him, but that was no good. Not from here. They would trace the call in minutes the moment they started checking. She went back to bed and switched off the lamp. If only she could sleep for an hour or two. The face surfaced in her consciousness: Cuchulain's bone-white face and dark eyes made sleep impossible.

She wore a gown in black velvet for the concert. It was by Balmain and very striking with a matching jacket. The pearls at her neck and the earrings were supposed to be lucky, a gift by the Maslovskys before the finals of the Tchaikovsky competition, her greatest triumph.

Natasha came in and stood behind her at the dressing table. 'Are you ready? Time's getting short.' She put her hands on Tanya's shoulders. 'You look lovely.'

'Thank you. I've packed my case.'

Natasha picked it up. 'Have you put a towel in? You always forget.' She zipped it open before Tanya could protest, then froze. She looked at the girl, eyes wide.

'Please?' Tanya said softly. 'If I ever meant anything to you.'

The older woman took a deep breath, went into the bathroom and returned with a towel. She folded it and placed it in the case and zipped it up. 'So,' she said. 'We are ready.'

'Is it still raining?'

'Yes.'

'Then I shan't wear the velvet cape. The trenchcoat, I think.'

Natasha took it from the wardrobe and draped it over her shoulders. Tanya felt her hands tighten for a moment. 'Now we must go.'

Tanya picked up the case and opened the door and went into the other room where Shepilov and Turkin waited. They both wore dinner jackets because of the reception after the performance.

'If I may be permitted the observation, you look superb, Comrade,' Turkin told her. 'A credit to our country.'

'Spare me the compliments, Captain,' she said frostily. 'If you wish to be of use, you can carry my case,' and she handed it to him and walked out.

The Conservatoire concert hall was packed for this occasion and when she walked on stage, the orchestra stood to greet her and there was a storm of applause, the audience standing also, following President Mitterand's example.

She sat down, all noise faded. There was complete silence as the conductor waited, baton ready and then it descended and as the orchestra started to play, Tanya Voroninova's hands rippled over the keyboard.

She was filled with a joy, an ecstasy almost, played as she had never played in her life before with a new, vibrant energy as if something which had been locked up in her for years was now released. The orchestra responded as if trying to match her so that at the end, in the dramatic finale to Rachmaninov's superb concerto, they fused into a whole that created an experience to be forgotten by few people who were there that night.

The cry from the audience was different from anything she had experienced in her life before. She stood facing them, the orchestra standing behind her, all clapping and someone threw a flower on the stage, and more followed as women unpinned their corsages.

She went off to the side and Natasha, waiting, tears streaming down her cheeks, flung her arms around her. 'Babushka, you were wonderful. The best I ever heard.'

Tanya hugged her fiercely. 'I know. My night, Natasha, the one night I can take on the whole world if need be and come out ahead of the game,' and she turned and went back on stage to an audience that refused to stop applauding.

François Mitterand, President of the Republic of France, took both her hands and kissed them warmly. 'Mademoiselle, I salute you. An extraordinary performance.'

'You are more than kind, *Monsieur le Président*,' she answered in his own language.

The crowd pressed close as champagne was offered and cameras flashed as the President toasted her and then introduced her to the Minister of Culture and others. She was aware of Shepilov and Turkin by the door, Nikolai Belov talking to them, handsome in velvet evening jacket and ruffled shirt. He raised his glass in a toast and moved towards her. She glanced at her watch. It was just after ten. If she was to go, it must be soon.

Belov reached for her right hand and kissed it. 'Tremendous stuff. You should get angry more often.'

'A point of view.' She took another glass of champagne from a waiter. 'Everyone who is anyone in the diplomatic corps seems to be here. You must be pleased. Quite a triumph.'

'Yes, but then, we Russians have always had a soul for music lacking in certain other peoples.'

She glanced around. 'Where's Natasha?'

'Over there with the Press. Shall I get her?'

'Not necessary. I need to go to the dressing room for a moment, but I can manage perfectly well on my own.'

'Of course.' He nodded to Turkin who came across. 'See Comrade Voroninova to her dressing room, Turkin. Wait for her and escort her back.' He smiled at Tanya. 'We don't want you to get hurt in the crush.'

The crowd opened for her, people smiling, raising their glasses, and Turkin followed her along the narrow corridor until they came to the dressing room.

She opened the door. 'I presume I'm permitted to go to the toilet?'

He smiled mockingly. 'If you insist, Comrade.'

He took out a cigarette and was lighting it as she closed the door. She didn't lock it, simply kicked off her shoes, pulled off the jacket and unzipped that lovely dress, allowing it to fall to the floor. She had the jumpsuit out of her case in a moment, was into it within seconds, zipping it up and pulling on the suede boots. She picked up the trenchcoat and handbag, moved into the toilet, closed the door and locked it.

She had checked the window earlier. It was large enough to get out of and opened into a small yard on the ground floor of the Conservatoire. She climbed up on the seat and wriggled through. It was raining hard now. She pulled on her trenchcoat, picked up her shoulderbag and ran to the gate. It was bolted on the inside and opened easily. A moment later, she was hurrying along the Rue de Madrid looking for a taxi.

8

Devlin was watching a late night movie on television when the phone rang. The line was surprisingly clear, so much so that at first he thought it must be local.

'Professor Devlin?'

'Yes.'

'It's Tanya – Tanya Voroninova.'

'Where are you?' Devlin demanded.

'The Gare du Nord. Paris. I've only got a couple of minutes. I'm catching the night train to Rennes.'

'To Rennes?' Devlin was bewildered. 'What in the world would you be going there for?'

'I change trains there for St Malo. I'll be there at breakfast time. There's a hydrofoil to Jersey. That's as good as being in England. Once there, I'm safe. I'll catch a plane for London. I only had minutes to give them the slip, so it seemed likely the other routes your people supplied would be blocked.'

'So, you changed your mind. Why?'

'Let's just say I've realized I like you and I don't like them. It doesn't mean I hate my country. Only some of the people in it. I must go.'

'I'll contact London,' Devlin said. 'Phone me from Rennes, and good luck.'

The line went dead. He stood there, holding the receiver, a slight ironic smile on his face, a kind of wonderment. 'Would you look at that now?' he said softly. 'A girl to take home to your mother and that's a fact.'

He dialled the Cavendish Square number and it was answered almost at once. 'Ferguson here.' He sounded cross.

'Would you by any chance be sitting in bed watching the old Bogart movie on the television?' Devlin enquired.

'Dear God, are you going into the clairvoyance business now?'

'Well, you can switch it off and get out of bed, you old bastard. The game's afoot with a vengeance.'

Ferguson's voice changed. 'What are you saying?'

'That Tanya Voroninova's done a bunk. She's just phoned me from the Gare du Nord. Catching the night train to Rennes. Change for St Malo. Hydrofoil to Jersey in the morning. She thought the other routes might be blocked.'

'Smart girl,' Ferguson said. 'They'll pull every trick in the book to get her back.'

'She's going to phone me when she gets to Rennes. I presume, at a guess, that would be about three-thirty or maybe four o'clock.'

Ferguson said, 'Stay by the phone. I'll get back to you.'

In his flat, Harry Fox was just about to get into the shower before going to bed when the phone rang. He answered it, cursing. It had been a long day. He needed some sleep.

'Harry?'

He came alert at once at the sound of Ferguson's voice. 'Yes, sir?'

'Get yourself over here. We've got work to do.'

Cussane was working in his study on Sunday's sermon when the sensor device linked to the apparatus in the attic was activated. By the time he was up there, Devlin was off the phone. He played the tape back, listening intently. When it was finished, he sat there, thinking about the implications which were all bad.

He went down to the study and phoned Cherny direct. When the Professor answered, he said, 'It's me. Are you alone?'

'Yes. Just about to go to bed. Where are you ringing from?'

'My place. We've got bad trouble. Now listen carefully.'

When he was finished, Cherny said, 'It gets worse. What do you want me to do?'

'Speak to Lubov now. Tell him to make contact with Belov in Paris at once. They may be able to stop her.'

'And if not?'

'Then I'll have to handle it myself when she gets here. I'll keep in touch, so stay by the phone.'

He poured himself a whiskey and stood in front of the fire. Strange, but he still saw her as that scrawny little girl in the rain all those years ago.

He raised his glass and said softly, 'Here's to you, Tanya Voroninova. Now, let's see if you can give those bastards a run for their money.'

Within five minutes, Turkin had realized something was badly wrong, had entered the dressing room and discovered the locked toilet door. The silence which was the only answer to his urgent knocking made him break down the door. The empty toilet, the window, told all. He clambered through, dropped into the yard and went into the Rue de Madrid. There was not a sign of her and he went round to the front of the Conservatoire and in through the main entrance, black rage in his heart. His career ruined, his very life on the line now because of that damned woman.

Belov was on another glass of champagne, deep in conversation with the Minister of Culture, when Turkin tapped him on the shoulder. 'Sorry to interrupt, Colonel, but could I have a word?' and he took him into the nearest corner and broke the bad news.

*　　*　　*

Nikolai Belov had always found that adversity brought out the best in him. He had never been one to cry over spilt milk. At his office at the Embassy, he sat behind the desk and faced Natasha Rubenova. Shepilov and Turkin stood by the door.

'I ask you again, Comrade,' he said to her. 'Did she say anything to you? Surely you of all people would have had some idea of her intentions?'

She was distressed and tearful, all quite genuine, and it helped her to lie easily. 'I'm as much at a loss as you are, Comrade Colonel.'

He sighed and nodded to Turkin who moved up behind her, shoving her down into a chair. He pulled off his right glove and squeezed her neck, pinching a nerve and sending a wave of appalling pain through her.

'I ask you again,' Nikolai Belov said gently. 'Please be sensible, I hate this kind of thing.'

Natasha, filled with pain, rage and humiliation, did the bravest thing of her life. 'Please! Comrade, I swear she told me nothing! Nothing!'

She screamed again as Turkin's finger found the nerve and Belov waved a hand. 'Enough. I'm satisfied she's telling the truth. What would her purpose be in lying?'

She sat there, huddled, weeping and Turkin said, 'What now, Comrade?'

'We have the airports fully covered. No possible flight she could have taken yet.'

'And Calais and Boulogne?'

'Our people are already on their way by road. The soonest she could leave from both places would be on one of the morning ferries and they will be there before those leave.'

Shepilov, who seldom spoke, said quietly, 'Excuse me, Comrade Colonel, but have you considered the fact that she may have sought asylum at the British Embassy?'

'Of course,' Belov told him. 'As it happens, since June of last year, we have a surveillance system operating at the entrance during the hours of darkness for rather obvious reasons. She has certainly not appeared there yet and if she does so . . .' he shrugged.

The door opened and Irana Vronsky hurried in. 'Lubov direct from Dublin for you, Comrade. Most urgent. The radio room have patched it through. Line one.'

Belov picked up the phone and listened. When he finally put it down, he was smiling. 'So far so good. She's on the night train to Rennes. Let's have a look at the map.' He nodded to Natasha. 'Take her out, Irana.'

Turkin said, 'But why Rennes?'

Belov found it on the map on the wall. 'To change trains for St Malo. From there she will catch the hydrofoil to Jersey in the Channel Islands.'

'British soil?'

'Exactly. Jersey, my dear Turkin, may be small, but it is very possibly the most important off-shore finance base in the world. They have an excellent airport, several flights a day to London and many other places.'

'All right,' Turkin said. 'We must drive to St Malo. Get there ahead of her.'

'Just a moment. Let's have a look in Michelin.' Belov found the red guide in the top left hand drawer of his desk and leafed through.

'Here we are – St Malo. Three hundred and seventy-two miles from Paris and a great deal of that through the Brittany countryside. Impossible to get there by car now, not in time. Go along to Bureau Five, Turkin. Let's see if they've got anyone we can use in St Malo. And you, Shepilov. Tell Irana I want all the information she has on Jersey. Airport, harbour, plane and boat schedules and so on – and hurry.'

At Cavendish Square, Kim was making up the fire in the sitting room while Ferguson, in an old towelling robe, sat at the desk working his way through a mass of papers.

The Gurkha stood up. 'Coffee, Sahib?'

'God, no, Kim. Tea, nice and fresh and keep it coming and some sort of sandwiches. Leave it to you.'

Kim went out and Harry Fox hurried in from the study. 'Right, sir, here's the score. She'll have a stopover at Rennes for almost two hours. From there to St Malo is seventy miles. She'll arrive at seven-thirty.'

'And the hydrofoil?'

'Leaves at eight-fifteen. Takes about an hour and a quarter. There's a time change, of course, so it arrives in Jersey at eight-thirty our time. There's a flight from Jersey to London, Heathrow, at ten minutes past ten. She'll have plenty of time to catch that. It's a small island, sir. Only fifteen minutes by cab from the harbour to the airport.'

'No, she can't be alone, Harry. I want her met. You'll have to go over first thing. There must be a breakfast plane.'

'Unfortunately it doesn't get into Jersey until nine-twenty.'

Ferguson said, 'Damnation!' and banged his fist on the desk as Kim entered carrying a tray containing tea things and a plate of newly cut sandwiches that gave off the unmistakable odour of grilled bacon.

'There is a possibility, sir.'

'What's that?'

'My cousin, Alex, sir. Alexander Martin. My second cousin actually. He lives in Jersey. Something in the finance industry. Married a local girl.'

'Martin?' Ferguson frowned. 'The name's familiar.'

'It would be, sir. We've used him before. When he was working for a merchant banker here in the city, he did a lot of travelling. Geneva, Zurich, Berlin, Rome.'

'He isn't on the active list?'

'No, sir. We used him as a bagman mainly, though there was an incident in East Berlin three years ago when things got out of hand and he behaved rather well.'

'I remember now,' Ferguson said. 'Supposed to pick up documents from a woman contact and when he found she was blown, he brought her out through Checkpoint Charlie in the boot of his car.'

'That's Alex, sir. Short service commission in the Welsh Guards, three tours in Ireland. Quite an accomplished musician. Plays the piano rather well. Mad as a hatter on a good day. Typically Welsh.'

'Get him!' Ferguson said. 'Now, Harry.' He had a hunch about Martin and suddenly felt much more cheerful. He helped himself to one of the bacon sandwiches. 'I say, these are really rather good.'

Alexander Martin was thirty-seven, a tall, rather handsome man with a deceptively lazy look to him. He was much given to smiling tolerantly, which he needed to do in the profession of investment broker which he had taken up on moving to Jersey eighteen months previously. As he had told his wife, Joan, on more than one occasion, the trouble with being in the investment business was that it threw you into the company of the rich and, as a class, he disliked them heartily.

Still, life had its compensations. He was an accomplished pianist if not a great one. If he had been, life might have been rather different. He was seated at the piano in the living room of his pleasant house in St Aubin overlooking the sea, playing a little Bach, ice-cold, brilliant stuff that required total concentration. He was wearing a dinner jacket, black tie undone at the neck. The phone rang for several moments before it penetrated his consciousness. He frowned, realizing the lateness of the hour and picked it up.

'Martin here.'

'Alex? This is Harry. Harry Fox.'

'Dear God!' Alex Martin said.

'How are Joan and the kids?'

'In Germany for a week, staying with her sister. Her husband's a major with your old mob. Detmold.'

'So, you're on your own? I thought you'd be in bed.'

'Just in from a late function.' Martin was very much awake now, all past experience telling him this was not a social call. 'Okay, Harry. What is this?'

'We need you, Alex, rather badly, but not like the other times. Right there in Jersey.'

Alex Martin laughed in astonishment. 'In Jersey? You've got to be joking.'

'Girl called Tanya Voroninova. Have you heard of her?'

'Of course I damn well have,' Martin told him. 'One of the best concert pianists to come along for years. I saw her perform at the Albert Hall in last season's promenade concerts. My office gets the Paris papers each day. She's there on a concert tour at the moment.'

'No she isn't,' Fox said. 'By now, she'll be half-way to Rennes on the night train. She's defecting, Alex.'

'She's what?'

'With luck, she'll be on the hydrofoil from St Malo, arriving Jersey at eight-twenty. She has a British passport in the name of Joanna Frank.'

Martin saw it all now. 'And you want me to meet her?'

'Exactly. Straight to the airport and bundle her on to

the ten-ten to Heathrow and that's it. We'll meet her this end. Will that give you any problem?'

'Certainly not. I know what she looks like. In fact, I think I've still got the programme from her concert at the Proms. There's a photo of her on that.'

'Fine,' Fox told him. 'She's phoning a contact of ours when she gets into Rennes. We'll warn her to expect you.'

Ferguson said, 'Give me the phone. Ferguson here.'

'Hello, sir,' Martin said.

'We're very grateful.'

'Nothing to it, sir. Just one thing. What about the opposition?'

'Shouldn't be any. KGB will be waiting at all the obvious bolt holes. Charles de Gaulle, Calais, Boulogne. Highly unlikely they'll be on to this one. I'll hand you back to Harry now.'

Fox said, 'We'll stay close, Alex. I'll give you this number in case of any problems.'

Martin wrote it down. 'Should be a piece of cake. Make a nice change from the investment business. I'll be in touch.'

He was totally awake now and decidedly cheerful. No hope of sleep. Things were looking up. He poured himself a vodka and tonic, and went back to his Bach at the piano.

Bureau Five was that section of the Soviet Embassy in Paris that dealt with the French Communist Party, infiltration of trade unions and so on. Turkin spent half an hour with their file on St Malo and the immediate area, but came up with nothing.

'The trouble is, Comrade,' he told Belov when he returned to the office, 'that the French Communist Party is extremely unreliable. The French tend to put country before party when the chips are down.'

'I know,' Belov said. 'It comes of an inborn belief in their own superiority.' He indicated the papers spread out on his desk. 'I've looked Jersey over pretty thoroughly. The solution is simple enough. You know that little airfield outside Paris we've used before?'

'Croix?' Turkin said. 'Lebel Air Taxis?'

'That's right. Jersey Airport opens early. You could land there at seven. Ample time to be down at the harbour to meet her. You have the usual selection of passports available. You could go as French businessmen.'

'But how do we bring her back?' Turkin asked. 'We'd have to pass through customs and immigration for the return flight from Jersey Airport. It would be an impossibility. Too easy for her to create a fuss.'

'Excuse me, Comrade Colonel,' Shepilov put in, 'but is it really necessary for us to bring her back at all since all that is needed in this affair is her silence, or have I got the wrong impression?'

'You certainly have,' Belov told him coldly. 'Whatever the circumstances, however difficult, General Maslovsky wants her back. I'd hate to be in your shoes if you reported that you had had to shoot her, Shepilov. I think there is an easy solution. According to the brochures, there is a yachting marina in St Helier Harbour. Boats for hire. Wasn't sailing something of a hobby of yours back home, Turkin?'

'Yes, Comrade.'

'Good, then I'm sure it's hardly beyond your abilities to sail a motor launch from Jersey to St Malo. You can hire a car there and bring her back by road.'

'Very well, Colonel.'

Irana came in with coffee on a tray. He said, 'Excellent. Now all that's needed is for someone to haul Lebel out of bed. The timing should just work nicely.'

Surprising herself, Tanya managed to sleep for most of the train journey and had to be prodded into wakefulness by two young students who had travelled next to her all the way from Paris. It was three-thirty and very cold on the station platform at Rennes although it had stopped raining. The students knew of an all-night café outside the station in the Boulevard Beaumont and showed her the way. It was warm and inviting in there, not too many people. She ordered coffee and an omelette and went to call Devlin on the public telephone.

Devlin, who had been waiting anxiously, said, 'Are you all right?'

'Fine,' she said. 'I even slept on the train. Don't worry. They can't have any idea where I am. When will I see you again?'

'Soon,' Devlin told her. 'We've got to get you to London safely first. Now listen to me. When the hydrofoil gets into Jersey, you'll be met by a man called Martin. Alexander Martin. Apparently he's a bit of a fan of yours so he knows what you look like.'

'I see. Anything else?'

'Not really.'

'Good, then I'll get back to my omelette, Professor.'

She rang off and Devlin replaced the receiver. A girl and a half, he told himself as he went into the kitchen. In the cottage, Harry Cussane was already phoning Paul Cherny.

Croix was a small airfield with a control tower, two hangars and three nissen huts, headquarters of an aero club but also used by Pierre Lebel to operate his air taxi service. Lebel was a dark, taciturn man who never asked questions if the price was right. He had flown for Belov on a number of occasions and knew Turkin and Shepilov well. He hadn't the slightest idea that they were Russian. Something illegal about them, he'd always thought, but as long as it didn't involve drugs and the price was right, he didn't mind. He was waiting for the two men when they arrived, opened the door of the main hangar so that they could drive inside.

'Which plane?' Turkin asked.

'We'll use the Chieftain. Faster than the Cessna and there's a headwind all the way to Golfe St Malo.'

'When do we leave?'

'As soon as you like.'

'But I thought the airport at Jersey wasn't open until seven?'

'Whoever told you that got it wrong. It's officially seven-thirty for air taxis. However, the airport is open for the paper plane from five-thirty.'

'Paper plane?'

'Newspapers from England. Post and so on. They're usually sympathetic to a request for an early landing, especially if they know you. I did get the impression there was some urgency on this one?'

'There certainly is,' Turkin told him.

'Good, let's go up to the office and settle the business end of things.'

The office was up a flight of rickety stairs, small and cluttered, the desk untidy, the whole lit by a single bulb. Turkin handed Lebel an envelope. 'Better count it.'

'Oh, I will,' the Frenchman said, and then the phone rang. He answered it at once, then passed it to Turkin. 'For you.'

Belov said, 'She's made contact with Devlin from Rennes. There's a new complication. She's being met off the hydrofoil in Jersey by an Alexander Martin.'

'Is he a pro?' Turkin asked.

'No information on him at all. One wouldn't have

thought they'd have any of their people in a place like Jersey. Still . . .'

'No problem,' Turkin said. 'We'll handle it.'

'Good luck.'

The line went dead and Turkin turned to Lebel. 'All right, my friend. Ready when you are.'

It was just six o'clock when they landed at Jersey Airport, a fine, blustery morning, the sky already lightening in the east, an orange glow on the horizon as the sun came up. The officer on duty at customs and immigration was pleasant and courteous. No reason not to be, for their papers were in order and Jersey was well used to handling thousands of French visitors each year.

'Stopping over?' he asked Lebel.

'No, straight back to Paris,' the Frenchman told him.

'And you, gentlemen?'

'Three or four days. Business and pleasure,' Turkin said.

'And nothing to declare? You've read the notice?'

'Not a thing.' Turkin offered his holdall.

The officer shook his head. 'All right, gentlemen. Have a nice stay.'

They shook hands formally with Lebel and passed out into the arrival hall, which at that time of the morning was deserted. There were one or two cars parked outside, but the taxi rank was empty. There was a telephone on the wall, but just as Turkin was moving to use it, Shepilov touched his arm and pointed. A cab was drawing up at the entrance to the airport. Two air hostesses got out and went in. The Russians waited and the cab drew up beside them.

'Early start, gentlemen,' the driver said.

'Yes, we're just in from Paris,' Turkin told him. 'Private flight.'

'Oh, I see. Where can I take you?'

Turkin, who had spent much of the flight examining the Jersey guide book Irana had provided, particularly the town map of St Helier, said, 'The Weighbridge, isn't that right? By the harbour.'

The taxi drew away. 'You don't need an hotel, then?'

'We're meeting friends later. They're taking care of that sort of thing. We thought we'd get some breakfast.'

'You'll be all right there. There's a café close to the Weighbridge opens early. I'll show you.'

The roads, at that time in the morning, were far from busy and the run down to Bel Royal and along the dual carriageway of Victoria Avenue took little more than ten minutes. The sun was coming up now and the view across St Aubin's Bay was spectacular, the tide in so that Elizabeth Castle on its rock was surrounded by water. Ahead of them was the town, the harbour breakwater, cranes lifting into the sky in the distance.

The driver turned in by the car park at the end of the esplanade. 'Here we are, gentlemen. The weighbridge. There's the tourist office. Open later if you need information. The café is just across the road over there around the corner. We'll call that three pounds.'

Turkin, who had been supplied with several hundred pounds in English banknotes by Irana, took a fiver from his wallet. 'Keep it. You've been very kind. Where's the marina from here?'

The driver pointed. 'Far end of the harbour. You can walk round.'

Turkin nodded to the breakwater stretching out into the bay. 'And the boats come in there?'

'That's right. Albert Quay. You can see the car ferry ramp from here. Hydrofoils berth further along.'

'Good,' Turkin said. 'Many thanks.'

They got out and the cab moved away. There was a public toilet a few yards away; without a word, Turkin led the way in and Shepilov followed. Turkin opened his holdall and burrowed under the clothing it contained, prising up the false bottom to reveal two handguns. He slipped one in his pocket and gave Shepilov the other. The weapons were automatics, each gun fitted with a silencer.

Turkin zipped up his holdall. 'So far so good. Let's take a look at the marina.'

There were several hundred boats moored there of every shape and size: yachts, motor cruisers, speedboats. They found the office of a boat hire firm easily enough, but it was not open yet.

'Too early,' Turkin said. 'Let's go down and have a look round.'

They walked along one of the swaying pontoons, boats moored on either side, paused, then turned into another. Things had always worked for Turkin. He was a great believer in his destiny. The nonsense over Tanya Voroninova had been an unfortunate hiccup in his career, but soon to be put right, he was confident of that. And now, fate took a hand in the game.

There was a motor cruiser moored at the end of the pontoon, dazzlingly white with a blue band above the watermark. The name on the stern was *L'Alouette*, registered Granville, which he knew was a port along the coast from St Malo. A couple came out on deck talking in French, the man tall and bearded with glasses. He wore a dark reefer coat. The woman wore jeans and a similar coat, a scarf around her head.

As the man helped her over the rail, Turkin heard him say, 'We'll walk round to the bus station. Get a taxi from there to the airport. The flight to Guernsey leaves at eight.'

'What time are we booked back?' she asked.

'Four o'clock. We'll have time for breakfast at the airport.'

They walked away. Shepilov said, 'What is Guernsey?'

'The next island,' Turkin told him. 'I read about it in the guide book. There's an inter-island flying service several times a day. It only takes fifteen minutes. A day out for tourists.'

'Are you thinking what I am?' Shepilov enquired.

'It's a nice boat,' Turkin said. 'We could be in St Malo and on our way hours before those two get back this afternoon.' He took out a pack of French cigarettes and offered one to his companion. 'Give them time to move away, then we'll check.'

They took a walk around the pontoons, returning in ten minutes and going on board. The door to the companionway which led below was locked. Shepilov produced a spring blade knife and forced it expertly. There were two cabins neatly furnished, a saloon and a galley. They went back on deck and tried the wheelhouse. The door to that was open.

'No ignition key,' Shepilov said.

'No problem. Give me your knife.' Turkin worked his way up behind the control panel and pulled down several wires. It took only a moment to make the right connection and when he pressed the starter button, the engine turned over at once. He checked the fuel gauge. 'Tank's three quarters full.' He unfastened the wires again. 'You know, I think this is our day, Ivan,' he said to Shepilov.

They walked back round to the other side of the harbour and turned along the top of the Albert Quay, pausing at the end to look down at the hydrofoil berth.

'Excellent.' Turkin looked at his watch. 'Now all we have to do is wait. Let's find that café and try some breakfast.'

* * *

At St Malo, the Condor hydrofoil moved out of the harbour past the Mole des Noires. It was almost full, mainly French tourists visiting Jersey for the day to judge from the conversations Tanya overheard. Once out of harbour, the hydrofoil started to lift, increasing speed, and she gazed out into the morning feeling exhilarated. She'd done it. Beaten all of them. Once in Jersey, she was as good as in London. She leaned back in the comfortable seat and closed her eyes.

Alex Martin turned his big Peugeot estate car on to the Albert Quay and drove along until he found a convenient parking place, which wasn't easy for the car ferry was in from Weymouth and things were rather busy. He had not slept at all and was beginning to feel the effects, although a good breakfast had helped and a cold shower. He wore navy-blue slacks, a polo neck sweater in the same colour and a sports jacket in pale blue tweed by Yves St Laurent. Partly this was a desire to make an impression on Tanya Voroninova. His music meant an enormous amount to him and the chance to meet a performer he admired so much was of more importance to him than either Ferguson or Fox could have imagined.

His hair was still a little damp and he ran his fingers through it, suddenly uneasy. He opened the glove compartment of the Peugeot and took out the handgun he found there. It was a .38 Smith and Wesson Special, the Airweight model with the two inch barrel, a weapon much favoured by the CIA. Six years before, he'd taken it from the body of a Protestant terrorist in Belfast, a member of the outlawed UVF. The man had tried to kill Martin, had almost succeeded. Martin had killed him instead. It had never worried him, that was the strange thing. No regrets, no nightmares.

'Come off it, Alex,' he said softly. 'This is Jersey.'

But the feeling wouldn't go away, Belfast all over again, that touch of unease. Remembering an old trick from undercover days, he slipped the gun into the waistband at the small of his back. Frequently even a body search missed a weapon secreted there.

He sat smoking a cigarette, listening to Radio Jersey on the car radio, until the hydrofoil moved in through the harbour entrance. Even then, he didn't get out. There were the usual formalities to be passed through, customs and so on. He waited until the first passengers emerged from the exit of the passenger terminal then got out and moved forward. He recognized Tanya at once in her black jumpsuit, the trenchcoat over her shoulders like a cloak.

He moved forward to meet her. 'Miss Voroninova?'

She examined him warily. 'Or should I say Miss Frank?'

'Who are you?'

'Alexander Martin. I'm here to see you get on your plane safely. You're booked on the ten-past-ten to London. Plenty of time.'

She put a hand on his arm, relaxing completely, unaware of Turkin and Shepilov on the other side of the road against the wall, backs partially turned. 'You've no idea how good it is to see a friendly face.'

'This way.' He guided her to the Peugeot. 'I saw you

play the Emperor at the Proms at the Albert Hall last year. You were amazing.'

He put her into the passenger seat, went round to the other side and got behind the wheel.

'Do you play yourself?' she asked, as if by instinct.

'Oh, yes.' He turned the ignition key. 'But not like you.'

Behind them, the rear doors opened on each side and the two Russians got in, Turkin behind Tanya. 'Don't argue, there's a silenced pistol against your spine and hers. These seats aren't exactly body armour. We can kill you both without a sound and walk away.'

Tanya went rigid. Alex Martin said calmly, 'You know these men?'

'GRU. Military Intelligence.'

'I see. What happens now?' he asked Turkin.

'She goes back if we can take her. If not, she dies. The only important thing is that she doesn't talk to the wrong people. Any nonsense from you and she'll be the first to go. We know our duty.'

'I'm sure you do.'

'Because we are strong and you are weak, pretty boy,' Turkin told him. 'That's why we'll win in the end. Walk right up to Buckingham Palace.'

'Wrong time of the year, old son,' Alex said. 'The Queen's at Sandringham.'

Turkin scowled. 'Very amusing. Now get this thing moving round to the Marina.'

*   *   *

They walked along the pontoon towards *L'Alouette*, Martin with a hand on the girl's elbow, the two Russians walking behind. Martin helped Tanya over the rail. She was trembling, he could feel it.

Turkin opened the companionway door. 'Down below, both of you.' He followed close behind, his gun in his hand now. 'Stop!' he said to Martin when they reached the saloon. 'Lean on the table, legs spread. You sit down,' he told Tanya.

Shepilov stood on one side, gun in hand. Tanya was close to tears. Alex said gently, 'Keep smiling. Always pays.'

'You English really take the biscuit,' Turkin said as he searched him expertly. 'You're nothing any more. Yesterday's news. Just wait till the Argentinians blow you out of the water down there in the South Atlantic.' He lifted Martin's jacket at the rear and found the Airweight. 'Would you look at that?' he said to Shepilov. 'Amateur. I noticed some cord in the galley. Get it.'

Shepilov was soon back. 'And once at sea, it's the deep six?' Martin enquired.

'Something like that.' Turkin turned to Shepilov. 'Tie him up. We'd better get out of here fast. I'll get the engine started.'

He went up the companionway. Tanya had stopped trembling, her face pale, rage in her eyes and desperation. Martin shook his head a fraction and Shepilov kneed him painfully in the rear. 'Up you come, hands

186

behind you.' Martin could feel the muzzle of the silencer against his back. The Russian said to Tanya, 'Tie his wrists.'

Martin said, 'Don't they ever teach you chaps anything? You never stand that close to anyone.'

He swung, pivoting to the left, away from the barrel of the gun. It coughed once, drilling a hole in the bulkhead. His right hand caught the Russian's wrist, twisting it up and round, taut as a steel bar. Shepilov grunted and dropped the weapon and Martin's clenched left fist descended in a hammer blow, snapping the arm.

Shepilov cried out, dropping to one knee. Martin bent down and picked up the gun and miraculously, the Russian's other hand swung up, the blade of the spring knife flashing. Martin blocked it, aware of the sudden pain as the blade sliced through his sleeve, drawing blood. He punched Shepilov on the jaw, knuckles extended and kicked the knife under the seat.

Tanya was on her feet, but already there were hurried steps on deck. 'Ivan?' Turkin called.

Martin put a finger to his lips to the girl, brushed past her and went into the galley. A small ladder led to the forward hatch. He opened it and went out on deck as he heard Turkin start down.

It had begun to rain, a fine mist drifting in from the sea as he stepped lightly across the deck to the entrance of the companionway. Turkin had reached the bottom and stood there, gun in his right hand as he peered cautiously into the saloon. Martin didn't make a sound, gave him no chance at all. He simply extended his pistol and shot him neatly through the right arm. Turkin cried out, dropped his weapon and staggered into the saloon and Martin went down the companionway.

Tanya moved to join him. Martin picked up Turkin's gun and put it in his pocket. Turkin leaned against the table, clutching his arm, glaring at him. Shepilov was just pulling himself up and sank on to the bench with a groan. Martin swung Turkin round and searched his pockets until he found his gun. He turned to Turkin again.

'I was careful with the arm. You aren't going to die – yet. I don't know who owns this boat, but you obviously meant to leave in it, you and chummy here. I'd get on with it if I were you. You'd only be an embarrassment to our people and I'm sure they'd like you back in Moscow. You ought to be able to manage between you.'

'Bastard!' Peter Turkin said in despair.

'Not in front of the lady,' Alex Martin told him. He pushed Tanya Voroninova up the companionway and turned. 'As a matter of interest, you two wouldn't last one bad Saturday night in Belfast,' then he followed the girl up to the deck.

When they reached the Peugeot, he took off his jacket gingerly. There was blood on his shirt sleeve and he fished out his handkerchief. 'Would you mind doing what you can with that?'

She bound it around the slash tightly. 'What kind of a man are you?'

'Well, I prefer Mozart myself,' Alex Martin said as he pulled on his jacket. 'I say, would you look at that?'

Beyond, on the outer edge of the marina, *L'Alouette* was moving out of the harbour. 'They're leaving,' Tanya said.

'Poor sods,' Martin told her. 'Their next posting will probably be the Gulag after this.' He handed her into the Peugeot and smiled cheerfully as he got behind the wheel. 'Now let's get you up to the airport, shall we?'

At Heathrow Airport's Terminal One, Harry Fox sat in the security office, drank a cup of tea and enjoyed a cigarette with the duty sergeant. The phone rang, the sergeant answered, then passed it across.

'Harry?' Ferguson said.

'Sir.'

'She made it. She's on the plane. Just left Jersey.'

'No problems, sir?'

'Not if you exclude a couple of GRU bogeymen snatching her and Martin off the Albert Quay.'

Fox said, 'What happened?'

'He managed, that's what happened. We'll have to use that young man again. You did say he was Guards?'

'Yes, sir. Welsh.'

'Thought so. One can always tell,' Ferguson said cheerfully and rang off.

'No, Madame, nothing to pay,' the steward said to Tanya as the one-eleven climbed into the sky away from Jersey. 'The bar is free. What would you like? Vodka and tonic, gin and orange? Or we have champagne.'

Free champagne. Tanya nodded and took the frosted glass he offered her. To a new life, she thought and then she said softly, 'To you, Alexander Martin,' and emptied the glass in a long swallow.

Luckily, the housekeeper had the day off. Alex Martin disposed of his shirt, pushing it to the bottom of the garbage in one of the bins, then went to the bathroom and cleaned his arm. It really needed stitching, but to go to the hospital would have meant questions and that would never do. He pulled the edges of the cut together with neat butterflies of tape, an old soldier's trick, and bandaged it. He put on a bathrobe, poured himself a large Scotch and went into the sitting room. As he sat down, the phone rang.

His wife said, 'Darling, I phoned the office and they said you were taking the day off. Is anything wrong? You haven't been overdoing it again, have you?'

She knew nothing of the work he'd done for Ferguson in the past. No need to alarm her now. He smiled ruefully, noting the slash in the sleeve of the Yves St Laurent jacket on the chair next to him.

'Certainly not,' he said. 'You know me? Anything for a quiet life. I'm working at home today, that's all. Now tell me – how are the children?'

9

At Cavendish Square, Ferguson was seated at the desk holding the telephone, face grave when Harry Fox came in from the study with a telex message. Ferguson made a quick gesture with one hand, then said, 'Thank you, Minister,' and replaced the receiver.

'Trouble, sir?' Fox asked.

'As far as I'm concerned it is. The Foreign Office have just informed me that the Pope's visit is definitely on. The Vatican will make an announcement within the next few hours. What have you got?'

'Telex, sir. Information on the Task Force's progress. The bad news is that HMS *Antelope* has finally sunk. She was bombed by Skyhawks yesterday. The good news is that seven Argentinian jets have been brought down.'

'I'd be happier about that if I saw the wreckage, Harry. Probably half that figure in actuality. Battle of Britain all over again.'

'Perhaps, sir. Everybody claims a hit in the heat of the moment. It can be confusing.'

Ferguson stood up and lit one of his cheroots. 'I don't know, sometimes the bloody roof just seems to fall in. I've got the Pope coming, which we could well have done without. Cuchulain still on the loose over there, and now this nonsense about the Argentinians trying to buy Exocet missiles on the black market in Paris. Orders have gone through to pull Tony Villiers from behind enemy lines in the Falklands?'

'No problem, sir. He's being off-loaded by submarine in Uruguay. Flying from Montevideo by Air France direct to Paris. Should be there tomorrow.'

'Good. You'll have to go over on the shuttle. Brief him thoroughly, then get straight back here.'

'Will that be enough, sir?'

'Good God, yes. You know what Tony's like when he gets moving. Hell on wheels. He'll sort the opposition out over there, no problem. I need you here, Harry. What about the Voroninova girl?'

'As I told you, sir, we stopped off at Harrods on the way from Heathrow to get her a few things. Only had what she stood up in.'

'She'll be broke, of course,' Ferguson said. 'We'll have to tap the contingency fund.'

'As a matter of fact that won't be necessary, sir. It seems she has a very substantial bank account here. Record royalties and so on. She certainly won't have any difficulty in earning her living. They'll be clamouring for her, all the impresarios, when they know she's available.'

'That will have to wait. She's very definitely to stay under wraps until I say so. What's she like?'

'Very nice indeed, sir. I settled her into the spare room and she was having a bath.'

'Yes, well don't let's make her too comfortable, Harry. We want to get on with this thing. I've heard from Devlin and it seems another of McGuiness's hatchet men, the one who was supposed to be keeping an eye on Cherny, has turned up in the Liffey. He doesn't waste time, our friend.'

'I see, sir,' Fox said. 'So what are you suggesting?'

'We'll get her over to Dublin now – this afternoon. You can escort her, Harry. Hand her over to Devlin at the airport, then get back here. You can go to Paris on the morning shuttle.'

Fox said mildly, 'She might just feel like sitting down for a moment. Taking a deep breath. That sort of thing.'

'So would we all, Harry, and if that's a subtle way of telling me how you feel, then all I can say is you should have taken that job they offered you at your uncle's merchant bank. Start at ten, finish at four.'

'And terribly, terribly boring, sir.'

Kim opened the door at that moment and ushered in Tanya Voroninova. Her eyes were slightly hollowed, but she looked surprisingly well, the general effect enhanced by the blue cashmere sweater and neat tweed skirt she had purchased at Harrods. Fox made the introductions.

'Miss Voroninova. A great pleasure,' Ferguson said. 'You've certainly had an active time of it. Please sit down.'

She sat on the couch by the fire. 'Have you any idea what's happening in Paris?' she asked.

'Not yet,' Fox said. 'We'll find out in the end, but if you want an educated guess, the KGB never care for failure at the best of times and if we consider your foster-father's special interest in this case . . .' He shrugged. 'I wouldn't care to be in Turkin or Shepilov's shoes.'

'Even such a shrewd old campainer as Nikolai Belov will have difficulty surviving this one,' Ferguson put in.

'So, what happens now?' she asked. 'Do I see Professor Devlin again?'

'Yes, but that means flying over to Dublin. I know your feet have hardly touched the ground, but time is of the essence. I'd like you to go later on this afternoon if that's all right. Captain Fox will escort you and we'll arrange for Devlin to meet you at Dublin Airport.'

She was still on a high, and somehow it seemed a part of what had already happened. 'When do we leave?'

'The early evening plane,' Devlin said. 'Sure, I'll be there. No problem.'

'You'll make your own arrangements about the necessary meeting with McGuiness so that she can look at whatever photos or other material they want to show her?'

'I'll take care of it,' Devlin said.

'Sooner rather than later,' Ferguson told him firmly.

'I hear and obey, O Genie of the lamp,' Devlin said. 'Now let me talk to her.'

Ferguson handed her the phone. Tanya said, 'Professor Devlin? What is it?'

'I've just heard from Paris. The Mona Lisa is smiling all over her face. See you soon.'

And in Moscow important things had been happening that morning. Events that were to affect the whole of Russia and world politics generally, for Yuri Andropov, head of the KGB since 1967, was named Secretary of the Communist Party Central Committee. He still inhabited his old office at KGB headquarters at Dzerhinsky Square and it was there that he summoned Maslovsky just after noon. The General stood in front of the desk, filled with foreboding, for Andropov was possibly the only man he had ever known of whom he was genuinely afraid. Andropov was writing, his pen scratching the paper. He ignored Maslovsky for a while, then spoke without looking up.

'There is little point in referring to the gross inefficiency shown by your department in the matter of the Cuchulain affair.'

'Comrade.' Maslovsky didn't attempt to defend himself.

'You have given orders that he is to be eliminated together with Cherny?'

'Yes, Comrade.'

'The sooner the better.' Andropov paused, removed his glasses and ran a hand over his forehead. 'Then there is the matter of your foster-daughter. She is now safely in London due to the bungling of your people.'

'Yes, Comrade.'

'From which city Brigadier Ferguson is having her flown to Dublin, where the IRA intend to give her any help she needs to identify Cuchulain?'

'That would appear to be the case,' Maslovsky said weakly.

'The Provisional IRA is a fascist organization as far as I am concerned, hopelessly tainted by its links with the Catholic Church, and Tanya Voroninova is a traitor to her country, her party and her class. You will send an immediate signal to the man Lubov in Dublin. He will eliminate her as well as Cherny and Cuchulain.'

He replaced his glasses, picked up his pen and started to write again. Maslovsky said in a hoarse voice, 'Please, Comrade, perhaps . . .'

Andropov glanced up in surprise. 'Does my order give you some sort of problem, Comrade General?'

Maslovsky, wilting under those cold eyes, shook his head hurriedly. 'No, of course not, Comrade,' and he turned and went out, feeling just the slightest tremor in his limbs.

At the Soviet Embassy in Dublin, Lubov had already received a signal from Paris informing him that Tanya

Voroninova had slipped the net. He was still in the radio room digesting this startling piece of news when the second signal came through, the one from Maslovsky in Moscow. The operator recorded it, placed the tape in the machine and Lubov keyed in his personal code. When he read the message he felt physically sick. He went to his office, locked the door and got a bottle of Scotch from the cupboard. He had one and then another. Finally he phoned Cherny.

'Costello, here.' It was the code name he used on such occasions. 'Are you busy?'

'Not particularly,' Cherny told him.

'We must meet.'

'The usual place?'

'Yes, I must talk to you first. Very important. However, we must also arrange to see our mutual friend this evening. Dun Street, I think. Can you arrange that?'

'It's very unusual.'

'As I said, matters of importance. Ring me back to confirm this evening's meeting.'

Cherny was definitely worried. Dun Street was a code name for a disused warehouse on City Quay which he had leased under a company name some years previously, but that wasn't the point. What was really important was the fact that he, Cussane and Lubov had never all met together in the same place before. He phoned Cussane at the cottage without success, so he tried the Catholic Secretariat offices in Dublin. Cussane answered at once.

'Thank God,' said Cherny. 'I tried the cottage.'

'Yes, I've just got in,' Cussane told him. 'Is there a problem?'

'I'm not sure. I feel uneasy. Can I speak freely?'

'You usually do on this line.'

'Our friend Costello has been in touch. Asked me to meet him at three-thirty.'

'Usual place?'

'Yes, but he's also asked me to arrange for the three of us to meet at Dun Street tonight.'

'That *is* unusual.'

'I know. I don't like it.'

'Perhaps he has instructions for us to pull out,' Cussane said. 'Did he say anything about the girl?'

'No. Should he have done?'

'I just wondered what was happening there, that's all. Tell him I'll see you at Dun Street at six-thirty. Don't worry, Paul. I'll handle things.'

He rang off and Cherny got straight back to Lubov. 'Six-thirty, is that all right?'

'Fine,' Lubov told him.

'He asked me if you'd heard anything about the girl in Paris.'

'No, not a word,' Lubov lied. 'I'll see you at three-thirty.' He rang off, poured himself a drink, then unlocked the top drawer of his desk, took out a case and opened it. It contained a Stechkin automatic pistol and a silencer. Gingerly, he started fitting them together.

*   *   *

In his office at the Secretariat, Harry Cussane stood at the window, looking down into the street. He had listened in to Devlin's conversations with Ferguson before leaving the cottage and knew that Tanya Voroninova was due that evening. It was inconceivable that Lubov would not have heard, either from Moscow or Paris, so why hadn't he mentioned it?

The meeting at Dun Street was unusual enough in itself, but in view of that meeting, why meet Cherny in the usual back row at the cinema first? What could possibly be the need? It didn't fit, any of it, and every instinct that Cussane possessed, honed by his years in the trenches, told him so. Whatever Lubov wanted to see them for, it was not conversation.

Paul Cherny was reaching for his raincoat when there was a knock at the door of his rooms. When he opened it, Harry Cussane was standing outside. He wore a dark trilby hat and raincoat of the kind affected by priests and looked agitated.

'Paul, thank God I caught you.'

'Why, what is it?' Cherny demanded.

'The IRA man who followed you, the one I disposed of the other day. They've set another one on. This way.'

Cherny's rooms were on the first floor of the old grey-stone college building. Cussane went up the stairs quickly to the next floor and turned at once up another flight of stairs.

'Where are we going?' Cherny called.

'I'll show you.'

On the top landing, the tall Georgian window at the end had its bottom half pushed up. Cussane peered out. 'Over there,' he said. 'On the other side of the quad.'

Cherny looked down to the stone flags and the green grass of the quadrangle. 'Where?' he asked.

There was the hand in the small of his back, a sudden violent push. He managed to cry out, but only just as he overbalanced across the low windowsill and plunged head first towards the stone flags eighty-feet below.

Cussane ran along the corridor and descended the back stairs hurriedly. In a sense, he had been telling the truth. McGuiness had indeed replaced Murphy with a new watchdog, in fact two of them this time, sitting in a green Ford Escort near the main entrance, not that it was going to do them much good now.

Lubov had the back row to himself. In fact, there were only five or six people in the cinema at all as far as he could see in the dim light. He was early, but that was by intention, and he fingered the silenced Stechkin in his pocket, his palms damp with sweat. He'd brought a flask with him and took it out now and swallowed deep. More Scotch to give him the courage he needed. First Cherny and then Cussane, but that should be easier if he was at the warehouse first and waiting in ambush.

He took another swig at the flask, had just replaced it in his pocket when there was a movement in the darkness and someone sat down beside him.

'Paul?' he turned his head.

An arm slid round his neck, a hand clamped over his mouth. In the second that he recognized Cussane's pale face under the brim of the black hat, the needle point of the stiletto the other held in his right hand probed in under his ribs, thrusting up into the heart. There was not even time to struggle. A kind of blinding light, no pain, then only darkness.

Cussane wiped the blade carefully on Lubov's jacket, eased him back in the seat as if asleep. He found the Stechkin in the dead man's pocket, took it out and slipped it into his own. He had been right, as usual. The final proof. He got up, went down the aisle, a shadow only in his black coat, and left through one of the exit doors.

He was back at the office in the Secretariat within half an hour, had hardly sat down when Monsignor Halloran came in. Halloran was very cheerful and obviously excited.

'Have you heard? Just had the confirmation from the Vatican. The Pope's visit is on.'

'So they've decided. You'll be going across?'

'Yes indeed. Seat booked in Canterbury Cathedral.

An historic occasion, Harry. Something for people to tell their grandchildren about.'

'For those who have any,' Cussane smiled.

Halloran laughed. 'Exactly, which hardly applies to us. I must be off. I've got a dozen things to organize.'

Cussane sat there thinking about it, then reached for his raincoat where he'd thrown it on a chair and took the poniard out in its leather sheath. He put it in one of the desk drawers then took out the Stechkin. What a bungling amateur Lubov had been to use a weapon of Russian manufacture. But it was the proof that he had needed. It meant that to his masters he was not only expendable. He was now a liability.

'So what now, Harry Cussane?' he asked himself softly. 'Where do you go?'

Strange that habit, when speaking to himself, of addressing Cussane by his full name. It was as if he were another person which, in a way, he was. The phone rang and when he answered, Devlin spoke to him.

'There you are.'

'Where are you?'

'Dublin airport. I'm picking up a house-guest. A very pretty girl, actually. I think you'll like her. I thought we all might have supper tonight.'

'That sounds nice,' Cussane said calmly. 'I've agreed to take evening Mass, though, at the village church. I'll be finished at eight. Is that all right?'

'Fine. We'll look forward to seeing you.'

Cussane put the phone down. He could run, of course,

but where and to what purpose? In any event, the play had at least one more act to go, all his instincts told him that.

'No place to hide, Harry Cussane,' he said softly.

When Harry Fox and Tanya came through the gate into the arrival hall, Devlin was waiting, leaning against a pillar, smoking a cigarette, wearing the black felt hat and trenchcoat. He came forward, smiling.

'*Cead mile failte,*' he said and took the young woman's hands. 'That's Irish for a hundred thousand welcomes.'

'*Go raibh maith agat.*' Fox gave him the ritual thanks.

'Stop showing off.' Devlin took her bag. 'His mother was a decent Irishwoman, thank the Lord.'

Her face was shining. 'I'm so excited. All this is so – so unbelievable.'

Fox said, 'Right, you're in safe hands now. I'm off. There's a return flight in an hour. I'd better book in. We'll be in touch, Liam.'

He went off through the crowd and Devlin took her elbow and led her to the main entrance. 'A nice man,' she said. 'His hand? What happened?'

'He picked up a bag with a bomb in it in Belfast one bad night and didn't throw it fast enough. He gets by very well with the electronic marvel they've given him.'

'You say that so calmly,' she said as they crossed to the carpark.

'He wouldn't thank you for the wrong kind of

sympathy. Comes of his particular kind of upbringing. Eton, the Guards. They teach you to get on with it, not cry in your beer.' He handed her into his old Alfa Romeo sports car. 'Harry's a special breed, just like that ould bastard Ferguson. What's known as a gentleman.'

'Which you are not?'

'God save us, my ould mother would turn in her grave to hear you even suggest it,' he said as he drove away. 'So, you decided to give things some more thought after I left Paris? What happened?'

She told him everything. Belov, the phone conversation with Maslovsky, Shepilov and Turkin, and finally, Alex Martin in Jersey.

Devlin was frowning thoughtfully as she finished. 'So they were on to you? Actually waiting in Jersey? How in the hell would they know that?'

'I asked about the train times at hotel reception,' she told him. 'I didn't give my name or room number. I thought that covered it. Perhaps Belov and his people were able to make the right sort of enquiries.'

'Maybe. Still, you're here now. You'll be staying with me at my cottage in Kilrea. It isn't far. I've got a call to make when we get in. With luck, we'll be able to set up the right kind of meeting for you tomorrow. Lots of photos for you to plough through.'

'I hope something comes of it,' she said.

'Don't we all? Anyway, a quiet night. I'll make the supper and a good friend of mine is joining us.'

'Anyone interesting?'

'The kind of man you'd find rather thin on the ground where you come from. A Catholic priest. Father Harry Cussane. I think you'll like him.'

He phoned McGuiness from his study. 'The girl is here. Staying with me at my place. How soon can you set up the right meeting?'

'Never mind that,' McGuiness told him. 'Have you heard about Cherny?'

'Devlin was immediately alert. 'No.'

'Took a very long fall from a very high window at Trinity College this afternoon. The thing is, did he fall or was he pushed?'

'I suppose one could say his end was fortuitous,' Devlin said.

'For one person only,' McGuiness told him. 'Jesus, I'd like to get my hands on that sod.'

'Set up the meeting with the girl then,' Devlin said. 'Maybe she'll recognize him.'

'I'd go to confession again if I thought that could be guaranteed. Okay, leave it with me. I'll get back to you.'

Cussane robed for Mass in the sacristy, very calm, very cold. It wasn't like a play any longer. More like an improvisation in which the actors created a story for themselves. He had no idea what was going to happen.

The four acolytes who waited for him were village

boys, clean and neat and angelic in their scarlet cassocks and white cottas. He settled the stole around his neck, picked up his prayer book and turned to them.

'Let's make it special tonight, shall we?'

He pressed the bellpush at the door. A moment later, the organ started to play. One of the boys opened the door and they moved through into the small church in procession.

Devlin was working in the kitchen preparing steaks. Tanya opened the French windows and was immediately aware of the organ music drifting across the garden from the other side of the wall. She went in to Devlin. 'What's that?'

'There's a convent over there and a hospice. Their chapel is the village church. That'll be Harry Cussane celebrating Mass. He won't be long.'

She went back into the living room and stood listening at the French windows. It was nice and not only peaceful. The organ playing was really rather good. She crossed the lawn and opened the door in the wall. The chapel, on the end of the convent, looked picturesque and inviting, soft light flooding from the windows. She went up the path and opened the oaken door.

There were only a handful of villagers, two people in wheelchairs who were obviously patients from the hospice and several nuns. Sister Anne-Marie played the organ.

It was not much of an instrument and the damp atmosphere had a bad effect on the reeds, but she was good, had spent a year at the Conservatoire in Paris as a young girl before heeding God's call and turning to the religious life.

The lights were very dim, mainly candles, and the church was a place of shadows and calm peace, the nuns' voices sweet as they sang the offertory: '*Domine Jesu Christ, Rex Floriae* . . .' At the altar, Harry Cussane prayed for all sinners everywhere whose actions only cut them off from the fact of God's infinite mercy and love. Tanya took a seat to one side on her own, moved by the atmosphere. The truth was that she had never attended a church service like this in her life. She couldn't see much of Cussane's face. He was simply the chief figure down there at the altar in the dim light, fascinating to her in his robes as was the whole business.

The Mass continued, most of those in the congregation went forward to the rail to receive the body and blood of Christ. She watched, as he moved from one person to the other, the head bending to murmur the ritual words and she was filled with a strange unease. It was as if she knew this man, some trick of physical movement that seemed familiar.

When the Mass was over, the final absolution given, he paused on the steps to address the congregation. 'And in your prayers during the coming days, I would ask each one of you to pray for the Holy Father, soon to visit England at a most difficult time.' He moved forward a little, the candlelight falling on his face. 'Pray for him that your prayers, added to his own, grant him the strength to accomplish his mission.'

His gaze passed over the entire congregation and for a moment it was as if he was looking at her directly, then he moved on. Tanya froze in horror, the shock, the most terrible she had ever known in her life. When he spoke the words of the benediction, it was as if his lips moved with no sound. The face – the face which had haunted her dreams for years. Older, of course, kinder even, and yet unmistakably the face of Mikhail Kelly, the man they had named Cuchulain.

What happened then was strange, yet perhaps not so strange if one considered the circumstances. The shock was so profound that it seemed to drain all strength from her and she remained in the half-darkness at the back of the church while people moved out and Cussane and the acolytes disappeared into the sacristy. It was very quiet in the church and she sat there, trying to make sense of things. Cuchulain was Father Harry Cussane, Devlin's friend, and it explained so many things. Oh, my God, she thought, what am I going to do? And then the sacristy door opened and Cussane stepped out.

Things were almost ready in the kitchen. Devlin checked the oven, whistling softly to himself and called, 'Have you laid the table in there?'

There was no reply. He went into the living room. Not only was the table not laid but there was no sign of Tanya. Then he noticed the French window ajar, took off his apron and moved forward.

'Tanya?' he called into the garden, and in the same moment saw that the door in the garden wall stood open.

Cussane wore a black suit and clerical collar. He paused for a moment, aware of her presence although he made no sign. He'd noticed her almost at once during the Mass. The fact that she was a stranger would have made her stand out, but in the circumstances it had been obvious who she must be. Knowing that, there was the ghost of the child there in the face, the child who had struggled as he held her that day in Drumore, all those years ago. Eyes never changed, and the eyes he had always remembered.

He turned at the altar rail, dropping to one knee to genuflect, and Tanya, in a panic now and terribly afraid, forced herself to her feet and moved along the aisle. The door to one of the confessional boxes stood partially open and she slipped inside. When she pulled it close, there was a slight creaking. She heard him walk down the aisle, the steps slow, distinct on the stone flags. They came closer. Stopped.

He said softly in Russian, 'I know you are there, Tanya Voroninova. You can come out now.'

*　　*　　*

211

She stood there, shivering, very cold. He was quite calm, his face grave. Still in Russian, he said, 'It's been a long time.'

She said, 'So, do you kill me like you killed my father? As you have killed so many others?'

'I hoped that wouldn't be necessary.' He stood there looking at her, his hands in the pockets of his jacket, and then he smiled gently and there was a kind of sadness there. 'I've heard you on records. You have a remarkable talent.'

'So have you.' She felt stronger now. 'For death and destruction. They chose you well. My foster-father knew what he was doing.'

'Not really,' he said. 'Nothing is ever that simple. I happened to be available. The right tool at the right time.'

She took a deep breath. 'What happens now?'

'I thought we were supposed to be having dinner together, you, I and Liam,' he said.

The porch door banged open and Devlin walked in. 'Tanya?' he called and then paused. 'Oh, there you are. So you two have met?'

'Yes, Liam, a long, long time ago,' Harry Cussane told him, and his hand came out of the right pocket of his jacket holding the Stechkin he had taken from Lubov.

At the cottage, he found cord in the kitchen drawer. 'The steaks smell good, Liam. Better turn the oven off.'

'Would you look at that?' Devlin said to the girl. 'He thinks of everything.'

'The only reason I've got this far,' Cussane said calmly.

They went into the living room. He didn't tie them up, but motioned them to sit on the sofa by the fire. He stepped on to the hearth, reached up inside the chimney and found the Walther hanging on its nail that Devlin always kept there for emergencies.

'Keeping you out of temptation, Liam.'

'He knows all my little secrets,' Devlin said to Tanya. 'But then he would. I mean, we've been friends for twenty years now.' The bitterness was there in the voice, the shake of raw anger, and he helped himself to a cigarette from the box on the side table without asking permission and lit it.

Cussane sat some distance away at the dining table and held up the Stechkin. 'These things make very little sound, old friend. No one knows that better than you. No tricks. No foolish Devlin gallantry. I'd hate to have to kill you.'

He laid the Stechkin on the table and lit a cigarette himself.

'Friend, is it?' Devlin said. 'About as true a friend as you are priest.'

'Friend,' Cussane insisted, 'and I've been a good priest. Ask anyone who knew me on the Falls Road in Belfast in sixty-nine.'

'Fine,' Devlin said. 'Only even an idiot like me can make two and two make four occasionally. Your masters put you in deep. To become a priest was your cover. Would I be right in thinking that you chose that seminary outside Boston for your training because I was English Professor there?'

'Of course. You were an important man in the IRA in those days, Liam. The advantages that the relationship offered for the future were obvious, but friends we became and friends we stayed. You cannot avoid that fact.'

'Sweet Jesus!' Devlin shook his head. 'Who are you, Harry? Who are you really?'

'My father was Sean Kelly.'

Devlin stared at him in astonishment. 'But I knew him well. We served in the Lincoln Washington Brigade in the Spanish Civil War. Just a minute. He married a Russian girl he met in Madrid.'

'My mother. My parents returned to Ireland where I was born. My father was hanged in England in nineteen-forty for his part in the IRA bombing campaign of that time. My mother and I lived in Dublin till nineteen-fifty-three, then she took me to Russia.'

Devlin said, 'The KGB must have fastened on you like leeches.'

'Something like that.'

'They discovered his special talents,' Tanya put in. 'Murder, for example.'

'No,' Cussane answered mildly. 'When I was first processed by the psychologists, Paul Cherny indicated that my special talent was for the stage.'

214

'An actor, is it?' Devlin said. 'Well, you're in the right job for it.'

'Not really. No audience, you see.' Cussane concentrated on Tanya. 'I doubt whether I've killed more than Liam. In what way are we different?'

'He fought for a cause,' she told him passionately.

'Exactly. I am a soldier, Tanya. I fight for my country – our country. As a matter of interest, I'm not an officer of the KGB. I am a lieutenant-colonel in Military Intelligence.' He smiled deprecatingly at Devlin. 'They kept promoting me.'

'But the things you've done. The killing,' she said. 'Innocent people.'

'There cannot be innocence in this world, not with Man in it. The Church teaches us that. There is always iniquity in this life – life is unfair. We must deal with the world as it is, not as it might have been.'

'Jesus!' Devlin said. 'One minute you're Cuchulain, the next you're a priest again. Have you any idea who you really are?'

'When I am priest, then priest I am,' Cussane told him. 'There is no avoiding that. The Church would be the first to say it in spite of what I have been. But the other me fights for his country. I have nothing to apologize for. I'm at war.'

'Very convenient,' Devlin said. 'So, the Church gives you your answer or is it the KGB – or is there a difference?'

'Does it matter?'

'Damn you, Harry, tell me one thing? How did you

know we were on to you? How did you know about Tanya? Was it me?' he exploded. 'But how could it have been me?'

'You mean you checked your telephone as usual?' Cussane was at the drinks cabinet now, the Stechkin in his hand. He poured Bushmills into three glasses, carried them on a tray to the table in front of the sofa, took one and stepped back. 'I was using special equipment up there in the attic of my place. Directional microphone and other stuff. There wasn't much that went on here that I missed.'

Devlin took a deep breath, but when he lifted his glass, his hand was steady. 'So much for friendship.' He swallowed the whiskey. 'So, what happens now?'

'To you?'

'No, to you, you fool. Where do you go, Harry? Back home to dear old Mother Russia?' He shook his head and turned to Tanya. 'Come to think of it, Russia isn't his home.'

Cussane didn't feel anger then. There was no despair in his heart. All his life, he had played each part that was required of him, cultivated the kind of professional coolness necessary for a well-judged performance. There had been little room for real emotion in his life. Any action, even the good ones, had been simply a reaction to the given situation, an essential part of the performance. Or so he told himself. And yet he truly liked Devlin, always had. And the girl? He looked at Tanya now. He did not want to harm the girl.

Devlin, as if sensing a great deal of this, said softly, 'Where do you run, Harry? Is there anywhere?'

'No,' Harry Cussane said calmly. 'Nowhere to go. No place to hide. For what I have done, your IRA friends would dispose of me without hesitation. Ferguson certainly would not want me alive. Nothing to be gained from that. I would only be a liability.'

'And your own people? Once back in Moscow, it would be the Gulag for sure. At the end of the day, you're a failure and they don't like that.'

'True,' Cussane nodded. 'Except in one respect. They don't even want me back, Liam. They just want me dead. They've already tried. To them also I would only be an embarrassment.'

There was silence at his words, then Tanya said, 'But what happens? What do you do?

'God knows,' he said. 'I am a dead man walking, my dear. Liam understands that. He's right. There is no place for me to run. Today, tomorrow, next week. If I stay in Ireland McGuiness and his men will have my head, wouldn't you agree, Liam?'

'True enough.'

Cussane stood up and paced up and down, holding the Stechkin against his knee. He turned to Tanya. 'You think life was cruel to a little girl back there in Drumore in the rain? You know how old I was? Twenty years of age. Life was cruel when they hanged my father. When my mother agreed to take me back to Russia. When Paul Cherny picked me out at the age of fifteen as a specimen with interesting possibilities for the KGB.' He sat down again. 'If my mother and I had been left alone in Dublin, who knows what might have happened to that one great talent I possessed. The Abbey Theatre, London, the Old Vic, Stratford?' He shrugged. 'Instead . . .'

Devlin was conscious of a great sadness, forgot for the moment everything else except that, for years, he had liked this man more than most.

'That's life,' he said. 'Always some bugger telling you what to do.'

'Living our lives for us, you mean?' Cussane said. 'School-teachers, the police, union leaders, politicians, parents?'

'Even priests,' Devlin said gently.

'Yes, I think I see now what the anarchists mean when they say "Shoot an authority figure today".' The evening paper was on a chair with a headline referring to the Pope's visit to England. Cussane picked it up. 'The Pope, for instance.'

Devlin said, 'A bad joke, that.'

'But why should I be joking?' Cussane asked him. 'You know what my brief was all those years ago, Liam? You know what Maslovsky told me my task was? To create chaos, disorder, fear and uncertainty in the West. I've helped keep the Irish conflict going, by hitting counter-productive targets, causing great harm on occasion to both Catholic and Protestant causes; IRA, UVF, I've pulled everyone in. But here.' He held up the newspaper with the photo of Pope John Paul on the front page. 'How about this for the most counter-productive target of all time? Would they like that in Moscow?' He nodded to Tanya. 'You must know Maslovsky well enough by now. Would it please him, do you think?'

'You're mad,' she whispered.

'Perhaps.' He tossed a length of cord across to her. 'Tie his wrists behind his back. No tricks, Liam.'

He stood well back, covering them with the Stechkin. There was little for Devlin to do except submit. The girl tied his hands awkwardly. Cussane pushed him down on his face beside the fire.

'Lie down beside him,' he told Tanya.

He pulled her arms behind her and tied her hands securely, then her ankles. Then he checked Devlin's wrists and tied his ankles also.

'So, you're not going to kill us?' Devlin said.

'Why should I?'

Cussane stood up, walked across the room, and with one swift jerk, pulled the telephone wire out of the wall.

'Where are you going?'

'Canterbury,' Cussane said. 'Eventually, that is.'

'Canterbury?'

'That's where the Pope will be on Saturday. They'll all be there. The cardinals, the Archbishop of Canterbury, Prince Charles. I know these things, Liam. I run the press office at the Secretariat, remember.'

'All right, let's be sensible,' Devlin said. 'You'll never get near him. The last thing the Brits want is the Pope

219

dead on their hands. They'll have security at Canterbury that would make even the Kremlin sit up and take notice.'

'A real challenge,' Cussane said calmly.

'For God's sake, Harry, shoot the Pope. To what end?'

'Why not?' Cussane shrugged. 'Because he's there. Because I've nowhere else to go. If I've got to die, I might as well go down doing something spectacular.' He smiled down. 'And you can always try and stop me, Liam, you and McGuiness and Ferguson and his people in London. Even the KGB would move heaven and earth to stop me if they could. It would certainly leave them with a lot of explaining to do.'

Devlin exploded. 'Is that all it is to you, Harry? A game?'

'The only one in town,' Cussane said. 'For years, I've been manipulated by other people. A regular puppet on a string. This time, I'm in charge. It should be an interesting change.'

He moved away and Devlin heard the French window open and close. There was silence. Tanya said, 'He's gone.'

Devlin nodded and struggled into a sitting position. He forced his wrists against the cord, but was wasting his time and knew it.

Tanya said, 'Liam, do you think he means it? About the Pope?'

'Yes,' Devlin said grimly. 'I believe he does.'

* * *

Once at his cottage, Cussane worked quickly and methodically. From a small safe hidden behind books in his study he took his Irish passport in his usual identity. There were also two British ones in different names. In one he was still a priest, in another a journalist. There was also two thousand pounds in notes of varying sizes, English not Irish.

He got a canvas holdall from his wardrobe of a type favoured by army officers and opened it. There was a board panel in the bottom which he pressed open. Inside he placed most of the money, the false passports, a Walther PPK with a Carswell silencer and several additional clips of ammunition, a block of plastic explosive, and two timing pencils. As an afterthought, he got a couple of Army field dressing packs from the bathroom cupboard and some morphine ampoules and put them in also. Like the soldier he thought himself to be, he had to be ready for anything. He replaced the panel, rolled up one of his black cassocks and placed it in the bottom of the bag. A couple of shirts and what he thought of as civilian ties, socks, toilet articles. His prayer book went in as a reflex habit as did the other things. The Host in the silver pyx, the holy oils. As a priest it had been second nature to travel with them for years now.

He went downstairs to the hall and pulled on his black raincoat, then took one of the two black felt hats from the hall cupboard and went into the study. Inside the crown of the hat he had sewn two plastic clips. He opened a drawer in his desk and took out a .38 Smith

221

and Wesson revolver with a two inch barrel. It fitted snugly into the clips and he put the hat into his holdall. The Stechkin he put in the pocket of his raincoat.

So, he was ready. He glanced once around the study of the cottage which had been his home for so long, then turned and went out. He crossed the yard to the garage, opened the door and switched on the light. His motorcycle stood beside the car, an old 350cc BSA in superb condition. He strapped his holdall on the rear, took the crash helmet from the peg on the wall and put it on.

When he kicked the starter, the engine roared into life at once. He sat there for a moment adjusting things, then he crossed himself and rode away. The sound of the engine faded into the distance and after a while there was only silence.

At that moment in Dublin, Martin McGuiness was watching one of his men put the receiver back on the phone rest.

'The line's dead, that's certain.'

'That seems more than a little strange to me, son,' McGuiness said. 'Let's pay Liam a visit, and let's drive fast.'

It took McGuiness and a couple of his men forty minutes to get there. He stood watching while his men released Devlin and the girl and shook his head.

'Christ, Liam, it would be funny seeing the great Liam Devlin trussed up like a chicken if it wasn't so bloody tragic. Tell me again? Tell me what it's about, then.'

He and Devlin went into the kitchen and Devlin filled him in on what had happened. When he was finished, McGuiness exploded. 'The cunning bastard. On the Falls Road in Belfast City they remember him as a saint, and him a sodding Russian agent pretending to be a priest.'

'I shouldn't think the Vatican will be exactly over-joyed,' Devlin told him.

'And you know what's worse? What really sticks in my throat? He's no fucking Russian at all. Jesus, Liam, his father died on an English gallows for the cause.' McGuiness was shaking with rage now. 'I'm going to have his balls.'

'And how do you propose to do that?'

'You leave that to me. The Pope at Canterbury, is it? I'll close Ireland up so tight that not even a rat could find a hole to sneak out.'

He bustled out, calling to his men and was gone. Tanya came into the kitchen. She looked pale and tired. 'Now what happens?'

'You put on the kettle and we'll have a nice cup of tea. You know, they say that in the old days a messenger bearing bad news was usually executed. Thank God for the telephone. You'll excuse me for a few minutes while I go across the road and ring Ferguson.'

10

Ballywalter on the coast just south of Dundalk Bay near Clogher Head could hardly be described as a port. A pub, a few houses, half-a-dozen fishing boats and the tiniest of harbours. It was a good hour and a half after Devlin's phone call to Ferguson that Cussane turned his BSA motorcycle into a wood on a hill overlooking the place. He pushed his machine up on its stand and went and looked down at Ballywalter, clear in the moonlight below, then he went back to the bike and unstrapped his holdall and took out the black trilby which he put on his head instead of the crash helmet.

He started down the road, bag in hand. What he intended now was tricky, but clever if it worked. It was like chess really; trying to think not just one move, but three moves ahead. Certainly now was the time to see if all that information so carefully extracted from the dying Danny Malone would prove worthwhile.

*   *   *

Sean Deegan had been publican in Ballywalter for eleven years. It was hardly a full-time occupation in a village that boasted only forty-one men of the legal age to drink, which explained why he was also skipper of a forty-foot motor fishing boat *Mary Murphy*. Added to this, on the illegal side of things, he was not only a member of the IRA, but very much on the active list, having only been released from Long Kesh prison in Ulster in February after serving three years' imprisonment for possession of illegal weapons. The fact that Deegan had personally killed two British soldiers in Derry had never been traced to him by the authorities.

His wife and two children were away visiting her mother in Galway and he had closed the bar at eleven, intending fishing early. He was still awake when Cussane came down the street. He had been awakened from his bed by a phone call from one of McGuiness's men. Deegan offered an illegal way out of the country to the Isle of Man, a useful staging post for England. The description of Cussane which he had been given was brief and to the point.

Deegan had hardly put the phone down when there was a knock at the door. He opened it and found Cussane standing there. He knew at once who his nocturnal caller was, although the clerical collar and black hat and raincoat would have been enough in themselves.

'What can I do for you, Father?' Deegan asked, stepping back so that Cussane might come in.

They went into the small bar and Deegan stirred the fire. 'I got your name from a parishioner, Danny Malone,' Cussane said. 'My name is Daly, by the way.'

'Danny, is it?' Deegan said. 'I heard he was in a bad way.'

'Dying, poor soul. He told me you could do a run to the Isle of Man if the price was right or the cause.'

Deegan went behind the bar and poured a whiskey. 'Will you join me, Father?'

'No thanks.'

'You're in trouble? Political or police?'

'A little of both.' Cussane took ten English fifty pound notes from his pocket and laid them on the bar. 'Would this handle it?'

Deegan picked the notes up and weighed them thoughtfully. 'And why not, Father? Look, you sit by the fire and keep yourself warm and I'll make a phone call.'

'A phone call?'

'Sure and I can't manage the boat on my own. I need at least one crew and two is better.'

He went out, closing the door. Cussane went round the bar to the phone there and waited. There was a slight tinkle from the bell and he lifted the receiver gently.

The man was talking urgently. 'Deegan here at Ballywalter. Have you Mr McGuiness?'

'He's gone to bed.'

'Jesus, man, will you get him? He's here at my place now. That fella Cussane your people phoned about.'

'Hold right there.' There was a delay, then another voice said, 'McGuiness. Is it yourself, Sean?'

'And none other. Cussane's here at my pub. Calls himself Daly. He's just given me five hundred quid to take him to the Isle of Man. What do I do, hold him?'

McGuiness said, 'I'd like nothing better than to see to him myself, but that's childish. You've got some good men there?'

'Phil Egan and Tadgh McAteer.'

'So – he dies, this one, Sean. If I told you what he'd done in the past, the harm he's done the movement, you'd never believe it. Take him in that boat of yours, nice and easy, no fuss, then a bullet in the back of the head three miles out and over the side with him.'

'Consider it done,' Deegan told him.

He put down the phone, left the living room, went upstairs and dressed fully. He went into the bar, pulling on an old pilot coat. 'I'll leave you for a while, Father, while I go and get my lads. Help yourself to anything you need.'

'That's kind of you,' Cussane told him.

He lit a cigarette and read the evening paper for something to do. Deegan was back in half an hour, two men with him. 'Phil Egan, Father, Tadgh McAteer.'

They all shook hands. Egan was small and wiry, perhaps twenty-five. McAteer was a large man in an old reefer coat with a beer belly heavy over his belt. He was older than Deegan. Fifty-five at least, Cussane would have thought.

'We'll get going then, Father.' Cussane picked up his bag and Deegan said, 'Not so fast, Father. I like to know what I'm handling.'

He put Cussane's bag on the bar, opened it and quickly sifted through the contents. He zipped it up, turned and nodded to McAteer, who ran his hands roughly over the priest and found the Stechkin. He took it out and placed it on the bar without a word.

Deegan said, 'What you need that for is your business. You get it back when we land you in the Isle of Man.' He put it in his pocket.

'I understand,' Cussane said.

'Good, then let's get going,' and Deegan led the way out.

Devlin was in bed when McGuiness rang him. 'They've got him,' he said.

'Where?'

'Ballywalter. One of our own, a man called Sean Deegan. Cussane turned up there saying he was a friend of Danny Malone and needed an undercover run to the Isle of Man. Presumably Danny had told him a thing or two he shouldn't.'

'Danny's a dying man. He wouldn't know what he was saying half the time,' Devlin said.

'Anyway, Cussane, or Father Daly as he's now calling himself, is in for a very unpleasant shock. Three miles out, Deegan and his boys nail the coffin lid on him and over he goes. I told you we'd get the sod.'

'So you did.'

'I'll be in touch, Liam.'

Devlin sat there thinking about it. Too good to be true. Cussane had obviously discovered from Danny Malone that Deegan offered the kind of service he did. Fair enough, but to turn up as he had done, no attempt at disguise beyond a change of name . . . He might have assumed that it would be morning before Devlin and Tanya would be found, but even so . . . It didn't make any kind of sense – or did it?

There was a light mist rolling in from the sea as they moved out, but the sky was clear and the moon touched things with a luminosity that was vaguely unreal. McAteer busied himself on deck, Egan had the hatch to the small engine room off and was down the ladder and Deegan was at the wheel. Cussane stood beside him, peering out through the window.

'A fine night,' Deegan observed.

'Indeed it is. How long will it take?'

'Four hours and that's taking it easy. It means we can time it to catch the local fishing boats going back to the Isle of Man with their night catches. We'll land you on the west coast. Little place I know near Peel. You can get

230

a bus across to Douglas, the capital. There's an airport, Ronaldsway. You can get a plane to London from there or just across the water to Blackpool on the English coast.'

'Yes, I know,' Cussane told him.

'Might as well go below. Get your head down for a while,' Deegan suggested.

The cabin had four bunks and a fixed table in the centre, a small galley at one end. It was very untidy, but warm and snug in spite of the smell of diesel oil. Cussane made himself tea in a mug and sat at the table drinking it and smoking a cigarette. He lay on one of the bottom bunks, his hat beside him, eyes closed. After a while, McAteer and Egan came down the companionway.

'Are you all right, Father?' McAteer enquired. 'Cup of tea or anything?'

'I've had one, thank you,' Cussane said. 'I think I'll get some sleep.'

He lay there, eyes almost closed, one hand negligently reaching under the hat. McAteer smiled at Egan and winked and the other man spooned instant coffee into three mugs and added boiling water and condensed milk. They went out. Cussane could hear their steps on deck, the murmur of conversation, a burst of laughter. He lay there, waiting for what was to come.

It was perhaps half an hour later that the engine stopped and they started to drift. Cussane got up and put his feet to the floor.

Deegan called down the companionway, 'Would you come up on deck, Father?'

Cussane settled his hat on his head at a neat angle and went up the ladder. Egan sat on the engine hatch, McAteer leaned out of the open wheelhouse window and Deegan stood at the stern rail, smoking a cigarette and looking back towards the Irish coast two or three miles away.

Cussane said, 'What is it? What's happening?'

'The jig's up!' Deegan turned, holding the Stechkin in his right hand. 'You see, we know who you are, old son. All about you.'

'And your wicked ways,' McAteer called.

Egan rattled a length of heavy chain. Cussane glanced towards him, then turned to Deegan, taking off his hat and holding it across his chest. 'There's no way we can discuss this, I suppose?'

'Not a chance,' Deegan told him.

Cussane shot him in the chest through the hat and Deegan was punched back against the rail. He dropped the Stechkin on the deck, overbalanced, grabbed for the rail unsuccessfully and went into the sea. Cussane was already turning, firing up at McAteer in the wheelhouse as he tried to draw back, the bullet catching the big man just above the right eye. Egan lashed out at him with the length of chain. Cussane avoided the awkward blow with ease.

'Bastard!' Egan cried, and Cussane took careful aim and shot him in the heart.

He moved fast now. Pocketing the Stechkin Deegan

had dropped he launched the inflatable with its outboard motor which was stowed amidships. He tied it to the rail and went into the wheelhouse where he had left his bag, stepping over McAteer's body to get it. He opened the false bottom, took out the plastic explosive and sliced a piece off with his pocket knife. He stuck one of the pencil timers in it, primed to explode in fifteen minutes and dropped it down the engine hatch, then got into the inflatable, started the motor and moved back to shore at speed. Behind him, Sean Deegan, still alive in spite of the bullet in his chest, watched him go and kicked slowly to keep afloat.

Cussane was well on his way when the explosion rent the night, yellow and orange flames flowering like petals. He glanced back only briefly. Things couldn't have worked out better. Now he was dead and McGuiness and Ferguson would call off the hounds. He wondered how Devlin would feel when he finally realized the truth.

He landed on a small beach close to Ballywalter and dragged the inflatable up into the shelter of a clump of gorse bushes. Then he retraced his steps up to the wood where he had left the motorcycle. He strapped his bag on the rear, put on his crash helmet and rode away.

It was another fishing boat from Ballywalter, the *Dublin Town*, out night-fishing, which was first on the scene. The crew, on deck handling their nets about a mile away, had seen the explosion as it occurred. By the time they reached the position where the *Mary Murphy* had gone down, about half an hour had elapsed. There was a considerable amount of wreckage on the surface and a life-jacket with the boat's name stencilled on it told them the worst. The skipper notified the coastguard of the tragedy on his radio and continued the search for survivors or at least the bodies of the crew; but he had no success and a thickening sea mist made things even more difficult. By five o'clock, a coastguard cutter was there from Dundalk, also several other small fishing craft, and they continued the search as dawn broke.

The news of the tragedy was passed on to McGuiness at four o'clock in the morning and he, in turn, phoned Devlin.

'Christ knows what happened,' McGuiness said. 'She blew up and went down like a stone.'

'And no bodies, you say?'

'Probably inside her, or what's left of her on the bottom. And it seems there's a bad rip tide in that area. It would carry a body a fair distance. I'd like to know what happened. A good man, Sean Deegan.'

'So would I,' Devlin said.

'Still, no more Cussane. At least that bastard has met his end. You'll tell Ferguson?'

'Leave it with me.'

Devlin put on a dressing gown, went downstairs and made some tea. Cussane was dead and yet he felt no pain for the man who, whatever else, had been his friend for more than twenty years. No sense of mourning. Instead a feeling of unease like a lump in the gut that refused to go away.

He rang the Cavendish Square number in London. It was picked up after a slight delay and Ferguson's voice answered, still half asleep. Devlin gave him the news and the Brigadier came fully awake with some rapidity.

'Are you sure about this?'

'That's how it looks. God knows what went wrong on the boat.'

'Ah well,' Ferguson said. 'At least Cussane's out of our hair for good and all. The last thing I needed was that madman on the rampage.' He snorted. 'Kill the Pope indeed.'

'What about Tanya?'

'She can come back tomorrow. Put her on the plane and I'll meet her myself. Harry will be in Paris to brief Tony Villiers on this Exocet job.'

'Right,' Devlin said. 'That's it then.'

'You don't sound happy, Liam. What is it?'

'Let's put it this way. With this one, I'd like to see the body,' Devlin said and rang off.

The Ulster border with the Irish Republic, in spite of road blocks, a considerable police presence and the British Army, has always been wide open to anyone who knows it. In many cases, farms on both sides have land breached

235

by the border's imaginary line and the area is criss-crossed by hundreds of narrow country lanes, field paths and tracks.

Cussane was safely in Ulster by four o'clock. Any kind of a vehicle on the road at that time in the morning was rare enough to make it essential that he drop out of sight for a while, which he did on the other side of Newry, holing up in a disused barn in a wood just off the main road.

He didn't sleep, but sat comfortably against a wall and smoked, the Stechkin ready to hand just in case. He left just after six, a time when there would be enough early workers on the road to make him inconspicuous, taking the AI through Banbridge to Lisburn.

It was seven-fifteen when he rode into the carpark at Aldergrove Airport and parked the motorcycle. The Stechkin joined the Walther in the false bottom of the bag. The holiday season having started, there was a flight to the Isle of Man leaving at eight-fifteen, with flights to Glasgow, Edinburgh and Newcastle as possible altern-atives if there was difficulty in obtaining a seat, all leaving within a period of one hour. The Isle of Man was his preference because it was a soft route, used mainly by holiday makers. In the event, there was space available and he had no difficulty in obtaining a ticket.

All hand baggage would be x-rayed, but that was true at most international airports these days. At Belfast, most baggage destined for the hold was x-rayed also, but this did not always apply to the softer routes during the holiday season. In any case, the false bottom of his bag, which was only three inches deep, was lined with lead. The contents would not show. Any difficulty he might have would present itself at Customs in the Isle of Man.

It was approximately eight-thirty and Cussane had been airborne for a good ten minutes when the *Dublin Town*, running low on fuel, gave up the fruitless search for survivors from the *Mary Murphy* and turned towards Ballywalter. It was the youngest member of the crew, a fifteen-year-old boy coiling rope in the prow, who noticed the wreckage to starboard and called to the skipper, who altered course at once. A few minutes later, he cut the engines and coasted in beside one of the *Mary Murphy's* hatches.

Sean Deegan was sprawled across it on his back. His head turned slowly and he managed a ghastly smile. 'Took your sweet time about it, didn't you?' he called in a hoarse voice.

At Ronaldsway Airport, Cussane had no difficulty with the Customs. He retrieved his bag and joined the large number of people passing through. No one made any attempt to stop him. As with all holiday resorts, the accent was on making things as painless for the tourist as possible. Islander aircraft made the short flight to Blackpool on the English coast numerous times during the day, but they were busy that morning and the earliest flight he could get was at noon. It could have been worse, so he purchased a ticket and went along to the cafeteria to have something to eat.

It was eleven-thirty when Ferguson answered the phone and found Devlin on the line. He listened, frowning in horror. 'Are you certain?'

'Absolutely. This man Deegan survived the explosion only because Cussane shot him into the water before-hand. It was Cussane who caused the explosion, then took off back to the shore in the fishing boat's inflat-able. Almost ran Deegan down.'

'But why?' Ferguson demanded.

'The clever bastard has been beating me at chess for years. I know his style. Always three moves ahead of the game. By staging his apparent death last night, he pulled off the hounds. There was no one looking for him. No need.'

Ferguson was filled with a dreadful foreboding. 'Are you trying to say what I think you are?'

'What do you think? He's on your side of the water now, not ours, Brigadier.'

Ferguson swore softly. 'Right, I'll get some official help from Special Branch in Dublin. They can turn over that cottage of his for us. Photos, fingerprints. Anything useful.'

'You'll need to inform the Catholic Secretariat,' Devlin told him. 'They're going to love this one at the Vatican.'

'The lady at number ten isn't likely to be too ecstatic about it either. What plane had you booked the Voroninova girl on?'

'Two o'clock.'

'Come with her. I need you.'

'There is just one item of minor importance, but worth mentioning,' Devlin told him. 'On your side of the water, I'm still a wanted man from way back. A member of an illegal organization is the least of it.'

'I'll take care of that, for God's sake,' Ferguson said. 'Just get your backside on that plane,' and he hung up.

Tanya Voroninova brought tea in from the kitchen. 'What happens now?'

'I'm going with you to London,' he said, 'and we'll take it from there.'

'And Cussane? Where is he, would you say?'

'Anywhere and everywhere.' He sipped some of his tea. 'He has one problem however. The Pope arrives Friday according to the morning paper. Visits Canterbury the next day.'

'Saturday the twenty-ninth?'

'Exactly. So Cussane has some time to fill. The question is, where does he intend to go?'

The phone rang. McGuiness was on the other end. 'You've spoken to Ferguson?'

'I have.'

'What does he intend to do?'

'God knows. He's asked me to go over.'

'And will you?'

'Yes.'

'Jesus, Liam, did you hear about this Russian, Lubov, turning up dead in the cinema? He preaches a hell of a sermon this priest of yours.'

'He's developed a slightly different attitude to the job since he discovered his own people were trying to knock him off,' Devlin said. 'Interesting to see where it takes him.'

'To Canterbury is where it's taking the mad bastard,' McGuiness said. 'And we can't help with that. It's up to British Intelligence to handle this one. Nothing more the IRA can do for them. Watch your back, Liam.'

He rang off and Devlin sat there, frowning thoughtfully. He stood up. 'I'm going out for a little while,' he said to Tanya. 'Shan't be long,' and he went out through the French windows.

The Customs at Blackpool were just as courteous as they had been at Ronaldsway. Cussane actually paused, smiling, and offered his bag as the stream of passengers moved through.

'Anything to declare, Father?' the Customs officer asked.

Cussane unzipped his bag. 'A bottle of Scotch and two hundred cigarettes.'

The Customs officer grinned. 'You could have had a litre of wine as well. It isn't your day, Father.'

'Obviously not.' Cussane zipped up his bag and moved on.

He hesitated outside the entrance of the small airport. There were several taxi cabs waiting, but he decided to walk down to the main road instead. He had, after all, all the time in the world. There was a newsagents across the road and he crossed over and bought a paper. As he came out, a bus pulled in at the stop a few paces away. Its indicator said Morecambe, which he knew was another seaside resort some miles up the coast. On impulse, he ran forward and scrambled on board as it drew away.

He purchased a ticket and went up on the top deck. It was really very pleasant and he felt calm and yet full of energy at the same time. He opened the newspaper and saw that the news from the South Atlantic was not good. HMS *Coventry* had been bombed and a Cunard container ship, the *Atlantic Conveyor*, had been hit by an Exocet missile. He lit a cigarette and settled down to read about it.

When Devlin went into the ward at the hospice, Sister Anne Marie was at Danny Malone's bed. Devlin waited and she finally whispered something to the nurse, then turned and noticed him. 'And what do you want?'

'To talk to Danny.'

'He isn't really up to conversation this morning.'

'It's very important.'

She frowned in exasperation. 'It always is with you. All right. Ten minutes.' She started to walk away, then turned.

'Father Cussane didn't come in last night. Do you know why?'

'No,' Devlin lied. 'I haven't seen him.'

She walked away and he pulled a chair forward. 'Danny, how are you?'

Malone opened his eyes and said hoarsely, 'Is it you, Liam? Father Cussane didn't come.'

'Tell me, Danny, you talked to him of Sean Deegan of Ballywalter who handles the Isle of Man run, I understand.'

Malone frowned. 'Sure, I talked to him about a lot of things.'

'But mainly of IRA matters.'

'Sure, and he was interested in me telling him how I managed things in the old days.'

'Particularly across the water?' Devlin asked.

'Yes. You know how long I lasted without getting caught, Liam. He wanted to know how I did it.' He frowned. 'What's the problem?'

'You were always the strong one, Danny. Be strong now. He wasn't one of our own.'

Malone's eyes widened. 'You're having me on, Liam.'

'And Sean Deegan in hospital with a bullet in him and two good men dead?'

Danny sat there, staring at him. 'Tell me.' So Devlin did. When he was finished, Danny Malone said softly, 'Bastard!'

'Tell me what you can remember, Danny. Anything that particularly interested him.'

Malone frowned, trying to think. 'Yes, the business of how I stayed ahead of Special Branch and those Intelligence boys for so long. I explained to him that I never used the IRA network when I was over there. Totally unreliable, you know that, Liam.'

'True.'

'I always used the underworld myself. Give me an honest crook any day of the week or a dishonest one if the price is right. I knew a lot of people like that.'

'Tell me about them,' Devlin said.

Cussane liked seaside towns, especially the ones that catered for the masses. Honest, working class people out for a good time. Lots of cafés, amusement arcades and fairgrounds and plenty of bracing air. Morecambe certainly had that. The dark waters of the bay were being whipped into whitecaps and on the far side he could see the mountains of the Lake District.

He walked across the road. It was not the height of the season yet, but there were plenty of tourists about and he threaded his way through the narrow streets until he found his way to the bus station.

It was possible to travel to most of the major provincial cities by high speed bus, mainly on the motorways. He consulted the timetables and found what he was looking for, a bus to Glasgow via Carlisle and Dumfries. It left in one hour. He booked a ticket and went in search of something to eat.

11

Georgi Romanov was senior attaché in charge of public relations at the Russian Embassy in London. He was a tall, amiable-looking man of fifty, secretly rather proud of his aristocratic name. He had worked for the KGB in London for eleven years now, and had been promoted to lieutenant-colonel the previous year. Ferguson liked him and he liked Ferguson. When Ferguson phoned him just after his final telephone conversation with Devlin and suggested a meeting, Romanov agreed at once.

They met in Kensington Gardens by the Round Pond, a rendezvous so convenient to the Embassy that Romanov was able to walk. Ferguson sat on a bench reading *The Times*. Romanov joined him.

'Hello, Georgi,' Ferguson said.

'Charles. To what do I owe the honour?'

'Straight talking, Georgi. This one is about as bad as

it could be. What do you know about a KGB agent, code name Cuchulain, put in deep in Ireland a good twenty years ago?'

'For once I can answer you with complete honesty,' Romanov said. 'Not a thing.'

'Then listen and learn,' Ferguson told him.

When he was finished, Romanov's face was grave. 'This really is bad.'

'You're telling me. The important thing is this. This madman is somewhere in the country having boasted of his intention of shooting the Pope at Canterbury on Saturday and frankly, with his track record, we have to take him seriously. He isn't just another nutter.'

'So what do you want me to do?'

'Get in touch with Moscow at the highest level. I should imagine the last thing they want is the Pope dead, at the hands of someone who can be proved to be a KGB agent, especially after that botched attempt in Rome. Which is exactly what Cussane wants. Warn them that, on this one, we'll brook no interference. And if, by some wild chance, he gets in touch with you, Georgi, you tell me. We're going to get this bastard, make no mistake and he dies, Georgi. No nonsense about a trial or anything like that. There again, I'm sure that's what your people in Moscow will want to hear.'

'I'm sure it is.' Romanov stood up. 'I'd better get back and send a signal.'

'Take a tip from an old chum,' Ferguson told him. 'Make sure you go higher than Maslovsky.'

In view of the importance of the matter, Ferguson had to go to the Director General, who in turn spoke to the Home Secretary. The result was a summons to Downing Street when Ferguson was half-way through his lunch. He rang for his car at once and was there within ten minutes. There was the usual small crowd at the end of the street behind barriers. The policeman on the door saluted. It was opened the moment Ferguson raised a hand to the knocker.

There was a hum of activity inside, but then there would be with the Falklands affair beginning to hot up. He was surprised that she was seeing him personally. His guide led the way up the main staircase to the first floor and Ferguson followed. On the top floor, the young man knocked at a door and led the way in.

'Brigadier Ferguson, Prime Minister.'

She looked up from her desk, elegant as always in a grey tweed dress, blonde hair groomed to perfection, and laid down her pen. 'My time is limited, Brigadier. I'm sure you understand.'

'I would have thought that an understatement, Ma'am.'

'The Home Secretary has filled me in on the relevant facts. I simply want an assurance from you that you will stop this man.'

'I can give you that without the slightest hesitation, Prime Minister.'

'If there was any kind of attempt on the Pope's life while he is here, even an unsuccessful one, the consequences in political terms would be disastrous for us.'

'I understand.'

'As head of Group Four, you have special powers, direct from me. Use them, Brigadier. If there is anything else you need, do not hesitate to ask.'

'Prime Minister.'

She picked up her pen and returned to work and Ferguson went out to find the young man waiting for him. As they went downstairs, it occurred to Ferguson, not for the first time in his career, that it was his own head that was on the block as much as Cussane's.

In Moscow, Ivan Maslovsky received another summons to the office of the Minister for State Security, still occupied by Yuri Andropov, whom he found sitting at his desk considering a typed report.

He passed it across. 'Read it, Comrade.'

Maslovsky did so and his heart seemed to turn to stone. When he was finished he handed it back, hands shaking.

'Your man, Maslovsky, is now at large in England, intent on assassinating the Pope, his sole idea apparently being to embarrass us seriously. And there is nothing we can do except sit back and hope that British

Intelligence will be one hundred per cent efficient in this matter.'

'Comrade, what can I say?'

'Nothing, Maslovsky. This whole sorry affair was not only ill-advised. It was adventurism of the worst kind.' Andropov pressed a button on his desk, the door opened behind Maslovsky and two young KGB captains in uniform entered. 'You will vacate your office and hand over all official keys and files to the person I designate. You will then be taken to the Lubianka to await trial for crimes against the State.'

The Lubianka, how many people had he sent there himself? Suddenly, Maslovsky found difficulty in breathing and there was a pain in both arms, his chest. He started to fall and clutched at the desk. Andropov jumped back in alarm and the two KGB officers rushed and grabbed Maslovsky's arms. He didn't bother to struggle, he had no strength, but he tried to speak as the pain got worse, tried to tell Andropov that there would be no cell in the Lubianka, no state trial. Strangely enough, the last thing he thought of was Tanya, his beloved Tanya seated at the piano playing his favourite piece, Debussy's *La Mer*. Then the music faded and there was only darkness.

Ferguson had a meeting with the Home Secretary, the Commander of C13, Scotland Yard's anti-terrorist squad and the Director General of the Security Services. He was tired when he got back to the flat and found Devlin sitting by the fire reading *The Times*.

'The Pope seems to be taking over from the Falklands at the moment,' Devlin said and folded the paper.

'Yes, well that's as maybe,' Ferguson said. 'He can't go back fast enough for me. You should have been with me at this meeting I've just attended, Liam. Home Secretary himself, Scotland Yard, the Director, and you know what?' He warmed himself, back against the fire. 'They aren't taking it all that seriously.'

'Cussane, you mean?'

'Oh, don't get me wrong. They accept his existence, if you follow me. I showed them the record and his activities in Dublin during the past few days have been bad enough, God knows. Levin, Lubov, Cherny, two IRA gunmen. The man's a butcher.'

'No,' Devlin said. 'I don't think so. To him, it's just part of the job. Something that has to be done. He gets it over with cleanly and expeditiously. He has frequently spared lives over the years. Tanya and myself were a case in point. He goes for the target, that's all.'

'Don't remind me.' Ferguson shuddered, and then the door opened and Harry Fox came in.

'Hello, sir. Liam. I believe things have been happening while I've been away.'

'I think one could say that,' Ferguson told him. 'Did things go well in Paris?'

'Yes, I saw Tony. He's in control.'

'You can tell me later. I'd better fill you in on the latest events.'

Which he did, as quickly as possible, Devlin occasionally making a point. When Ferguson was finished, Harry Fox said, 'What a man. Strange.' He shook his head.

'What is?'

'When I met him the other day, I rather liked him, sir.'

'Not a difficult thing to do,' Devlin said.

Ferguson frowned. 'Let's have no more of that kind of bloody nonsense.' The door opened and Kim entered with tea things on a tray and a plate of toasted crumpets. 'Excellent,' Ferguson said. 'I'm famished.'

Fox said, 'What about Tanya Voroninova?'

'I've fixed her up with a safe house for the moment.'

'Which one, sir?'

'The Chelsea Place apartment. The Directorate supplied a woman operative to stay with her till we get sorted.'

He handed them each a cup of tea. 'So, what's the next move?' Devlin asked.

'The Home Secretary and the Director, and I must say I agree with them, don't feel we should make too public an issue of this at the moment. The whole purpose of the Pope's visit is sweetness and light. A genuine attempt to help bring about the end of the war in the South Atlantic. Imagine how it would look on the front pages of the nationals. The first visit ever of a Pope to England and a mad-dog killer on the loose.'

'And a priest to boot, sir.'

'Yes, well we can discount that, especially as we know what he really is.'

Devlin said, 'Discount nothing. Let me, as a not very good Catholic, fill you in on a few things. In the eyes of the Church, Harry Cussane was ordained priest at Vine Landing, Connecticut, twenty-one years ago and still is a priest. Haven't you read any Graham Greene lately?'

'All right,' Ferguson said testily. 'Be that as it may, the Prime Minister doesn't see why we should give Cussane front-page publicity. It won't do any of us any good.'

'It could catch him quickly, sir,' Fox said mildly.

'Yes, well they all expect us to do that anyway. Special Branch in Dublin have lifted his prints for us at his cottage. They've gone into the Dublin computer which, as you know, is linked with the security services' computer at Lisburn which, in turn, is linked to our computer here and at Central Records, Scotland Yard.'

'I didn't realize you had that kind of hook-up,' Devlin said.

'Miracle of the micro-chip,' Ferguson said. 'Eleven million people in there. Criminal records, schooling, professions, sexual preferences. Personal habits. Where they buy their furniture.'

'You've got to be joking.'

'No. Caught one of your lot over here from Ulster last year because he always shopped at the Co-Op. Had an excellent cover, but couldn't change the habit of a lifetime. Cussane is in there now and not only his fingerprints but everything we know about him, and as most of the big provincial police forces have what we call visual display characteristics on their computer system, they can plug in to our central bank and punch out his photo.'

'God Almighty!'

'Actually, they can do the same with you. As regards Cussane, I've instructed them to insert a deliberately amended record. No mention of the KGB or anything like that. Poses as a priest, known connections with the IRA. Extremely violent – approach with care. You get the picture.'

'Oh, I do.'

'To that end, we're releasing his picture to the press and quoting very much the details I've just given you. Some evening papers will manage to get it out, but all the national newspapers will have it in tomorrow's editions.'

'And you think that will be enough, sir?' Fox asked.

'Very possibly. We'll have to wait and see, won't we? One thing is certain.' Ferguson walked to the window and glanced out. 'He's out there somewhere.'

'And the thing is,' Devlin said, 'no one can do a damn thing about it till he surfaces.'

'Exactly.' Ferguson went back to the tray and picked up the pot. 'This tea is really quite delicious. Anyone like another cup?'

*　　*　　*

A little later that afternoon His Holiness Pope John Paul II sat at a desk in the small office adjacent to his bedchamber and examined the report which had just been handed to him. The man who stood before him wore the plainest of black habits and in appearance might have been a simple priest. He was, in fact, Father General of the Society of Jesus, that most illustrious of all orders within the Catholic Church. The Jesuits were proud to be known as Soldiers of Christ and had been responsible, behind the scenes, for the Pope's security for centuries now. All of which explained why the Father General had hastened from his office at the Collegio di San Roberto Bellarmino on the Via del Seminario to seek audience with His Holiness.

Pope John Paul put the report down and looked up. He spoke in excellent Italian, only a trace of his Polish native tongue coming through. 'You received this when?'

'The first report from the Secretariat in Dublin came three hours ago, then the news from London a little later. I have spoken personally to the British Home Secretary who has given me every assurance for your safety and referred me to Brigadier Ferguson, mentioned in the report as being directly responsible.'

'But are you worried?'

'Holiness, it is almost impossible to prevent a lone assassin from reaching his target, especially if he does not care about his own safety and this man Cussane has proved his abilities on too many occasions in the past.'

'Father Cussane.' His Holiness got up and paced to

the window. 'Killer he may have been, may still be, but priest he is and God, my friend, will not allow him to forget that.'

The Father General looked into that rough hewn face, the face that might have belonged to any one of a thousand ordinary working men. It was touched with a strange simplicity, a certainty. As had happened on other occasions the Father General, for all his intellectual authority, wilted before it.

'You will go to England, Holiness?'

'To Canterbury, my friend, where Blessed Thomas Beckett died for God's sake.'

The Father General reached to kiss the ring on the extended hand. 'Then your Holiness will excuse me. There is much to do.'

He went out. John Paul stood at the window for a while, then crossed the room, opened a small door and entered his private chapel. He knelt at the altar, hands clasped, a certain fear in his heart as he remembered the assassin's bullet that had almost ended his life, the months of pain. But he pushed that away from him and concentrated on all that was important: his prayers for the immortal soul of Father Harry Cussane and for all sinners everywhere, whose actions only cut them off from the infinite blessing of God's love.

Ferguson put down the phone and turned to Devlin and Fox. 'That was the Director General. His Holiness has been informed in full about Cussane and the threat he poses. It makes no difference.'

'Well, it wouldn't, would it?' Devlin said. 'You're talking about a man who worked for years in the Polish underground against the Nazis.'

'All right,' Ferguson said. 'Point taken. Anyway, you'd better get kitted out. Take him along to the Directorate, Harry. Grade A Security Pass. Not just another piece of plastic with your photo on it,' he said to Devlin. 'Very few people have this particular one. It'll get you in anywhere.'

He moved to his desk and Devlin said, 'Will it entitle me to a gun? A Walther wouldn't come amiss. I'm one of nature's pessimists, as you know.'

'Out of favour with most of our people since that idiot tried to shoot Princess Anne and her bodyguard's Walther jammed. Revolvers never do. Take my advice.'

He picked up some papers and they went into the study and got their coats. 'I still prefer a Walther,' Devlin said.

'One thing's for sure,' Fox said. 'Whatever it is, it had better not jam, not if you're facing Harry Cussane,' and he opened the door and they went out to the lift.

Harry Cussane had a plan of sorts. He knew the end in view on Saturday at Canterbury, but that left the best part of three days and three nights, in which he had to hide out. Danny Malone had mentioned a number of people in the criminal world who provided the right kind of help at a price. Plenty in London of course or Leeds or Manchester, but the Mungo brothers and their farm in Galloway had particularly interested him. It was the remoteness which appealed. The last place anyone would look for him would be Scotland and yet the British Airways shuttle from Glasgow to London took only an hour and a quarter.

Time to fill, that was the thing. No need to be in Canterbury until the last moment. Nothing to organize. That amused him, sitting there in the bus speeding up the motorway to Carlisle. One could imagine the preparation at Canterbury Cathedral, every possible entry point guarded, police marksmen everywhere, probably even the SAS in plain clothes dispersed in the crowd. And all for nothing. It was like chess, as he used to tell Devlin, the world's worst player. It wasn't the present move that counted. It was the final move. It was rather like a stage magician. You believed what he did with his right hand, but it was what he did with his left that was important.

He slept for quite a while and, when he awakened, there was the sea shining in the afternoon light on his left. He leaned over and spoke to the old woman in front of him. 'Where are we?'

'Just past Annan.' She had a thick Glasgow accent. 'Dumfries next. Are you a Catholic?'

'I'm afraid so,' he said warily. The Scottish Lowlands had always been traditionally Protestant.

'That's lovely. I'm Catholic myself. Glasgow-Irish, Father.' She took his hand and kissed it. 'Bless me, Father. You're from the old country.'

'I am indeed.'

He thought she might prove a nuisance, but strangely enough, she simply turned her head and settled back in her seat. Outside, the sky was very dark and it started to rain, thunder rumbling ominously and soon the rain had increased into a monsoon-like force that drummed loudly on the roof of the bus. They stopped in Dumfries to drop two passengers and then moved on through streets washed clean of people, out into the country again.

Not long now. No more than fifteen miles to his dropping-off point at Dunhill. From there, a few miles on a side road to a hamlet called Larwick and the Mungos' place, a mile or two outside Larwick in the hills.

The driver had been speaking into the mike on his car radio and now he switched over to the coach's loudspeaker system. 'Attention, ladies and gentlemen. I'm afraid we've got trouble up ahead just before Dunhill. Bad flooding on the road. A lot of vehicles already stuck in it.'

The old woman in front of Cussane called, 'What are we supposed to do? Sit in the bus all night?'

'We'll be in Corbridge in a few minutes. Not much of a place, but there's a milk stop there on the railway line. They're making arrangements to stop the next train for Glasgow.'

'Three times the fare on the railway,' the old woman called.

'The company pays,' the driver told her cheerfully. 'Don't worry, love.'

'Will the train stop at Dunhill?' Cussane asked.

'Perhaps. I'm not sure. We'll have to see.'

Lag's Luck, they called it in prison circles. Danny Malone had told him that. No matter how well you planned, it was always something totally unforeseeable that caused the problem. No point in wasting energy in dwelling on that. The thing to do was examine alternatives.

A white sign, Corbridge etched on it in black, appeared on the left and then the first houses loomed out of the heavy rain. There was a general store, a newsagents, the tiny railway station opposite. The driver turned the coach into the forecourt.

'Best wait in here while I check things out.' He jumped down and went into the railway station.

The rain poured down relentlessly. There was a gap between the pub and the general store, beams stretching between to shore them up. Obviously the building which had stood there had just been demolished. A small crowd had gathered. Cussane watched idly, reached for the packet of cigarettes in his pocket and found it empty. He hesitated, then picked up his bag, got off the coach and ran across the road to the newsagents. He asked the young woman standing in the entrance for a couple of packs of cigarettes and an ordnance survey map of the area if she had it. She did.

'What's going on?' Cussane asked.

'They've been pulling down the old grain store for a week now. Everything was fine until this rain started. They've got trouble in the cellars. A roof fall or something.'

They moved out into the entrance again and watched. At that moment, a police car appeared from the other end of the village and pulled in. There was only one occupant, a large heavily-built man who wore a navy-blue anorak with sergeant's stripes on it. He forced his way through the crowd and disappeared.

The young woman said, 'The cavalry's arrived.'

'Isn't he from round here?' Cussane asked.

'No police station in Corbridge. He's from Dunhill. Sergeant Brodie – Lachlan Brodie.' The tone of her voice was enough.

'Not popular?' Cussane asked.

'Lachlan's the kind who likes nothing better than finding three drunks together at the same time on a Saturday night to beat up. He's built like the rock of ages and likes to prove it. You wouldn't be Catholic, by any chance?'

'I'm afraid so.'

'To Lachlan, that means antichrist. He's the kind of Baptist who thinks music is a sin. A lay preacher as well.'

A workman came through the crowd in helmet and orange safety jacket. His face was streaked with mud and water. He leaned against the wall, 'It's a sod down there.'

'That bad?' the woman said.

'One of my men is trapped. A wall collapsed. We're doing our best, but there isn't much room to work in and the water's rising.' He frowned and said to Cussane, 'You wouldn't be Catholic by any chance?'

'Yes.'

The man grabbed his arm. 'My name's Hardy. I'm the foreman. The man down there is as Glaswegian as me, but Italian. Gino Tisini. He thinks he's going to die. Begged me to get him a priest. Will you come, Father?'

'But of course,' Cussane said without hesitation, and handed his bag to the woman. 'Would you look after that for me?'

'Certainly, Father.'

He followed Hardy through the crowd and down into the excavation. There was a gaping hole, cellar steps descending. Brodie, the police sergeant, was holding people back. Hardy started down and as Cussane followed, Brodie caught his arm. 'What's this?'

'Let him by,' Hardy called. 'He's a priest.'

The hostility was immediate in Brodie's eyes, the dislike plain. It was an old song to Cussane, Belfast all over again. 'I don't know you,' Brodie said.

'My name's Fallon. I came in on the bus on the way to Glasgow,' Cussane told him calmly.

He took the policeman's wrist, loosening the grip on his arm, and Brodie winced at the strength of it as Cussane pushed him to one side and went down the steps. He was knee-deep in water at once and ducked under a low roof and followed Hardy into what must have been a narrow passageway. There was a certain amount of light from an extension lamp and it illuminated a chaos of jumbled masonry and planking. There was a narrow aperture and as they reached it, two men stumbled out, both soaked to the skin and obviously at exhaustion point.

'It's no good,' one of them said. 'His head will be under the water in a matter of minutes.'

Hardy brushed past and Cussane went after them. Gino Tisini's white face loomed out of the darkness as they crouched to go forward. Cussane put out a hand to steady himself and a plank fell and several bricks.

'Watch it!' Hardy said. 'The whole thing could go like a house of cards.'

There was the constant gurgle of water as it poured in. Tisini managed a ghastly smile. 'Come to hear my confession, Father? It would take a year and a day.'

'We haven't got that long. Let's get you out,' Cussane said.

There seemed to be a sudden extra flow of water; it washed over Tisini's face and he panicked. Cussane moved behind him, supporting the man's head above the water, crouching over him protectively.

Hardy felt under the water. 'There's a lot moved here,' he said. 'That's where the inflow of water helps. There's just one beam pinning him down now, but it leads into the wall. If I put any kind of force on it, it could bring the lot in on us.'

'If you don't, he drowns within the next couple of minutes,' Cussane said.

'You could be in trouble too, Father.'

'And you,' Cussane said, 'so get on with it.'

'Father!' Tisini cried. 'In the name of God, absolve me!'

Cussane said in a firm clear voice, 'May Our Lord Jesus Christ absolve you and I, by His authority, absolve you from your sins in the name of the Father and the Son and of the Holy Spirit.' He nodded to Hardy. 'Now!'

The foreman took a breath and dipped under the surface, his hands gripping the edges of the beam. His shoulders seemed to swell, he came up out of the water, the beam with him and Tisini screamed and floated free in Cussane's hands. The wall started to bulge. Hardy pulled Tisini up and dragged him towards the entrance, Cussane pushing from the rear as the walls crumbled around them. He put an arm up to protect his head and shoulders, was aware that they were at the steps now, willing hands reaching down to help, and then a brick struck him a glancing blow on the head. He tried to go up the steps, fell on his knees, and there was only darkness.

12

He came awake slowly to find the young woman from the shop crouching over him. He was lying on a rug in front of a coal fire and she was wiping his face.

'Easy,' she said. 'You'll be fine. Remember me? I'm Moira McGregor. You're in my shop.'

'What about the Italian and that fellow Hardy?'

'They're upstairs. We've sent for a doctor.'

He was still confused and found it difficult to think straight. 'My bag?' he said slowly. 'Where is it?'

The big policeman, Brodie, loomed over them. 'Back in the land of the living, are we?' There was an edge to his voice. An unpleasantness. 'Worth a couple of dozen candles to the Virgin, I suppose.'

He went out. Moira McGregor smiled at Cussane. 'Take no notice. You saved that man's life, you and Hardy. I'll get you a cup of tea.'

She went into the kitchen and found Brodie standing

by the table. 'I could do with a touch of something stronger myself,' he said.

She took a bottle of Scotch and a glass from a cupboard and put them on the table without a word. He reached for a chair and pulled it forward, not noticing Cussane's bag which fell to the floor. The top being unzipped, several items tumbled out, a couple of shirts and the pyx and the violet stole amongst them.

'This his bag?' Brodie asked.

She turned from the stove, a kettle in her hand. 'That's right.'

He dropped to one knee, stuffing the items back into the bag and frowned. 'What's this?'

By some mischance, the false bottom of the bag had become dislodged in the fall. The first thing Brodie discovered was an English passport and he opened it. 'He told me his name was Fallon.'

'So?' Moira said.

'Then how come he has a passport in the name of Father Sean Daly? Good likeness too.' His hand groped further and came up, holding the Stechkin. 'God Almighty!'

Moira McGregor felt sick. 'What does it mean?'

'We'll soon find out.'

Brodie went back into the other room and put the bag down on a chair. Cussane lay quietly, eyes closed. Brodie knelt down beside him, took out a pair of handcuffs and, very gently, eased one bracelet over Cussane's left wrist. Cussane opened his eyes and Brodie seized the other wrist and snapped the steel cuff in place. He pulled the priest to his feet, then shoved him down into a chair.

'What's all this then?' Brodie had the false base up completely now and sifted through the contents. 'Three handguns, assorted passports and a sizeable sum in cash. Bloody fine priest you are. What's it all about?'

'You are the policeman, not me,' Cussane said.

Brodie cuffed him on the side of the head. 'Manners, my little man. I can see I'm going to have to chastise you.'

Watching from the door, Moira McGregor said, 'Don't do that.'

Brodie smiled contemptuously. 'Women – all the same. Fancy him, do you, just because he played the hero?'

He went out. She said to Cussane desperately, 'Who are you?'

He smiled. 'I wouldn't bother your head about that. I could manage a cigarette, though, before bully-boy gets back.'

Brodie had been a policeman for twenty years after five years in the military police. Twenty undistinguished years. He was a sour and cruel man whose only real authority was the uniform, and his religion had the same purpose as the uniform, to give him a spurious authority. He could have rung headquarters in Dumfries, but there was something special about this, he felt it in his bones, so instead, he rang police headquarters in Glasgow.

Glasgow had received photo and full details on Harry Cussane only one hour previously. The case was marked Priority One with immediate referral to Group Four in London. Brodie's telephone call was transferred at once to Special Branch. Within two minutes he found himself talking to a Chief Inspector Trent.

'Tell me all about it again,' Trent told him. Brodie did so. When he was finished, Trent said, 'I don't know how much time you've got in, but you've just made the biggest collar of your career. This man's called Cussane. A real IRA heavy. You say the passengers on the bus he was on are being transferred to the train?'

'That's right, sir. Flooding on the road. This is only a milk stop, but they're going to stop the Glasgow express.'

'When is it due?'

'About ten minutes, sir.'

'Get on it, Brodie, and bring Chummy with you. We'll meet you in Glasgow.'

Brodie put down the phone, choking with excitement, then he went into the sitting room.

Brodie walked Cussane along the platform, one hand on his arm, the other clutching Cussane's bag. People turned to watch curiously as the priest passed, wrists handcuffed in front of him. They reached the guards van at the rear of the train, the guard standing on the platform beside the open door.

'What's this?'

'Special prisoner for Glasgow.' Brodie pushed Cussane inside. There were some mailbags in the corner and he shoved him down on to them. 'Now you stay quiet like a good boy.'

There was a commotion and Hardy appeared at the door, Moira McGregor behind him. 'I came as soon as I could,' the foreman said. 'I just heard.'

'You can't come in here,' Brodie told him.

Hardy ignored him. 'Look, I don't know what this is about, but if there's anything I can do.'

On the platform, the guard blew his whistle. Cussane said, 'Nothing anyone can do. How is Tisini?'

'Looks like a broken leg.'

'Tell him his luck is good.'

There was a lurch as the train started. 'It suddenly occurs to me that if I hadn't drawn you in to help, you wouldn't be here now,' Hardy said.

He moved out to join Moira on the platform as the guard jumped inside. 'Luck of the draw,' Cussane called. 'Don't worry about it.'

And then Hardy and the woman were swept away into the past as the guard pulled the sliding door shut and the train surged forward.

*　　*　　*

Trent couldn't resist phoning Ferguson in London and the Directorate-General patched him in to the Cavendish Square phone. Fox and Devlin were out and Ferguson answered himself.

'Trent here, sir, Chief-Inspector, Special Branch, Glasgow. We think we've got your man, Cussane.'

'Have you, by God?' Ferguson said. 'What shape is he in?'

'Well, I haven't actually seen him, sir. He's been apprehended in a village some miles south of here. He's arriving by train in Glasgow within the hour. I'll pick him up myself.'

'Pity the bugger didn't turn up dead,' Ferguson said. 'Still, one can't have everything. I want him down here on the first available plane in the morning, Chief-Inspector. Bring him yourself. This one's too important for any slip-ups.'

'Will do, sir,' said Trent eagerly.

Ferguson put down the receiver, reached for the red phone, but some innate caution stopped him. Much better to phone the Home Secretary when the fish was actually in the net.

Brodie sat on a stool, leaning back in the corner watching Cussane and smoking a cigarette. The guard was checking a list on his desk. He totalled it and put his pen away. 'I'll make my rounds. See you later.'

He went out and Brodie pulled his stool across the

270

baggage car and sat very close to Cussane. 'I've never understood it. Men in skirts. It'll never catch on.' He leaned forward. 'Tell me, you priests – what do you do for it?'

'For what?' Cussane said.

'You know. Is it choirboys? Is that the truth of it?' There were beads of perspiration on the big man's forehead.

'That's a hell of a big moustache you're wearing,' Cussane said. 'Have you got a weak mouth or something?'

Brodie was angry now. 'Cocky bastard. I'll show you.'

He reached forward and touched the end of the lighted cigarette to the back of Cussane's hand. Cussane cried out and fell back against the mailbags.

Brodie laughed and leaned over him. 'I thought you'd like that,' he said and reached to touch the back of the hand again. Cussane kicked him in the crutch. Brodie staggered back clutching at himself and Cussane sprang to his feet. He kicked out expertly, catching the right kneecap, and as Brodie keeled forward, raised his knee into the face.

The police sergeant lay on his back moaning and Cussane searched his pockets, found the key and unlocked his handcuffs. He got his bag, checked that the contents were intact and slipped the Stechkin into his pocket. He pulled back the sliding door and rain flooded in.

The guard, entering the baggage car a moment later, caught a brief glimpse of him landing in heather at the side of the track and rolling over and over down the slope. And then there was only mist and rain.

* * *

When the train coasted into Glasgow Central, Trent and half-a-dozen uniformed constables were waiting on platform one. The door of the baggage car slid open and the guard appeared.

'In here.'

Trent paused at the entrance. There was only Lachlan Brodie nursing a bloody and swollen face, sitting on the guard's stool. Trent's heart sank. 'Tell me,' he said wearily. Brodie did the best he could. When he was finished, Trent said, 'He was handcuffed, you say, and you let him take you?'

'It wasn't as simple as it sounds, sir,' Brodie said lamely.

'You stupid, stupid man,' Trent said. 'By the time I'm finished with you, you'll be lucky if they put you in charge of a public lavatory.'

He turned away in disgust and went back along the platform to phone Ferguson.

Cussane at that precise moment was halted in the shelter of some rocks on top of a hill north of Dunhill. He had the ordnance survey map open that he'd purchased from Moira McGregor. He found Larwick with no trouble and the Mungos' farm was just outside. Perhaps fifteen miles and most of that over hill country, and yet he felt cheerful enough as he pressed on.

The mist curling in on either hand, the heavy rain, gave him a safe, enclosed feeling, remote from the world outside, a kind of freedom. He moved on through birch trees and wet bracken that soaked his trouser legs. Occasionally grouse or plover lifted from the heather, disturbed by his passing. He kept on the move, for by now his raincoat was soaked through and he was experienced enough to know the dangers of being in hill country like this in the wrong clothing.

He came over the edge of an escarpment perhaps an hour after leaving the train and looked down into a valley glen below. Darkness was falling, but there was a clearly defined man-made track a few yards away ending at a cairn of rough stones. It was enough; he hurried on with renewed energy and plunged down the hillside.

Ferguson was looking at a large ordnance survey map of the Scottish Lowlands. 'Apparently he got the coach in Morecambe,' he said. 'We've established that.'

'A neat way of getting to Glasgow, sir,' Fox said.

'No,' Ferguson said. 'He took a ticket to a place called Dunhill. What in the hell would he be doing there?'

'Do you know the area?' Devlin asked.

'Had a week's shooting on some chap's estate about twenty years ago. Funny place, the Galloway hills. High forests, ridgebacks and secret little lochs everywhere.'

'Galloway, you said?' Devlin looked closer at the map. 'So that's Galloway?'

Ferguson frowned. 'So what?'

'I think that's where he's gone,' Devlin said. 'I think that's where he was aiming to go all along.'

Fox said, 'What makes you think that?'

He told them about Danny Malone and when he was finished, Ferguson said, 'You could very well have something.'

Devlin nodded. 'Danny mentioned a number of safe houses used by the underworld in various parts of the country, but the fact that he's in the Galloway area must have some connection with this place run by the Mungo brothers.'

'What do we do now, sir?' Fox asked Ferguson. 'Get Special Branch, Glasgow, to lay on a raid on this Mungo place?'

'No, to hell with that,' Ferguson said. 'We've already had a classic example of just how efficient the local police can be; they had him and let him slip through their fingers.' He glanced out of the window at the darkness outside. 'Too late to do anything tonight. Too late for him as well. He'll still be on foot in those hills.'

'Bound to be,' Devlin said.

'So – you and Harry fly up to Glasgow tomorrow. You check out this Mungo place personally. I'm invoking special powers. On this one, Special Branch will do what you want.'

He went out. Fox gave Devlin a cigarette. 'What do you think?'

'They had him, Harry, in handcuffs,' Devlin said, 'and he got away. That's what I think. Now give me a light.'

*   *   *

Cussane went down through birch trees following the course of a pleasant burn which splashed between a jumble of granite boulders. He was beginning to feel tired now in spite of the fact that the going was all downhill.

The burn disappeared over an edge of rock, cascading into a deep pool as it had done several times before and he slithered down through birch trees through the gathering dusk rather faster than he had intended, landing in an untidy heap, still holding on to his bag.

There was a startled gasp and Cussane, coming up on one knee, saw two children crouched at the side of the pool. The girl, on a second look, was older than he had thought, perhaps sixteen, and wore wellingtons and jeans and an old reefer coat that was too big for her. She had a pointed face, wide dark eyes, and a profusion of black hair flowed from beneath a knitted Tam O'Shanter.

The boy was younger, no more than ten, with ragged jersey, cut-down tweed trousers and rubber and canvas running shoes that had seen better days. He was in the act of withdrawing a gaff from the water, a salmon spitted on it.

Cussane smiled. 'Where I come from that wouldn't be considered very sporting.'

'Run, Morag!' the boy cried and lunged at Cussane with the gaff, the salmon still wriggling on the end.

A section of the bank crumbled under his foot and he fell back into the pool. He surfaced, still clutching the gaff, but in an instant, the swift current, swollen by the heavy rain, had him in its grasp and carried him away.

'Donal!' the girl screamed and ran to the edge.

Cussane got a hand to her shoulder and pulled her back, just in time as another section of the bank crumbled. 'Don't be a fool. You'll go the same way.'

She struggled to break free and he dropped his bag, shoved her out of the way, and ran along the bank, pushing through the birches. At that point the water poured through a narrow slot in the rocks with real force, taking the boy with it.

Cussane plunged on, aware of the girl behind him. He pulled off his raincoat and threw it to one side. He cut out across the rocks, trying to get to the end of the slot before the boy, reaching out to grab one end of the outstretched gaff which the boy still clutched, minus the salmon now.

He managed it, was aware of the enormous force of the current and then went in headfirst, a circumstance impossible to avoid. He surfaced in the pool below, the boy a yard or so away and reached out and secured a grip on the jersey. A moment later, the current took them in to a shingle strand. As the girl ran down the bank, the boy was on his feet, shook himself like a terrier and scrambled up to meet her.

A sudden eddy brought Cussane's black hat floating in. He picked it up, examined it and laughed. 'Now that will certainly never be the same again,' and he tossed it out into the pool.

He turned to go up the bank and found himself looking into the muzzle of a sawn-off shotgun held by an old man of at least seventy who stood at the edge of the birch trees, the girl, Morag, and the young Donal beside him. He wore a shabby tweed suit, a Tam O'Shanter that was twin to the girl's, and badly needed a shave.

'Who is he, Granda?' the girl asked. 'No water baillie.'

'With a minister's collar, that would hardly be likely.' The old man's speech was tinged with the soft *blâs* of the highlander. 'Are you a man of the cloth?'

'My name is Fallon,' Cussane told him. 'Father Michael Fallon.' He recalled the name of a village in the area from his examination of the ordnance survey map. 'I was making for Whitechapel, missed the bus and thought I'd try a short-cut over the hill.'

The girl had walked back to pick up his raincoat. She returned and the old man took it from her. 'Away you now, Donal, and get the gentleman's bag.'

So, he must have seen everything from the beginning. The boy scampered away and the old man weighed the raincoat in his hand. He felt in a pocket and produced the Stechkin. 'Would you look at that now? No water baillie, Morag, that's for sure, and a damn strange priest.'

'He saved Donal, Granda?' the girl touched his sleeve.

He smiled slowly down at her. 'And so he did. Away to the camp then, girl. Say that we have company and see that the kettle is on the fire.'

He put the Stetchkin back in the raincoat and handed it to Cussane. The girl turned and darted away through the trees and the boy came back with the bag.

'My name is Hamish Finlay and I am in your debt.' He rumpled the boy's hair. 'You are welcome to share what we have. No man can say more.'

They moved up through the trees and started through the plantation. Cussane said, 'This is strange country.'

The old man took out a pipe and filled it from a worn pouch, the shotgun under his arm. 'Aye, the Galloway is that. A man can lose himself here, from other men, if you take my meaning?'

'Oh, I do,' Cussane said. 'Sometimes we all need to do that.'

There was a cry of fear up ahead, the girl's voice raised high. Finlay's gun was in his hands in an instant and as they moved forward, they saw her struggling in the arms of a tall, heavily-built man. Like Finlay, he carried a shotgun and wore an old, patched, tweed suit. His face was brutal and badly needed a shave and yellow hair poked from beneath his cap. He was staring down at the girl as if enjoying her fear, a half smile on his face. Cussane was conscious of real anger, but it was Finlay who handled it.

'Leave her, Murray!'

The other man scowled, hanging on to her, then pushed her away with a forced smile. 'A bit of sport only.' The girl turned and ran away behind him. 'Who's this?'

'Murray, my dead brother's child you are and my responsibility, but did I ever tell you there's a stink to you like bad meat on a summer day?'

The shotgun moved slightly in Murray's grasp and there was hot rage in the eyes. Cussane slipped a hand in his raincoat pocket and found the Stechkin. Calmly, almost contemptuously, the old man lit his pipe and something went out of Murray. He turned on his heel and walked away.

'My own nephew.' Finlay shook his head. 'You know what they say. "Our friends we choose ourselves, but our relations are chosen for us."'

'True,' Cussane said as they started walking again.

'Aye, and you can take your hand off the butt of that pistol. It won't be needed now, Father – or whatever ye are.'

The camp in the hollow was a poor sort of place. The three wagons were old with patched canvas tilts, and the only motor vehicle in view was a jeep of World War Two vintage, painted khaki green. A depressing air of poverty hung over everything, from the ragged clothes of the three women who cooked at the open fire, to the bare feet of the children who played tig amongst the half dozen horses that grazed beside the stream.

Cussane slept well, deep, dreamless sleep that was totally refreshing, and awakened to find the girl, Morag, sitting on the opposite bunk watching him.

Cussane smiled. 'Hello there.'

'That's funny,' she said. 'One minute you were asleep, the next your eyes were open and you were wide awake. How did you learn to do that?'

'The habit of a lifetime.' He glanced at his watch. 'Only six-thirty.'

'We rise early.' She nodded outside the wagon. He could hear voices and smell bacon frying.

'I've dried your clothes,' she said. 'Would you like some tea?'

There was an eagerness to her as if she desperately wanted to please, something infinitely touching. He reached to pull the Tam O'Shanter down more over one ear. 'I like that.'

'My mother knitted it for me.' She pulled it off and looked at it, her face sad.

'That's nice. Is she here?'

'No.' Morag put the Tam O'Shanter back on. 'She ran away with a man called McTavish last year. They went to Australia.'

'And your father?'

'He left her when I was a baby.' She shrugged. 'But I don't care.'

'Is young Donal your brother?'

'No. His father is my cousin, Murray. You saw him earlier.'

'Ah, yes. You don't like him, I think.'

She shivered. 'He makes me feel funny.'

Cussane was conscious of the anger again, but

controlled it. 'That tea would be welcome, plus the chance to get dressed.'

Her reply, cynical and far too adult for her age, surprised him. 'Frightened I might corrupt you, Father?' She grinned. 'I'll fetch your tea.' And she darted out.

His suit had been thoroughly brushed and dried. He dressed quickly, omitting the vest and clerical collar and pulling a thin black polo neck sweater over his head instead. He pulled on his raincoat because it was still raining and went out.

Murray Finlay leaned against the side of a wagon smoking a clay pipe, Donal crouched at his feet.

Cussane said, 'Good morning,' but Murray could only manage a scowl.

Morag turned from the fire to offer Cussane tea in a chipped enamel mug and Murray called, 'Don't I get one?'

She ignored him and Cussane asked, 'Where's your grandfather?'

'Fishing by the loch. I'll show you. Bring your tea.'

There was something immensely appealing, a *gamine* quality that was somehow accentuated by the Tam O'Shanter. It was as if she was putting out her tongue at the whole world in spite of her ragged clothes. It was not pleasant to think of such a girl brutalized by contact with the likes of Murray and the squalor of the years to come.

They went over the rise and came to a small loch, a pleasant place where heather flowed down to the shore-line. Old Hamish Finlay stood thigh deep, rod in hand, making one extremely expert cast after another. A wind stirred the water, small black fins appeared and suddenly, a trout came out of the deep water beyond the sandbar, leapt in the air and vanished.

The old man glanced at Cussane and chuckled. 'Would you look at that now? Have you noticed how often the good things in life tend to pop up in the wrong places?'

'Frequently.'

Finlay gave Morag his rod. 'You'll find three fat ones in the basket. Off with you and get the breakfast going.'

She turned back to the camp and Cussane offered the old man a cigarette. 'A nice child.'

'Aye, you could say that.'

Cussane gave him a light. 'This life you lead is a strange one and yet you aren't gypsies, I think?'

'People of the road. Tinkers. People have many names for us and some of them none too kind. The last remnants of a proud clan broken at Culloden. Mind, we have links with other road people on occasion. Morag's mother was an English gypsy.'

'No resting place?' Cussane said.

'None. No man will have us for long enough. There's a village constable at Whitechapel who'll be up here no later than tomorrow. Three days – that's all we get and he'll move us on. But what about you?'

'I'll be on my way this morning as soon as I've eaten.'

The old man nodded. 'I shan't query the collar you

wore last night. Your business is your own. Is there nothing
I can do for you?'

'Better by far to do nothing,' Cussane told him.

'Like that, is it?' Finlay sighed heavily and, somewhere, Morag screamed.

Cussane came through the trees on the run and found
them in a clearing amongst the birches. The girl was
on her back, Murray was crouching on top, pinning
her down and there was only lust on his face. He groped
for one of her breasts, she cried out again in revulsion
and Cussane arrived. He got a handful of Murray's long
yellow hair, twisting it cruelly so that it was the big
man's turn to cry out. He came to his feet and Cussane
turned him round, held him for a moment, then pushed
him away.

'Don't touch her again!'

Old Hamish Finlay arrived at that moment, shotgun
at the ready. 'Murray, I warned you.'

But Murray ignored him and advanced on Cussane,
glaring ferociously. 'I'm going to smash you, you little
worm!'

He came in fast, arms raised to destroy. Cussane
pivoted to one side and delivered a left to Murray's
kidneys as he lurched past. Murray went down on one
knee, stayed there for a moment, then got up and swung
the wildest of punches. Cussane sank a left under his
ribs followed by a right hook to the cheek, splitting flesh.

'Murray, my God is a God of Wrath when the occasion warrants it.' He punched the big man in the face a second time. 'Touch this girl and I'll kill you, understand?'

Cussane kicked Murray under the kneecap. The big man went down on his knees and stayed there.

Old Finlay moved in. 'I've given you your last warning, you bastard.' He prodded Murray with the shotgun. 'You'll leave my camp this day and go your own way.'

Murray lurched painfully to his feet and turned and hobbled away towards the camp. Finlay said, 'By God, man, you don't do things by halves.'

'I could never see the point,' Cussane told him.

Morag had picked up the rod and fishbasket. She stood looking at him, a kind of wonder in her eyes. And then she backed away. 'I'll see to the breakfast,' she said in a low voice, turned and ran towards the camp.

There was the sound of the jeep's engine starting up, it moved away. 'He hasn't wasted much time,' Cussane said.

Finlay said, 'Good riddance. Now let's to breakfast.'

Murray Finlay pulled up the jeep in front of the newsagents in Whitechapel and sat there thinking. Young Donal sat beside him. He hated and feared his father, had not wanted to come, but Murray had given him no option.

'Stay there,' Murray told him. 'I need tobacco.'

He went to the door of the newsagents' shop which obstinately stayed closed when he tried to push it open. He cursed and started to turn away, then paused. The morning papers were stacked in the shop doorway and his attention was caught by a photo on the front page of one of them. He took out a knife, cut the string which tied the bundle and picked up the top copy.

'Would you look at that? I've got you now, you bastard.' He turned, hurried across the street to the police cottage and opened the garden gate.

Young Donal, puzzled, got out of the jeep, picked up the next paper and found himself looking at a reasonably good photo of Cussane. He stood staring for a moment at the photo of the man who had saved his life, then turned and ran up the road as fast as he could.

Morag was stacking the tin plates after breakfast when Donal arrived on the run.

'What is it?' she cried, for his distress was obvious.

'Where's the Father?'

'Walking in the woods with Granda. What is it?'

There was the sound of the jeep approaching. Donal showed her the paper wildly. 'Look at that. It's him.'

Which it undeniably was. The description, as Ferguson had indicated, had Cussane only posing as a priest and made him out to be not only IRA, but a thoroughly dangerous man.

The jeep roared into the camp, and Murray jumped out holding his shotgun, followed by the village constable who was in uniform but had obviously not had time to shave.

'Where is he?' Murray demanded, and grabbed the boy by the hair and shook him. 'Tell me, you little scut!'

Donal screamed in pain. 'In the wood.'

Murray pushed him away and nodded to the constable. 'Right, let's get him.' He turned and hurried towards the plantation.

Morag didn't think, simply acted. She ducked into the wagon, found Cussane's bag and threw it into the jeep. Then she climbed behind the wheel and pressed the starter. She had driven it often and knew what she was doing. She took the jeep away, wheels spinning across the rough ground. She turned away to one side of Murray and the constable. Murray turned, she was aware of the rage in his face, the flat bang of the shotgun. She swung the wheel, brushing him to one side and took the jeep straight into the forest of young birch trees. Cussane and Finlay, alerted by the commotion, were running towards the camp when the jeep came crashing through the trees and stopped.

'What is it, lass?' Finlay cried.

'Murray got the police. Get in! Get in!' she said to Cussane.

He didn't argue, simply vaulted in beside her, and she took the jeep round in a circle, crashing through the trees. Murray came limping towards them, the constable beside him and the two men dived to one side. The jeep burst out of the trees, bumped across the rough ground past the camp and turned on to the road.

She braked to a halt. 'Whitechapel won't be right. Won't they block the road?'

'They'll block all the bloody roads,' he said.

'So where do we go?'

'We?' Cussane said.

'Don't argue, Mr Cussane. If I stay, they'll arrest me for helping you.'

She passed him the newspaper Donal had given her. He looked at his photo and read the salient facts quickly. He smiled wryly. Someone had been on to him a damn sight more quickly than he would ever have imagined.

'So where to?' she asked impatiently.

He made his decision then. 'Turn left and keep climbing. We're going to try and reach a farm outside a village called Larwick on the other side of those hills. They tell me these things will go anywhere, so who needs roads? Can you handle it?'

'Just watch me!' she said, and drove away.

13

The glen was mainly national forest and they left the road and followed a track through pine trees, climbing higher and higher beside a burn swollen by the heavy rain. Finally, they came up out of the trees at the head of the glen and reached a small plateau.

He touched her arm. 'This will do,' he called above the roaring of the engine.

She braked to a halt and switched off. Rolling hills stretched on either side, fading into mist and heavy rain. He got out the ordnance survey map and went forward to study the terrain. The map was as accurate as only a government survey could make it. He found Larwick with no difficulty. Glendhu, that was where Danny Malone had said the Mungos' farm was, a couple of miles outside the village. The Black Glen it meant in Gaelic and there was only one farm marked. It had to be the place. He spent a few more minutes studying the lie of the land below him in conjunction with the map and then went back to the jeep.

Morag looked up from the newspaper. 'Is it true, all this stuff about you and the IRA?'

He got in out of the rain. 'What do you think?'

'It says here you often pose as a priest. That means you aren't one?'

It was a question as much as anything else and he smiled. 'You know what they say. If it's in the papers it must be true. Why, does it worry you being in the company of such a desperate character?'

She shook her head. 'You saved Donal at the burn and you didn't need to. You helped me – saved me from Murray.' She folded the paper and tossed it into the back of the jeep, a slight frown of bewilderment on her face. 'There's the man in the paper and then there's you. It's like two different people.'

'Most of us are at least three people,' he said. 'There's who I think I am, then the person you think I am.'

'Which only leaves who you really are,' she cut in.

'True, except that some people can only survive by continuously adapting. They become many people, but for it to work, they must really live the part.'

'Like an actor?' she said.

'That's it exactly, except that like any good actor, they must believe in the role they are playing at that particular time.'

She lay back in the seat, half-turned towards him, arms folded, listening intently and it struck him then that, in spite of her background and the sparseness of any formal education in her life, she was obviously highly intelligent.

'I see,' she said. 'So when you pose as a priest, you actually become a priest.'

The directness was disturbing. 'Something like that.' They sat there in silence for a few moments before he said softly, 'You saved my hide back there. If it hadn't been for you, I'd have been in handcuffs again.'

'Again?' she said.

'I was picked up by the police yesterday. They were taking me to Glasgow in the train, but I managed to jump for it. Walked over the hill from there and met you.'

'Lucky for Donal,' she said. 'Lucky for me, if it comes to that.'

'Murray, you mean? Has he been a problem for long?'

'Since I was about thirteen,' she said calmly. 'It wasn't so bad while my Mam was still with us. She kept him in check. But after she left . . .' She shrugged. 'He's never had his way with me, but lately, it got worse. I'd been thinking of leaving.'

'Running away? But where would you go?'

'My grandma. My mother's mother. She's a true gypsy. Her name's Brana – Brana Smith, but she calls herself Gypsy Rose.'

'I seem to have heard a name like that before,' Cussane said, smiling.

'She has the gift,' Morag told him seriously. 'Second

291

sight in all things, with the palm, the crystal or the Tarot cards. She has a house in Wapping in London, on the river, when she isn't working the fairgrounds with the travelling shows.'

'And you'd like to go to her?'

'Granda always said I could when I was older.' She pushed herself up. 'What about you? Do you intend to make for London?'

'Perhaps,' he said slowly.

'Then we could go together.' This she said to him calmly and without emotion, as if it was the most natural thing in the world.

'No,' he said flatly. 'I don't think so. For one thing, it would only get you deeper in trouble. For another, I have to travel light. No excess baggage. When I have to run, I have to run fast. No time to think of anyone but me.'

There was something in her eyes, a kind of hurt, but she showed no emotion, simply got out of the jeep and stood at the side of the track, hands in pockets. 'I understand. You go on from here. I'll walk back down the glen.'

He had a momentary vision of the wretched encampment, imagined the slow and inevitable brutalization of the years. And she was worth more than that. Much more.

'Don't be stupid,' he said. 'Get in!'

'What for?'

'I need you to drive the jeep, don't I, while I follow

the map? Down through the glen below and over that centre hill. There's a farm in a place called Glendhu outside Larwick.'

She got behind the wheel quickly, smiling. 'Have you friends there?'

'Not exactly.' He reached for his bag, opened it, pulled open the false bottom and took out the bundle of banknotes. 'This is the kind of stuff they like. What most people like if it comes to that.' He pulled several notes off, folded them and put them in the breast pocket of her old reefer coat. 'That should keep you going till you find your grannie.'

Her eyes were round in astonishment. 'I can't take that.'

'Oh yes, you can. Now get this thing moving.'

She selected a low gear and started down the track carefully. 'And what happens when we get there? To me, I mean?'

'We'll have to see. Maybe you could catch a train. On your own, you'd probably do very well. I'm the one they're really after, so your only real danger is in being with me.'

She didn't say anything to that and he studied the map in silence. Finally, she spoke again. 'The business about me and Murray. Does that disgust you? I mean, the wickedness of it?'

'Wickedness?' He laughed softly. 'My dear girl, you have no conception of what true wickedness, real evil, is like, although Murray is probably animal enough to come close. A priest hears more of sin in a week than most people experience in a lifetime.'

She glanced at him briefly. 'But I thought you said you only posed as a priest.'

'Did I?' Cussane lit another cigarette and leaned back in the seat, closing his eyes.

As the police car turned out of the carpark at Glasgow Airport, Chief Inspector Trent said to the driver, 'You know where we're going. We've only got thirty-five minutes so step on it.' Devlin and Fox sat in the rear of the car and Trent turned towards them. 'Did you have a good flight?'

'It was fast, that was the main thing,' Fox said. 'What's the present position?'

'Cussane turned up again, at a gypsy encampment in the Galloway Hills. I got the news on the car radio just before you got in.'

'And got away again, I fancy?' Devlin said.

'As a matter of fact, he did.'

'A bad habit he has.'

'Anyway, you said you wanted to be in the Dunhill area. We're going straight to Glasgow Central Railway Station now. The main road is still flooded, but I've made arrangements for us to board the Glasgow to London express. They'll drop us at Dunhill. We'll also have the oaf who had Cussane and lost him in the first place, Sergeant Brodie. At least he knows the local area.'

'Fine,' Devlin said. 'That takes care of everything from the sound of it. You're armed, I hope?'

'Yes. Am I permitted to know where we're going?' Trent asked.

Fox said, 'A village called Larwick not far from this Dunhill place. There's a farm outside which, according to our information, operates as a safe house for criminals on the run. We think our man could be there.'

'But in that case, you should let me call in reinforcements.'

'No,' Devlin told him. 'We understand the farm in question is in an isolated area. The movement of people in any kind of numbers, never mind men in uniform, would be bound to be spotted. If our man is there, he'd run for it again.'

'So we'd catch him,' Trent said.

Devlin glanced at Fox who nodded, and the Irishman turned back to Trent. 'The night before last, three gunmen of the Provisional IRA tried to take him on the other side of the water. He saw them all off.'

'Good God!'

'Exactly. He'd see off a few of your chaps, too, before they got to him. Better to try it our way, Chief Inspector,' Harry Fox said. 'Believe me.'

From the crest of the hill above Glendhu, Cussane and Morag crouched in the wet bracken and looked down. The track had petered out, but in any case, it had seemed politic to Cussane to leave the jeep up there out of sight. There was nothing like an ace in the hole if anything went sour. Better the Mungos didn't know about that.

'It doesn't look much,' Morag said.

Which was an understatement, for the farm presented an unlovely picture. One barn without its roof, tiles missing from the roof of the main building. There were potholes in the yard filled with water, a truck minus its wheels, a decaying tractor, red with rust.

The girl shivered suddenly. 'I've got a bad feeling. I don't like that place.'

He stood up, picked up his bag, and took the Stechkin from his pocket. 'I've got this. There's no need to worry. Trust me.'

'Yes,' she said and there was a kind of passion in her voice. 'I do trust you.'

She took his arm and together they started down through the bracken towards the farm.

Hector Mungo had driven down to Larwick early that morning, mainly because he'd run out of cigarettes although come to think of it, they'd run out of almost everything. He purchased bacon, eggs, various canned foods, a carton of cigarettes and a bottle of Scotch and told the old lady who ran the general store, to put it on the bill, which she did because she was afraid of Mungo and his brother. Everyone was afraid of them. On his way out, Hector helped himself to a morning paper as an afterthought, got into the old van and drove away.

He was a hard-faced man of sixty-two, sullen and morose in an old flying jacket and tweed cap, a grey stubble covering his chin. He turned the van into the yard, pulled up and got out with the cardboard box filled with his purchases and ran for the door through the rain, kicking it open.

The kitchen he entered was indescribably filthy, the old stone sink piled high with dirty pots. His brother, Angus, sat at the table, head in hands, staring into space. He was younger than his brother, forty-five, with cropped hair and a coarse and brutal face that was rendered even more ugly by the old scar that bisected the right eye which had been left milky white.

'I thought you'd never come.' He reached in the box as his brother put it down and found the whisky, opening it and taking a long swallow. Then he found the cigarettes.

'You idle bastard,' Hector told him. 'You might have put the fire on.'

Angus ignored him, simply took another pull at the bottle, lit a cigarette and opened the newspaper. Hector moved across to the sink and found a match to light the Calor gas stove beside it. He paused, looking out into the yard as Cussane and Morag appeared and approached the house.

'We've got company,' he said.

Angus moved to join him. He stiffened. 'Just a minute.'

He laid the newspaper down on the draining board. 'That looks damn like him right there on the front page to me.'

Hector examined the newspaper report quickly. 'Jesus, Angus, we've got a right one here. Real trouble.'

'Just another little Mick straight out of the bogs,' Angus said contemptuously. 'Plenty of room for him at the bottom of the well, just like the others.'

'That's true.' Hector nodded solemnly.

'But not the girl.' Angus wiped his mouth with the back of one hand. 'I like the look of her. She's mine, you old bastard. Just remember that. Now let them in,' he added, as there came a knock at the door.

'You know the Mungo brothers then, Sergeant?' Fox asked Brodie.

They were in the guard's van at the back of the speeding train, the four of them: Devlin, Fox, Trent and the big sergeant.

'They're animals,' Brodie said. 'Everyone in the district is terrified of them. I don't know how they make a living up there. They've both done prison time, Hector for operating an illegal whisky still. He's been inside three times for that. Angus has a string of minor offences to his name and then he killed a man in a fist fight some time back. Sentenced to five years, but they let him out in three. And twice he's been accused of rapes and then the women concerned have dropped the charges.

The suggestion that they operate a safe house doesn't surprise me, but I've no knowledge of it and it certainly has never been mentioned in their files.'

'How close can we get to their farm without being spotted?' Trent asked.

'About a quarter of a mile. The road up Glendhu only goes to their place.'

'No other way out?' Fox asked.

'On foot, I suppose, up the glen, over the hill.'

Devlin said, 'We've got to allow for one important point. If Cussane did mean to stay with the Mungos, his plans were badly disrupted. Being taken by the Sergeant here, jumping from the train, that gypsy encampment, were not on the agenda. That could have changed his plans.'

'True,' Harry Fox said. 'And there's the girl too.'

Trent said, 'They could still be back there in the hills. On the other hand, they've got to pass through Larwick to get to the farm if they're still in that jeep. In a village that size, somebody must have seen it.'

'Let's hope so,' Devlin said and the express started to slow as they came into Dunhill.

'Danny Malone.' Hector Mungo poured strong tea into dirty mugs and added milk. 'A long time since we had Danny here, isn't it, Angus?'

'Aye, it is that.' Angus sat with a glass in his hand, ignoring the other two and staring at Morag who did her best to avoid his gaze.

Cussane was already aware that he had made a big mistake. The service the Mungo brothers had offered people like Danny years before must have been very different from what was available now. He ignored the tea and sat there, one hand on the butt of the Stechkin. He wasn't sure what his next move should be. The script seemed to be writing itself this time.

'Actually, we were reading about you just before you arrived.' Hector Mungo shoved the paper across. 'No mention of the girl, you see.'

Cussane ignored the paper. 'There wouldn't be.'

'So what can we do for you? You want to hole up here for a while?'

'Just for the day,' Cussane said. 'Then tonight, when it's dark, one of you can take us south in that old van of yours. Fill it up with stuff from around the farm, hide us in the back.'

Hector nodded gravely. 'I don't see why not. Where to? Dumfries?'

'How far to Carlisle where the motorway begins?'

'Sixty miles. It'll cost you though.'

'How much?'

Hector glanced at Angus and licked dry lips nervously. 'A thousand. You're hot, my friend. Very hot.'

Cussane opened his case, took out the wad of banknotes and peeled ten off. He laid them on the table. 'Five hundred.'

'Well, I don't know,' Hector began.

'Don't be stupid,' Angus said. 'That's more money in

300

one piece than you've seen at any time during the past six months.' He turned to Cussane. 'I'll drive you to Carlisle myself.'

'That's settled then.' Cussane got up. 'You've got a room we can use, I suppose.'

'No problem.' Hector was all eagerness. 'One to spare for the young lady, too.'

'One will do just fine,' Cussane said as they followed him out into the stone-flagged corridor and up the rickety stairs.

He opened the first door on the landing and led the way into a large bedroom. There was a murky, unpleasant smell and the flowered wallpaper was stained with damp. There was an old brass double bed with a mattress that had seen better days, army surplus blankets stacked on top of it.

'There's a lavatory next door,' Hector said. 'I'll leave you to it then.'

He went out, closing the door. They heard him go back down stairs. There was an old rusting bolt on the door. Cussane rammed it home. There was another door on the opposite side of the room with a key in the lock. He opened it and looked out on a stone staircase against the side of the house going down to the yard. He closed the door and locked it again.

He turned to the girl. 'All right?'

'The one with the bad eye.' She shuddered. 'He's worse than Murray.' She hesitated. 'Can I call you Harry?'

'Why not?'

He quickly unfolded the blankets and spread them on the mattress. 'What are we going to do?' she asked.

'Rest,' he said. 'Get a little sleep. No one can get in. Not at the moment.'

'Do you think they'll take us to Carisle?'

'No, but I don't think they'll try anything until it's dark and we're ready to leave.'

'How can you be sure they will try?'

'Because that's the kind of men they are. Now lie down and try and get some sleep.'

He got on the bed without taking off his coat, the Stechkin in his right hand. She lay down on the other side of the bed. For a while, she stayed there and then she rolled over and cuddled against him.

'I'm frightened.'

'Hush.' His arm went around her. 'Be still now. I am here. Nothing will touch you in this place.'

Her breathing became slow and heavy. He lay there holding her, thinking about things. She was already a liability and how long he could sustain that, he wasn't sure. On the other hand, he owed her. There was a moral debt in that, surely. He looked down at the purity of the young face, still untouched by life. Something good in a bad world. He closed his eyes, thinking of that, and finally slept.

'Did you see all that cash?' Hector asked.

'Yes,' Angus said. 'I saw it.'

'He's locked the door. I heard him.'

'Of course he has. He's no fool. Not that it matters. He's got to come out sooner or later. We'll take him then.'

'Good,' Hector said.

His brother poured another whisky. 'And don't forget. I get the girl.'

Devlin, Fox, Trent and Brodie drove up to Larwick from Dunhill in an old blue Ford van which the police sergeant had borrowed from a local garage. He parked it outside the general store in the village and went in while the others waited. He returned five minutes later and got behind the wheel of the Ford.

'Hector Mungo was in earlier for groceries. The old girl in there runs the saloon bar at the pub in the evenings. She says both of them are around, but no strangers, and they'd stick out like a sore thumb in a place like this.'

Devlin looked out of one of the rear windows in the van doors. There was really only one street, a row of granite cottages, a pub, the store and the hills lifting steeply above. 'I see what you mean.'

Brodie started the engine and drove away, following a narrow road between grey stone walls. 'The only road and the farm at the end of it.' A few minutes later he said, 'Right, this is about as far as we can go without being seen.'

He pulled in under some trees and they all got out. 'How far?' Trent asked.

'Less than a quarter of a mile. I'll show you.'

He led the way up through the trees at the side of the road, scrambling up through ferns and bracken and paused cautiously on the ridge line. 'There you are.'

The farm was below in the hollow a few hundred yards away. 'Cannery Row,' Devlin murmured.

'Yes, it does look a bit like that,' Fox replied. 'No sign of life.'

'What's more important, no sign of the jeep,' Devlin said. 'Maybe I was wrong after all.'

At that moment, both the Mungo brothers came out of the kitchen door and crossed the yard. 'That's them presumably.' Fox took a small pair of Zeiss fieldglasses from his pocket and focused them. 'Nasty looking couple,' he added, as they went into the barn.

A moment later Morag Finlay came into view.

Trent said excitedly, 'It's the girl. Has to be. Reefer coat, Tam O'Shanter. Fits the description exactly.'

'Jesus, Mary and Joseph,' Devlin said softly. 'I was right. Harry must be in the house.'

Trent said, 'How are we going to handle this?'

'You've both got personal radios?' Fox asked.

'Sure.'

'Right, give me one of them. Devlin and I will go in from the rear of the farm. With any kind of luck, we'll take them by surprise. You go back and wait in the van.

The moment I give you the good word, you come up that road like an express train.'

'Fine.'

Trent and Brodie went back towards the road. Devlin took a Walther PPK from his pocket and cocked it. Fox did the same.

The Irishman smiled. 'Just remember one thing. Harry Cussane isn't the kind of man to give any kind of a chance to.'

'Don't worry,' Fox said grimly. 'I shan't.' He started down the slope through the wet bracken and Devlin followed.

Morag came awake and lay staring up at the ceiling blankly, and then she remembered where she was and turned to look at Cussane beside her. He slept quietly, his breathing light, the face in repose, very calm. He still clutched the Stetchkin in his right hand. She gently eased her feet to the floor, stood up and stretched, then she walked to the window. As she looked out, Hector and Angus Mungo crossed the yard and went into the barn opposite. She opened the door and stood at the top of the stone stairs and was aware of some sort of engine starting up. She frowned, listening intently and then quickly went down the steps and crossed the yard.

In the bedroom, Cussane stirred, stretched, then opened his eyes, instantly awake as usual. He was aware of the girl's absence at once, was on his feet in a second. Then he noticed the open door.

The barn was filled with the sour-sweet smell of mash for the Mungos operated their still in there. Hector switched on the old petrol engine and pump that provided their power supply, then checked the vat.

'We need more sugar,' he said.

Angus nodded. 'I'll get some.'

He opened a door that led into a hut built on the side of the barn. There were various supplies in there, all necessary ingredients of their illegal work, and several sacks of sugar. He was about to pick one up when through a broken plank, he saw Morag Finlay outside, peering in through a window at what was going on in the barn. He smiled delightedly, put down the sack and crept out.

Morag was not even aware of his approach. A hand was clamped over her mouth, stifling her cry and she was lifted in strong arms and carried, kicking and struggling, into the barn.

Hector turned from stirring the vat. 'What's this?'

'A little nosey-parker that needs teaching its manners,' Angus said.

He put her down and she struck at him wildly. He slapped her back-handed and then again with enough force to send her sprawling on a pile of sacks.

He stood over her and started to unbuckle his belt.

'Manners,' he said. 'That's what I'm going to teach you.'

'Angus!' Harry Cussane called from just inside the door. 'Are you a bastard by nature or do you really have to work at it?'

He stood there, hands negligently in the pockets of his raincoat, and Angus turned to face him. He bent down to pick up a shovel. 'You little squirt, I'm going to split your skull.'

'Something I picked up from the IRA,' Cussane said. 'A special punishment for special bastards like you.'

The Stechkin came out of his pocket, there was a dull thud and a bullet splintered Angus Mungo's right kneecap. He screamed, fell back against the petrol motor and rolled over, clutching at his knee with both hands, blood pumping between his fingers. Hector Mungo gave a terrible cry of fear, turned and ran headlong for the side door, arms up in a futile gesture of protection. He burst through and disappeared.

Cussane ignored Angus and pulled Morag to her feet. 'Are you all right?'

She turned and looked down at Angus, rage and humiliation on her face. 'No thanks to him.'

He took her arm and they went out and crossed the yard to the kitchen door. As the girl opened it, Harry Fox called, 'Hold it right there, Cussane!' and moved from behind the parked van.

Cussane recognized the voice instantly, sent the girl staggering through the door, turned and fired, all in one smooth motion. Fox fell back against the van, the gun jumping from his hand. In the same moment, Devlin came round the corner and fired twice. The first bullet ripped Cussane's left sleeve, the second caught him in the shoulder, spinning him round. He went through the kitchen door headfirst, kicked it closed behind him, turned and rammed home the bolt.

'You're hit!' Morag cried.

He shoved her ahead of him. 'Never mind that! Let's get out of here!' He pushed her up the stairs towards the bedroom. 'You take the bag,' he urged her, and ran across to the open door and peered out.

The van, with Fox and Devlin, was just round the corner. He put a finger to his lips, nodding to Morag, and went down the stone staircase quietly, the girl following. At the bottom, he led the way round to the back garden, ducked behind the wall and started along the track through the bracken that led to the head of Glendhu.

Devlin opened Fox's shirt and examined the wound just below the breast on the left. Fox's breathing was bad, his eyes full of pain. 'You were right,' he whispered. 'He's good.'

'Take it easy,' Devlin said. 'I've called in Trent and Brodie.'

He could already hear the Ford approaching. Fox said, 'Is he still in the house?'

'I doubt it.'

Fox sighed. 'We cocked it, Liam. There'll be hell to pay over this. We had him and he got away.'

'A bad habit he has,' Devlin said again, and the Ford entered the farmyard and skidded to a halt.

Cussane sat sideways in the passenger seat of the jeep, feet on the ground. He was stripped to the waist. There wasn't a great deal of blood, just the ugly puckered lips of the wound. He knew that was a bad sign, but there was no point in telling her that. She carefully poured sulfa powder on the wound from his small medical kit and affixed one of the field service dressing packs under his instructions.

'How do you feel?' she asked anxiously.

'Fine.' Which was a lie, for now that the initial shock was wearing off, he was in considerable pain. He found one of the morphine ampoules. They were of the kind used on the battlefield. He gave himself an injection and the pain started to ease quite quickly.

'Good,' he said. 'Now pass me a clean shirt. There should still be one left.'

She helped him on with it and then his jacket and raincoat. 'You'll be needing a doctor.'

'Oh, sure,' he said. 'Please help me. I've got a bullet in the shoulder. The first thing he'd reach for would be a telephone.'

'Then what do we do? They'll really start hunting you now. All the roads covered.'

'I know,' he said. 'Let's have a look at the map.' After a while, he said, 'The Solway Firth between us and England. Only one main route through to Carlisle via Dumfries and Annan. Not much road to plug.'

'So we're trapped?'

'Not necessarily. There's the railway. There might be some sort of chance there. Let's get moving and find out.'

Ferguson said, 'It's a mess. Couldn't be worse. How's Harry Fox?'

'He'll live, as they say. At least that's the local doctor's opinion. They've got him here in Dumfries at the general hospital.'

'I'll make arrangements to have him shipped down here to London as soon as possible. I want him to have the best. Where are you phoning from?'

'Police headquarters in Dumfries. Trent's here with me. They're turning out all the men they can. Road blocks and so on. The weather isn't helping. Still raining like hell.'

'What do you think, Liam?'

'I think he's gone.'

'You don't think they are going to net him up there?'

'Not a chance in the wide world.'

Ferguson sighed. 'Yes, frankly, that's how I feel. Stay for a while with Harry, just to make sure, then come back.'

'Now – this evening?'

'Get the night train to London. The Pope flies into Gatwick Airport at eight o'clock tomorrow morning. I want you with me.'

Cussane and Morag left the jeep in a small quarry in a wood above Dunhill and walked down towards the railway line. At that end of the small town, the streets were deserted in the heavy rain and they crossed the road, passed a ruined warehouse with boarded-up windows and squeezed through a gap in the fence above the railway line. A goods train stood in the siding. Cussane crouched down and watched as a driver in overalls walked along the track and pulled himself up into the engine.

'But we don't know where it's going,' Morag said.

Cussane smiled. 'It's pointing south, isn't it?' He grabbed her arm. 'Come on!'

They went down the bank through the gathering dusk, crossed the line as the train started to move. Cussane broke into a trot, reached up and pushed back a sliding door. He tossed in the bag, pulled himself up, turned and reached for the girl's hand. A moment later and she was with him. The wagon was almost filled with packing cases, some of them stencilled with the address of a factory in Penrith.

'Where's that?' Morag asked.

'South of Carlisle. Even if we don't go further than that, we're on our way.'

He sat down, feeling reasonably elated, and lit a cigarette. His left arm worked, but it felt as if it didn't belong to him. Still, the morphine had taken care of the pain. Morag snuggled beside him and he put an arm around her. A long time since he had felt protective towards anyone. To be even more blunt, a long time since he had cared.

She had closed her eyes and seemed to sleep. Thanks to the morphine, the pain had not returned and he could cope when it did. There were several ampoules in his kit. Certainly enough to keep him going. With the bullet in him and no proper medical attention, sepsis would only be a matter of time, but all he needed now was thirty-six hours. The Holy Father flew into Gatwick in the morning. And the day after that, Canterbury.

As the train started to coast along the track he leaned back, his good arm around the girl, and drifted into sleep.

14

Morag came awake with a start. The train seemed to be skidding to a halt. They were passing through some sort of siding and light from the occasional lamp drifted in through the slats, picking Cussane's face out of the darkness. He was asleep, the face wiped clean of any expression. When she gently touched his forehead it was damp with sweat. He groaned and turned on one side and his arm swung across his body. She saw that he was clutching the Stechkin.

She was cold. She turned up the collar of the reefer coat, put her hands in her pockets and watched him. She was a simple girl, uncomplicated in spite of the life she had known, but blessed with a quick mind and a fund of sound common sense.

She had never known anyone like Cussane. It was not just the gun in his hand, the quick, cold violence of the man. She had no fear of him. Whatever else he was, he was not cruel. Most important of all, he had helped her and that was something she was not used to. Even her grandfather had difficulty in protecting her from Murray's brutality. Cussane had saved her from that, and she was enough of a woman to realize he'd saved her from far worse. That she had helped him simply did not occur to her. For the first time in her life, she was filled with a sense of freedom.

The wagon jolted again, Cussane's eyes opened and he turned quickly, up on one knee, and checked his watch. 'One-thirty. I must have slept for a long time.'

'You did.'

He peered out through the slats and nodded. 'We must be moving into the sidings at Penrith. Where's my bag?'

She pushed it across. He rummaged inside, found the medical kit and gave himself another morphine injection. 'How is it?' she asked.

'Fine,' he said. 'No trouble. I'm just making sure.'

He was lying, for the pain, on waking, had been very real. He slid back the door and peered out and a sign for Penrith loomed out of the dark. 'I was right,' he said.

'Are we getting out here?'

'No guarantee this train goes any further and it's not much of a walk to the motorway.'

'Then what?'

'There'll be a service centre, a café, shops, parked cars, trucks. Who knows?' The pain had faded again now and he managed a smile. 'An infinite possibility to things. Now give me your hand, wait till we slow right down, and jump.'

It was a longer walk than Cussane had anticipated so that it was three o'clock when they turned into the carpark of the nearest service centre on the M6 and approached the café. A couple of cars moved in off the motorway and then a truck, a freightliner so massive that Cussane didn't see the police car until the last moment. He pulled Morag down behind a van and the police car stopped, the light on top of it lazily turning.

'What shall we do?' she whispered.

'Wait and see.'

The driver stayed behind the wheel, the other policeman got out and went in the café. They could see him clearly through the plate glass windows. There were perhaps twenty or thirty people in there, scattered amongst the tables. He took a good look round and came out again. He got back in the car and was speaking on the radio as it drove away.

'They were looking for us,' Morag said.

'What else?' He took the Tam O'Shanter off her head and stuffed it in a nearby waste bin. 'That's better. Too much like advertising.' He fumbled in his pocket and found a five pound note which he gave to her. 'They do take-outs in these places. Get some hot tea and sand-wiches. I'll wait here. Safer that way.'

She went up the ramp and into the café. He saw her hesitate at the end of the counter, then pick up a tray. He noticed a bench against a low wall nearby, half-hidden by a large van. He sat down and lit a cigarette and waited, thinking about Morag Finlay.

Strange how right it seemed to think of her. It occurred to him wryly, with the usual priest's habit of self-doubt, that he should not be doing so. She was only a child. He had been celibate for more than twenty years, had never found it in the slightest degree difficult to manage without women. How absurd it would be, to fall in love at the end of the day with a little sixteen-year-old gypsy girl.

She came round the van with a plastic tray and put it on the bench. 'Tea and ham sandwiches and what do you think of this? We're in the paper. There was a stand by the door.'

He drank the scalding hot tea carefully from one of the plastic cups and unfolded the paper on his knee, reading it in the dim light falling across the carpark from the café. The newspaper was a local paper, printed in Carlisle the previous evening. They had Cussane on the front page, a separate picture of Morag beside him.

'You look younger,' he said.

'That was a snap my mother took last year. Granda had it on the wall in his caravan. They must have taken it. He'd never have given it to them.'

'If a local paper had this last night, I'd say we'll be in every national newspaper's first edition later on this morning,' he said.

There was a heavy silence, he lit another cigarette and sat there smoking it, not saying anything.

'You're going to leave me, aren't you?' she asked.

He smiled gently. 'My God, you're about a thousand years old, aren't you? Yes, I'm going to leave you. We don't have any choice.'

'You don't have to explain.'

But he did. 'Newspaper photos can be meaningless to most people. It's the unusual that stands out, like you and me together. On your own, you'd stand a very good chance of going anywhere you want. You've got the money I gave you?'

'Yes.'

'Then go in the café. Sit in the warm and wait. The express buses stop in here. I should know. I came up on one the other day going the opposite way. You should get one to Birmingham and on to London from there with no trouble.'

'And you?'

'Never mind about me. If they do lay their hands on you, tell them I forced you to help me. Enough people will believe that to make it true.' He picked up his bag and put a hand to her face. 'You're a special person. Don't ever let anyone put you down again. Promise me?'

'I will.' She found herself choking, reached up to kiss his cheek, then turned and ran away.

She had learned, in a hard school, not to cry, but there was a hot prickly feeling at the back of her eyes as she went into the café. She brushed past a table. A hand caught her sleeve and she turned to look down at a couple of youths in motor cyclists' black leathers, hard, vicious looking young men with cropped hair. The one who had her sleeve was blond with a Nazi Iron Cross on his breast.

He said, 'What's your problem, darling? Nothing a ride on the back of my bike wouldn't fix.'

She pulled away, not even angry, went and got a cup of tea and sat at a table, hands wrapped around its healing warmth. He had come into her life, he had gone from it and nothing would ever be the same again. She started to cry, slow bitter tears, the first in years.

Cussane had two choices: to take his chance on thumbing a lift or to steal a car. The second gave him more freedom, more personal control, but it would only work if the vehicle wouldn't be missed for some time. There was a motel on the other side of the motorway. Anything parked there would belong to people staying overnight. Three to four hours at least before any of those would be missed, and by then he would be long gone.

He went up the steps to the flyover, thinking about Morag Finlay, wondering what would happen to her. But that wasn't his problem. What he had said to her made perfect sense. Together, they stuck out like a sore thumb. He paused on the bridge, lit another cigarette, trucks swishing past beneath him on the motorway. All perfectly sensible and logical, so why did he feel so rotten about it?

'Dear God, Harry,' he said softly, 'you're being corrupted by honesty and decency and innocence. It's not possible to soil that girl. She'll always remain untouched by the rottenness of life.'

And yet . . .

Someone moved up beside her and a soft voice said, 'You okay, kid? Anything I can do?'

He was West Indian, she knew that, with dark, curling hair, a little grey at the edges. He was perhaps forty-five and wore a heavy driving coat with fur collar, all much stained with grease, and carried a plastic sandwich box and a thermos flask. He smiled, the kind of smile that told her instantly that she was okay, and sat down.

'What's the problem?'

'Life,' she said.

'Heh, that's really profound for a chick as young as you.' But the smile was sympathetic. 'Can I do anything?'

'I'm waiting for the bus.'

'To where?'

'London.'

He shook his head. 'It's always London you kids make for when you run away from home.'

'My grandmother lives in London,' she said wearily. 'Wapping.'

He nodded and frowned as if considering the matter, then stood up. 'Okay, I'm your man.'

'What do you mean?'

'I drive a freightliner and London is my home base. The long way round, mind you, 'cause when I hit Manchester, I've got to take the Pennine motorway to Leeds to drop something off, but we should be in London by the early afternoon.'

'I don't know.' She hesitated.

'Bus won't be through here for another five hours, so what have you got to lose? If it helps, I've got three girls of my own, all older than you, and my name is Earl Jackson.'

'All right,' she said, making her decision, and went out at his side.

They walked down the ramp and started across the carpark. The freightliner also towed a huge trailer. 'Here we are,' he said. 'All the comforts of home.'

There was a footstep and as they turned, the blond biker from the café moved round from behind another truck. He came forward and stood there, hands on hips. 'Naughty girl,' he said. 'I told you you'd be better off on the back seat of my bike and what do I find? You're flying off into the night with Rastus here. Now that's definitely out of order.'

'Oh, dear,' Earl Jackson said. 'It talks and everything. Probably wets if you give it water.'

He leaned down to put his sandwich box and thermos on the ground and the other biker ducked from under the truck and booted him so that he staggered forward losing his balance. The blond one lifted a knee in his face. The one behind pulled Jackson to his feet, an arm round his throat and the other flexed his hands, tightening his gloves.

'Hold him, Sammy. He's my meat now.'

Sammy screamed as a fist swung into his kidneys. He jerked in agony, releasing his grip on Jackson and Cussane hit him again, sending him to his knees.

He slipped past Jackson to confront the other biker. 'You really should have stayed under your stone.'

The youth's hand came out of his pocket and, as Morag cried a warning, there was a click as a blade sprang into view, flashing in the pale light. Cussane dropped his bag, swayed to one side, grabbed for the wrist with both hands, twisted it round and up, locking the arm, and ran the blond headfirst into the side of the truck. The youth dropped to his knees, blood on his face, and Cussane pulled him up and reached for the other, who was now standing. He pulled them close.

'I could put you on sticks for a year, but perhaps you'd just rather go?'

They backed off in horror, turned and stumbled away. Cussane was aware of the pain then, so bad that it made him feel sick. He turned, clutching at the canvas side of the trailer, and Morag ran forward and put an arm around him.

'Harry, are you all right?'

'Sure, don't worry.'

Earl Jackson said, 'You saved my hide, man. I owe you.' He turned to Morag. 'I don't think I got the whole story.'

'We were together, then we got separated.' She glanced at Cussane. 'Now we're together again.'

Jackson said, 'Is his destination London, too?'

She nodded. 'Does the offer still hold good?'

He smiled. 'Why not. Climb up in the cab. You'll find a sliding panel behind the passenger seat. An improvement of mine. There's a bunk in there, blankets and so on. It means I can sleep in the carpark and save on hotel bills.'

Morag climbed up. As Cussane made to follow her, Jackson caught his sleeve. 'Look, I don't know what gives here, but she's a nice kid.'

'You don't need to worry,' Cussane told him. 'I think so too.' And he climbed up into the cab.

It was just after 8 a.m. on a fine, bright morning when the Alitalia jet which had brought Pope John Paul from Rome landed at Gatwick Airport. The Pontiff came down the ladder, waving to the enthusiastic crowd. His first act was to kneel and kiss English soil.

Devlin and Ferguson stood on the balcony looking down. The Brigadier said, 'It's at moments like this that I'd welcome my pension.'

'Face facts,' Devlin said. 'If a really determined assassin, the kind who doesn't mind committing suicide, sets his sights on getting the Pope or the Queen of England or whoever, the odds are heavily in his favour.'

Below, the Pope was welcomed by Cardinal Basil Hume and the Duke of Norfolk on behalf of the Queen. The Cardinal made a speech of welcome and the Pope replied. Then they moved to the waiting cars.

Devlin said, 'What happens now?'

'Mass at Westminster Cathedral. After lunch, a visit to Her Majesty at Buckingham Palace. Then St George's Cathedral at Southwark to anoint the sick. It's going to be all go, I can see that.' Ferguson was unhappy and it showed. 'Dammit, Liam, where is he? Where is that sod, Cussane?'

'Around,' Devlin said. 'Closer than we think, probably. The only certainty is that he'll surface within the next twenty-four hours.'

'And then we get him,' Ferguson said as they walked away.

'If you say so,' was Liam Devlin's only comment.

The yard of the warehouse in Hunslet, Leeds, quite close to the motorway, was packed with trucks. Cussane had the sliding panel open and Jackson said, 'Keep out of sight, man. Passengers are strictly *verboten*. I could lose my licence.'

He got out of the truck to see to the disengagement of the trailer, then went into the freight office to get a signature for it.

The clerk looked up from his desk. 'Hello, Earl, good run?'

'Not bad.'

'I hear they've been having fun over there on the M6. One of the lads rang in from outside Manchester. Had a breakdown. Said they'd had a lot of police activity.'

'I didn't notice anything,' Jackson said. 'What was it about?'

'Looking for some guy that's mixed up with the IRA. Has a girl with him.'

Jackson managed to stay calm and signed the sheets. 'Anything else?'

'No, that's fine, Earl. See you next trip.'

Jackson moved outside. He hesitated beside the truck, then followed his original intention and went out of the yard across the road to the transport café. He gave the girl behind the counter his thermos to fill, ordered some bacon sandwiches and bought a newspaper which he read slowly on the way back to the truck.

He climbed up behind the wheel and passed the thermos and sandwiches through. 'Breakfast and something to read while you eat.'

The photos were those which had appeared in the Carlisle paper and the story was roughly the same. The details on the girl were sparse. It simply said she was in his company.

As they entered the slip road leading up to the motorway, Cussane said, 'Well?'

Jackson concentrated on the road. 'This is heavy

stuff, man. Okay, I owe you, but not that much. If you're picked up . . .'

'It would look bad for you.'

'I can't afford that,' Jackson told him. 'I've got form. Been inside twice. Cars were my game till I got smart. I don't want trouble and I definitely don't want to see the inside of Pentonville again.'

'Then the simplest thing to do is keep driving,' Cussane told him. 'Once in London, we drop off and you go on about your business. No one will ever know.'

It was the only solution and Jackson knew it. 'Okay,' he sighed. 'I guess that's it.'

'I'm sorry, Mr Jackson,' Morag told him.

He smiled at her in the mirror. 'Never mind, kid. I should have known better. Now keep inside and close that panel,' and he turned the freightliner on to the motorway.

Devlin was on the phone to the hospital in Dumfries when Ferguson came in from the study.

As the Irishman put down the receiver, the Brigadier said, 'I could do with some good news. Just had advance notice that 2 Para under the command of Colonel H. Jones attacked some place called Goose Green in the Falklands. Turned out to be about three times the Argentinian troops there as anticipated.'

'What happened?'

'Oh, they won the day, but Jones died, I'm afraid.'

'The news on Harry Fox is comforting,' Devlin said. 'They are flying him down from Glasgow this evening. But he's in fair shape.'

'Thank God for that,' Ferguson said.

'I spoke to Trent. They can't get a word out of those tinkers. Nothing helpful anyway. According to the old grandfather, he's no idea where the girl might go. Her mother's in Australia.'

'They're worse than gypsies, tinkers,' Ferguson said. 'I know. I come from Angus, remember. Funny people. Even when they hate each other, they hate the police more. Wouldn't even tell you the way to the public toilet.'

'So what do we do now?'

'We'll go along to St George's to see what His Holiness is up to, then I think you can take a run down to Canterbury. I'm laying on a police car and driver for you, by the way. I think it will help for you to look as official as possible from now on.'

Morag sat in the corner of the bunk, her back against the wall. 'Why did you come back at Penrith? You haven't told me.'

Cussane shrugged. 'I suppose I decided you weren't fit to be out on your own or something like that.'

She shook her head. 'Why are you so afraid to admit to kindness?'

'Am I?' He lit a cigarette and watched her as she

took an old pack of cards from her pocket and shuffled them. They were Tarot. 'Can you use those things?'

'My grandma showed me how years ago when I was quite young. I'm not sure if I have the gift. It's hard to tell.'

She shuffled the cards again. He said, 'The police might be waiting at her place.'

She paused, surprise on her face. 'Why should they? They don't know she exists.'

'They must have asked questions at the camp and someone must have told them something. If not your grandad, there's always Murray.'

'Never,' she said. 'Even Murray wouldn't do a thing like that. You were different – an outsider – but me, that's not the same at all.'

She turned the first card. It was the Tower, the building struck by lightning, two bodies falling. 'The individual suffers through the forces of destiny being worked out in the world,' Morag commented.

'That's me. Oh, that's very definitely me,' Harry Cussane told her and he started to laugh helplessly.

Susan Calder was twenty-three, a small girl, undeniably attractive in the neat navy-blue police uniform with the hat with the black and white checks round the brim. She had trained as a schoolteacher, but three terms of that had very definitely been enough. She had volunteered for the Metropolitan Police and had been accepted. She had served for just over one year. Waiting beside the police car outside the Cavendish Square flat, she presented a pleasing picture, and Devlin's heart lifted. She was polishing the windscreen as he came down the steps.

'Good day to you, *a colleen*, God save the good work.'

She took in the black Burberry, the felt hat slanted across the ears, was about to give him a dusty answer, then paused. 'You wouldn't be Professor Devlin, would you?'

'As ever was. And you?'

'WPC Susan Calder, sir.'

'Have they told you you're mine until tomorrow?'

'Yes, sir. Hotel booked in Canterbury.'

'There *will* be talk back at the station. Let's get moving then,' and he opened the rear door and got in. She slipped behind the wheel and drove away and Devlin leaned back, watching her. 'Have they told you what this is about?'

'You're with Group Four, sir, that's all I know.'

'And that is?'

'Anti-terrorism; intelligence side of things as distinct from the Yard's anti-terrorist squad.'

'Yes, Group Four can employ people like me and get away with it.' He frowned. 'The next sixteen hours will see the making or breaking of this affair and you'll be with me every step of the way.'

'If you say so, sir.'

'So I think you deserve to know what it's about.'

'Should you be telling me, sir?' she asked calmly.

It was one way of getting it all straight in his head.

'No, but I'm going to,' he said and started to talk, telling her everything there was to know about the whole affair from the beginning and especially about Harry Cussane.

When he was finished, she said, 'It's quite a story.'

'And that's an understatement.'

'There is just one thing, sir.'

'And what would that be?'

'My elder brother was killed in Belfast three years ago while serving there as a lieutenant in the Marines. A sniper hit him from a place called the Divis flats.'

'Does that mean I pose a problem for you?' Devlin asked her.

'Not at all, sir. I just wanted you to know,' she said crisply and turned into the main road and drove down towards the river.

Cussane and Morag stood in the quiet street on the edge of Wapping and watched the freightliner turn the corner and disappear.

'Poor Earl Jackson,' Cussane said. 'I bet he can't get away fast enough. What's your grandma's address?'

'Cork Street Wharf. It's five or six years since I was there. I'm afraid I can't remember the way.'

'We'll find it.'

They walked down towards the river which seemed

the obvious thing to do. His arm was hurting again and he had a headache, but he made no sign of any of this to the girl. When they came to a grocery shop on a corner, she went in to make enquiries.

She came out quickly. 'It's not far. It's only a couple of streets away.'

They walked to the corner and there was the river and a hundred yards further on, a sign on the wall saying *Cork Street Wharf.*

Cussane said, 'All right, off you go. I'll stay back out of the way, just in case she has visitors.'

'I shan't be long.'

She hurried off down the street and Cussane stepped back through a broken door into a hard half-filled with rubble and waited. He could smell the river. Not many boats now though. This had once been the greatest port in the world, now it was a graveyard of rusting cranes pointing into the sky like primeval monsters. He felt lousy and when he lit a cigarette, his hand shook. There was the sound of running steps and Morag appeared. 'She isn't there. I spoke to the next door neighbour.'

'Where is she?'

'With a touring show. A fairground show. She's in Maidstone this week.'

And Maidstone was only thirty miles from Canterbury. There was an inevitability to things and Cussane said, 'We'd better get going then.'

'You'll take me?'

'Why not?' and he turned and led the way along the street.

He found what he was looking for within twenty minutes, a pay and display parking lot.

'Why is this so important?' she demanded.

'Because people pay in advance for however many hours of parking they want and stick the ticket on the windscreen. A wonderful aid to car thieves. You can tell just how long you've got before the car is missed.'

She scouted around. 'There's one here says six hours.'

'And what time was it booked in?' He checked and took out his pocket knife. 'That'll do. Four hours to go. Dark then anyway.'

He worked on the quarter-light with the knife, forced it and unlocked the door, then he reached under the dashboard and pulled the wires down.

'You've done this before,' she said.

'That's true.' The engine roared into life. 'Okay,' he said, 'Let's get out of here,' and as she scrambled into the passenger seat, he drove away.

15

'Of course, it's hardly surprising the Pope wants to come here, sir,' Susan Calder said to Devlin. 'This is the birthplace of English Christianity. It was St Augustine who founded the cathedral here in Saxon times.'

'Is it now?' They were standing in the magnificent Perpendicular nave of the cathedral, the pillars soaring to the vaulted ceiling high above them. The place was a hive of activity, workmen everywhere.

'It's certainly spectacular,' Devlin said.

'It was even bombed in nineteen-forty-two during the Canterbury blitz. The library was destroyed, but it's been rebuilt. Up here in the north-west transept is where Saint Thomas Beckett was murdered by the three knights eight hundred years ago.'

'I believe the Pope has a particular affinity for him,' Devlin said. 'Let's have a look.'

They moved up the nave to the place of Beckett's

martyrdom all those years ago. The precise spot where he was traditionally believed to have fallen was marked by a small square stone. There was a strange atmosphere. Devlin shivered, suddenly cold.

'The Sword's Point,' the girl said simply. 'That's what they call it.'

'Yes, well they would, wouldn't they? Come on, let's get out of here. I could do with a smoke and I've seen enough.'

They went out through the south porch past the police guard. There was plenty of activity outside also, workmen working on stands and a considerable police presence. Devlin lit a cigarette and he and Susan Calder moved out on to the pavement.

'What do you think?' she said. 'I mean, not even Cussane could expect to get in there tomorrow. You've seen the security.'

Devlin took out his wallet and produced the security card Ferguson had given him. 'Have you seen one of these before?'

'I don't think so.'

'Very special. Guaranteed to unlock all doors.'

'So?'

'Nobody has asked to see it. We were totally accepted when we walked in. Why? Because you are wearing police uniform. And don't tell me that's what you are. It isn't the point.'

'I see what you mean.' She was troubled and it showed.

'The best place to hide a tree is in a forest,' he said.

'Tomorrow, there'll be policemen all over the place and church dignitaries so what's another policeman or priest.'

At that moment someone called his name, and they turned to see Ferguson walking towards them with a man in a dark overcoat. Ferguson wore a greatcoat of the kind favoured by Guards officers, and carried a smartly rolled umbrella.

'Brigadier Ferguson,' Devlin told the girl hastily.

'There you are,' the Brigadier said. 'This your driver?'

'WPC Calder, sir,' she saluted smartly.

'This is Superintendent Foster, attached to Scotland Yard's anti-terrorist squad,' Ferguson said. 'I've been going over things with him. Seems pretty watertight to me.'

'Even if your man gets as far as Canterbury, there's no way he'll get in the cathedral tomorrow,' Foster said simply. 'I'd stake my reputation on it.'

'Let's hope you don't have to,' Devlin told him.

Ferguson tugged at Foster's sleeve impatiently. 'Right, let's get inside before the light fails. I'm staying here tonight myself, Devlin. I'll phone you at your hotel later.'

The two men walked up to the great door, a policeman opened it for them and they went inside. 'Do you think he knows them?' Devlin asked her gently.

'God, I don't know. You've got *me* wondering now, sir.' She opened the door of the car for him. He got in and she slid behind the wheel and started the engine. 'One thing.'

'What's that?'

'Even if he did get in and did something, he'd never get out again.'

'But that's the whole point,' Devlin said. 'He doesn't care what happens to him afterwards.'

'God help us then.'

'I wouldn't bank on it. Nothing we can do now, girl dear. We don't control the game any more, it controls us, so get us to that hotel in your own good time and I'll buy you the best dinner the place can offer. Did I tell you, by the way, that I have this terrible thing for women in uniform?'

As she turned out into the traffic she started to laugh.

The caravan was large and roomy and extremely well-furnished. The bedroom section was separate in its own small compartment, twin bunks. When Cussane opened the door and peered in, Morag appeared to be sleeping.

He started to close the door and she called, 'Harry?'

'Yes?' He moved back in. 'What is it?'

'Is Grandma still working?'

'Yes.'

He sat on the edge of the bunk. He was in considerable pain now. It even hurt to breathe. Something was badly wrong, he knew that. She reached up to touch his face and he drew back a little.

She said, 'Remember in Granda's caravan that first day? I asked if you were frightened I might corrupt you.'

'To be precise,' he told her, 'your actual words were: "Are you frightened I might corrupt you, *Father*?"'

She went very still. 'You are a priest then? A real priest? I think I always knew it.'

'Go to sleep,' he said.

She reached for his hand. 'You wouldn't leave without telling me?'

There was genuine fear in her voice. He said gently, 'Now would I do a thing like that to you?' He got up and opened the door. 'Like I said, get some sleep. I'll see you in the morning.'

He lit a cigarette, opened the door and went out. The Maidstone fairground was a comparatively small affair, a number of sideshows, various stalls, bingo stands, several carousels. There were still a number of people around, noisy and good-humoured in spite of the late hour, music loud on the night air. At one end of the caravan was the Land Rover which towed it, at the other the red tent with the illuminated sign that said *Gypsy Rose*. As he watched, a young couple emerged, laughing. Cussane hesitated, then went in.

Brana Smith was at least seventy, a highly-coloured scarf drawing back the hair from the brown parchment face. She wore a shawl over her shoulders, a necklace of gold coins around her neck. The table she was seated at had a crystal ball on it.

'You certainly look the part,' he said.

'That's the general idea. The public like a gypsy to look like a gypsy. Put up the closed sign and give me a cigarette.' He did as he was told, came back and sat opposite her like a client, the crystal between them. 'Is Morag asleep?'

'Yes.' He took a deep breath to control his pain. 'You must never let her go back to that camp, you understand me?'

'Don't worry.' Her voice was dry and very calm. 'We gypsies stick together and we pay our debts. I'll put the word out and one day soon Murray pays for what he's done, believe me.'

He nodded. 'When you saw her picture in the paper today and read the circumstances, you must have been worried. Why didn't you get in touch with the police?'

'The police? You must be joking.' She shrugged. 'In any case, I knew she was coming and I knew she would be all right.'

'Knew?' Cussane said.

She rested a hand lightly on the crystal. 'These are only the trappings, my friend. I have the gift as my mother did before me and hers before her.'

He nodded. 'Morag told me. She read the Tarot cards for me, but she isn't certain of her powers.'

'Oh, she has the gift.' The old woman nodded. 'As yet unformed.' She pushed a pack of cards to him. 'Cut them, then hand them back to me with your left hand.'

338

He did as he was told and she cut them in turn. 'The cards mean nothing without the gift. You understand this?'

He felt strangely light-headed. 'Yes.'

'Three cards, that will tell all.' She turned the first. It was the Tower. 'He has suffered through the forces of destiny,' she said. 'Others have controlled his life.'

'Morag drew that card,' he said. 'She told me something like that.'

She turned the second card. It showed a young man suspended upside down from a wooden gibbet by his right ankle.

'The Hanged Man. When he strives hardest, it is with his own shadow. He is two people. Himself and yet not himself. Impossible now to go back to the wholeness of youth.'

'Too late,' he said. 'Far too late.'

The third card showed Death in traditional form, his scythe mowing a crop of human bodies.

'But whose?' Cussane laughed a little too loud. 'Death, I mean? Mine or perhaps somebody else's?'

'The card means far more than its superficial image implies. He comes as a redeemer. In this man's death lies the opportunity for rebirth.'

'Yes, but for whom?' Cussane demanded, leaning forward. The light reflected from the crystal seemed very bright.

She touched his forehead, damp with sweat. 'You are ill.'

'I'll be all right. I need to lie down, that's all.' He got to his feet. 'I'll sleep for a while, if that's all right with you, then I'll leave before Morag wakes. That's important. Do you understand me?'

'Oh, yes,' she nodded. 'I understand you very well.'

He went out into the cool night. Most people had gone home now, the stalls, the carousels were closing down. His forehead was burning. He went up the steps into the caravan and lay on the bench seat, looking up at the ceiling. Better to take the morphine now than in the morning. He got up, rummaged in the bag and found an ampoule. The injection worked quite quickly and, after a while, he slept.

He came awake with a start, his head clear. It was morning, light coming in through the windows and the old woman was seated at the table smoking a cigarette and watching him. When he sat up, the pain was like a living thing. For a moment, he thought he was going to stop breathing.

She pushed a cup across to him. 'Hot tea. Drink some.'

It tasted good, better than anything he had ever known, and he smiled and helped himself to a cigarette from her packet, hand shaking. 'What time is it?'

'Seven o'clock.'

'And Morag's still asleep?'

'Yes.'

'Good. I'll get going.'

She said gravely, 'You're ill, Father Harry Cussane. Very ill.'

He smiled gently. 'You have the gift, so you would know.' He took a deep breath. 'Things to get straight before I go. Morag's position in all this. Have you got a pencil?'

'Yes.'

'Good. Take down this number.' She did as she was told. 'The man on the other end is called Ferguson – Brigadier Ferguson.'

'Is he police?'

'In a way. He'd dearly love to get his hands on me. If he isn't there, they'll know how to contact him wherever he is, which is probably Canterbury.'

'Why there?'

'Because I'm going to Canterbury to kill the Pope.' He produced the Stechkin from his pocket. 'With this.'

She seemed to grow small, to withdraw into herself. She believed him, of course, he could see that. 'But why?' she whispered. 'He's a good man.'

'Aren't we all?' he said, 'or at least were, at some time or other in our lives. The important thing is this. When I've gone, you phone Ferguson. Tell him I'm going to Canterbury Cathedral. You'll also tell him I forced Morag to help me. Say she was frightened for her life. Anything.' He laughed. 'Taking it all in all, that should cover it.'

He picked up his bag and walked to the door. She said, 'You're dying, don't you know that?'

'Of course I do.' He managed a smile. 'You said that Death on the Tarot cards means redemption. In my death lies the opportunity for rebirth. That child's in there. That's all that's important.' He opened the bag, took out the bundle of fifty pound notes and tossed them on the table. 'That's for her. I won't be needing it now.'

He went out. The door banged. She sat there listening, aware of the sound of the car starting up and moving away. She stayed like that for a long time, thinking about Harry Cussane himself. She had liked him more than most men she had known, but there was Death in his eyes, she had seen that at the first meeting. And there was Morag to consider.

There was a sound of movement next door where the girl slept – a faint stirring. Old Brana checked her watch. It was eight-thirty. Making her decision, she got up, let herself out of the caravan quietly. Hurried across the fairground to the public phone box and dialled Ferguson's number.

Devlin was having breakfast at the hotel in Canterbury with Susan Calder when he was called to the phone. He was back quite quickly.

'That was Ferguson. Cussane's turned up. Or at least his girl-friend has. Do you know Maidstone?'

'Yes, sir. It can't be more than sixteen or seventeen miles from here. Twenty at the most.'

'Then let's get moving,' he said. 'There really isn't much time for any of us now.'

In London, the Pope had left the Pro-Nunciature very early to visit more than 4000 religious: nuns, monks, and priests, Catholic and Anglican, at Digby Stuart Training College in London. Many of them were from enclosed orders. This was the first time they had gone into the outside world in many years. It was a highly emotional moment for all when they renewed their vows in the Holy Father's presence. It was after that that he left for Canterbury in the helicopter provided by British Caledonian Airways.

Stokely Hall was bounded by a high wall of red brick, a Victorian addition to the estate when the family still had money. The lodge beside the great iron gates was Victorian also, though the architect had done his best to make it resemble the early Tudor features of the main house. When Cussane drove by on the main road, there were two police cars at the gates and a police motor-cyclist who had been trailing behind him for the past mile, turned in.

Cussane carried on down the road, the wall on his left, fringed by trees. When the gate was out of sight, he scanned the opposite side of the road and finally noticed a five-barred gate and a track leading into a wood.

He drove across quickly, got out, opened the gate, then drove some little way into the trees. He went back to the gate, closed it and returned to the car.

He took off his raincoat, jacket and shirt, awkwardly because of his bad arm. The smell was immediately apparent, the sickly odour of decay. He laughed foolishly and said softly, 'Jesus, Harry, you're falling apart.'

He got his black vest from the bag, his clerical collar and put them on. Finally, the cassock. It seemed a thousand years since he had rolled it up and put it in the bottom of the bag at Kilrea. He reloaded the Stechkin with a fresh clip, put it in one pocket, a spare clip in the other and got in the car as it started to drizzle. No more morphine. The pain would keep him sharp. He closed his eyes and vowed to stay in control.

Brana Smith sat at the table in the caravan, an arm around Morag, who was crying steadily.

'Just tell me exactly what he said,' Liam Devlin told her.

'Grandma . . .' the girl started.

The old woman shook her head. 'Hush, child.' She turned to Devlin. 'He told me he intended to shoot the Pope. Showed me the gun. Then he gave me the telephone number to ring in London. The man Ferguson.'

'And what did he tell you to say?'

'That he would be at Canterbury Cathedral.'

'And that's all?'

'Isn't it enough?'

Devlin turned to Susan Calder standing at the door. 'Right, we'd better get back.'

She opened the door. Brana Smith said, 'What about Morag?'

'That's up to Ferguson.' Devlin shrugged. 'I'll see what I can do.'

He started to go out and she said, 'Mr Devlin?' He turned. 'He's dying.'

'Dying?' Devlin said.

'Yes, from a gunshot wound.'

He went out, ignoring the curious crowd of fairground workers, and got in the front passenger seat beside Susan. As she drove away, he called up Canterbury Police Headquarters on the car radio and asked to be patched through to Ferguson.

'Nothing fresh here,' he told the Brigadier. 'The message was for you and quite plain. He intends to be at Canterbury Cathedral.'

'Cheeky bastard!' Ferguson said.

'Another thing. He's dying. It would seem sepsis must be setting in from the bullet he took at the Mungos' farm.'

'Your bullet?'

'That's right.'

Ferguson took a deep breath. 'All right, get back here fast. The Pope should be here soon.'

* * *

345

Stokely Hall was one of the finest Tudor mansions in England and the Stokelys had been one of the handful of English aristocratic families to maintain its Catholicism after Henry VIII and the Reformation. The thing which distinguished Stokely was the family chapel, the chapel in the wood, reached by tunnel from the main house. It was regarded by most experts as being, in effect, the oldest Catholic church in England. The Pope had expressed a desire to pray there.

Cussane lay back in the passenger seat thinking it over. The pain was a living thing now, his face ice-cold and yet dripping sweat. He managed to find a cigarette and started to light it and then, in the distance, heard the sound of engines up above. He got out of the car and stood listening. A moment later, the blue and white painted helicopter passed overhead.

Susan Calder said, 'You don't look happy, sir.'

'It was Liam last night. And I'm not happy. Cussane's behaviour doesn't make sense.'

'That was then, this is now. What's worrying you?'

'Harry Cussane, my good friend of more than twenty years. The best chess player I ever knew.'

'And what was the most significant thing about him?'

'That he was always three moves ahead. That he had the ability to make you concentrate on his right hand when what was really important was what he was doing

346

with his left. In the present circumstances, what does that suggest to you?'

'That he hasn't any intention of going to Canterbury Cathedral. That's where the action is. That's where everyone is waiting for him.'

'So he strikes somewhere else. But how? Where's the schedule?'

'Back seat, sir.'

He found it and read it aloud. 'Starts off at Digby Stuart College in London, then by helicopter to Canterbury.' He frowned. 'Wait a minute. He's dropping in at some place called Stokely Hall to visit a Catholic chapel.'

'We passed it on the way to Maidstone,' she said. 'About three miles from here. But that's an unscheduled visit. It's not been mentioned in any of the newspapers that I've seen and everything else has. How would Cussane know?'

'He used to run the press office at the Catholic Secretariat in Dublin.' Devlin slammed a fist into his thigh. 'That's it. Has to be. Get your foot down hard and don't stop for anything.'

'What about Ferguson?'

He reached for the mike. 'I'll try and contact him, but it's too late for him to do anything. We'll be there in a matter of minutes. It's up to us now.'

He took the Walther from his pocket, cocked it, then put the safety catch on as the car shot forward.

*   *   *

The road was clear when Cussane crossed it. He moved into the shelter of the trees and walked along the base of the wall. He came to an old iron gate, narrow and rusting, fixed firm in the wall and as he tested it, heard voices on the other side. He moved behind a tree and waited. Through the bars he could see a path and rhododendron bushes. A moment later, two nuns walked by.

He gave them time to pass, then went back to where the ground under the trees rose several feet bringing him almost level with the wall. He reached for a branch that stretched across. It would have been ridiculously easy if it had not been for his shoulder and arm. The pain was appalling, but he hoisted the skirts of his cassock to give him freedom of movement and swung across, pausing on top of the wall for only a moment before dropping to the ground.

He stayed on one knee, fighting for breath, then stood up and ran a hand over his hair. Then he hurried along the path, aware of the nuns' voices up ahead, turned a corner by an old stone fountain and caught up with them. They turned in surprise. One of them was very old, the other younger.

'Good morning, Sisters,' he said briskly. 'Isn't it beautiful here? I couldn't resist taking a little walk.'

'Neither could we, Father,' the older one said.

They walked on side-by-side and emerged from the shrubbery on to an expansive lawn. The helicopter was parked a hundred yards to the right, the crew lounging beside it. There were several limousines in front of the

house and two police cars. A couple of policemen crossed
the lawn with an Alsatian guard dog on a lead. They
passed Cussane and the two nuns without a word and
continued down towards the shrubbery.

'Are you from Canterbury, Father?' the old nun
enquired.

'No, *Sister* . . .?' he paused.

'Agatha – and this is Sister Anne.'

'I'm with the Secretariat in Dublin. A wonderful thing
to be invited over here to see His Holiness. I missed
him during his Irish trip.'

Susan Calder turned in from the road at the front gate
and Devlin showed his security pass as two policemen
moved forward. 'Has anyone passed through here in
the last few minutes?'

'No, sir,' one officer said. 'A hell of a lot of guests
came before the helicopter arrived though.'

'Move!' Devlin said.

Susan went up the drive at some speed. 'What do
you think?'

'He's here!' Devlin said. 'I'd stake my life on it.'

'Have you met His Holiness yet, Father?' Sister Anne
enquired.

'No, I've only just arrived from Canterbury with a
message for him.'

They were crossing the gravel drive now, past the policemen standing beside the cars, up the steps and past the two uniformed security guards and in through the great oak door. The hall was spacious, a central staircase lifting to a landing. Double doors stood open to the right, disclosing a large reception room filled with visitors, many of them church dignitaries.

Cussane and the two nuns walked towards it. 'And where is this famous Stokely chapel?' he asked. 'I've never seen it.'

'Oh, it's so beautiful,' Sister Agatha said. 'So many years of prayer. The entrance is just down the hall, see where the Monsignor is standing?'

They paused at the door of the reception and Cussane said, 'If you'll excuse me for a moment. I may be able to give my message to His Holiness before he joins the reception.'

'We'll wait for you, Father,' Sister Agatha said. 'I think we'd rather go in with you.'

'Of course. I shan't be long.'

Cussane went past the bottom of the stairs and moved into the corner of the hall where the Monsignor was standing, resplendent in scarlet and black. He was an old man with silver hair and spoke with an Italian accent.

'What do you seek, Father?'

'His Holiness.'

'Impossible. He is at prayer.'

Cussane put a hand to the old man's face, turned the

handle of the door and forced him through. He closed the door behind him with a foot.

'I'm truly sorry, Father.' He chopped the old priest on the side of the neck and gently lowered him to the floor.

A long narrow tunnel stretched ahead of him, dimly lit, steps leading up to an oaken door at the end. The pain was terrible now, all consuming. But that no longer mattered. He fought for breath momentarily, then took the Stechkin from his pocket and went forward.

Susan Calder swung the car in at the bottom of the steps and as Devlin jumped out, she followed him. His security pass was already in his hand as a police sergeant moved forward.

'Anything out of the way happened? Anyone unusual gone in?'

'No, sir. Lots of visitors before the Pope arrived. Couple of nuns and a priest just went in.'

Devlin went up the steps on the run past the security guards, Susan Calder at his heels. He paused, taking in the scene, the reception on the right, the two nuns waiting by the door. *A priest, the sergeant had said.*

He approached Sisters Agatha and Anne. 'You've just arrived, Sisters?'

Beyond them, the guests talked animatedly, waiters moving amongst them.

'That's right,' Sister Agatha said.

'Wasn't there a priest with you?'

'Oh, yes, the good father from Dublin.'

Devlin's stomach went hollow. 'Where is he?'

'He had a message for His Holiness, a message from Canterbury, but I told him the Holy Father was in the chapel so he went to speak to the Monsignor on the door.' Sister Agatha led the way across the hall and paused. 'Oh, the Monsignor doesn't seem to be there.'

Devlin was running and the Walther was in his hand as he flung open the door and tumbled over the Monsignor on the floor. He was aware of Susan Calder behind him, was even more aware of the priest in the black cassock mounting the steps at the end of the tunnel and reaching for the handle of the oak door.

'Harry!' Devlin called.

Cussane turned and fired without the slightest hesitation, the bullet slamming into Devlin's right forearm, punching him back against the wall. Devlin dropped the Walther as he fell and Susan cried out and flattened herself against the wall.

Cussane stood there, the Stechkin extended in his right hand, but he did not fire. Instead, he smiled a ghastly smile.

'Stay out of it, Liam,' he called. 'Last act!' and he turned and opened the chapel door.

Devlin was sick, dizzy from shock. He reached for the Walther with his left hand, fumbled and dropped it as he tried to stand. He glared up at the girl.

'Take it! Stop him! It's up to you now!'

Susan Calder knew nothing of guns beyond a couple of hours of basic handling experience on her training course. She had fired a few rounds from a revolver on the range, that was all. Now, she picked up the Walther without hesitation and ran along the tunnel. Devlin got to his feet and went after her.

The chapel was a place of shadows hallowed by the centuries, the sanctuary lamp the only light. His Holiness Pope John Paul II knelt in his white robes before the simple altar. The sound of the silenced Stechkin, muffled by the door, had not alerted him, but the raised voices had. He was on his feet and turning as the door crashed open and Cussane entered.

He stood there, face damp with sweat, strangely medieval in the black cassock, the Stechkin against his thigh.

John Paul said calmly, 'You are Father Harry Cussane.'

'You are mistaken. I am Mikhail Kelly.' Cussane laughed wildly. 'Strolling player of sorts.'

'You are Father Harry Cussane,' John Paul said relentlessly. 'Priest then, priest now, priest eternally. God will not let go.'

'No!' Cussane cried in a kind of agony. 'I refuse it!'

The Stechkin swung up and Susan Calder stumbled in through the door, falling to her knees, skirt riding up, the Walther levelled in both hands. She shot him twice in the back, shattering his spine and Cussane cried out in agony and fell on his knees in front of the Pope. He stayed there for a moment then rolled on his back, still clutching the Stechkin.

Susan stayed on her knees, lowering the Walther to the floor, watching as the Pontiff gently took the Stechkin from Cussane's hand.

She heard the Pope say in English, 'I want you to make an act of contrition. Say after me: O my God who art infinitely good in thyself . . .'

'Oh my God,' Harry Cussane said and died.

The Pope, on his knees, started to pray, hands clasped.

Behind Susan, Devlin crawled in and sat with his back against the wall, holding his wound, blood on his fingers. She dropped the gun and eased against him as if for warmth.

'Does it always feel like this?' she asked him harshly. 'Dirty and ashamed?'

'Join the club, girl dear,' Liam Devlin said, and he put his good arm around her.

EPILOGUE

———

It was six o'clock on a grey morning, the sky swollen with rain, when Susan Calder turned her mini car in through the gate of St Joseph's Catholic Cemetery, Highgate. It was a poor sort of place with lots of Gothic monuments from an obviously more prosperous past, but now, everything overgrown, nothing but decay.

She was not in uniform and wore a dark headscarf, blue-belted coat and leather boots. She pulled in at the superintendent's lodge and found Devlin standing beside a taxi. He was wearing his usual dark Burberry and black felt hat and his right arm was in a black sling. She got out of the car and he came to meet her.

'Sorry I'm late. The traffic,' she said. 'Have they started?'

'Yes.' He smiled ironically. 'I think Harry would have appreciated this. Like a bad set for a second rate movie. Even the rain makes it another cliché,' he said, as it started to fall in heavy drops.

He told the taxi driver to wait and he and the girl went along the path between gravestones. 'Not much of a place,' she said.

'They had to tuck him away somewhere.' He took out a cigarette with his good hand and lit it. 'Ferguson and the Home Office people felt you should have had some sort of gallantry award.'

'A medal?' There was genuine distaste on her face. 'They can keep it. He had to be stopped, but that doesn't mean I liked doing it.'

'They've decided against it anyway. It would be too public; require an explanation and they can't have that. So much for Harry wanting to leave the KGB with the blame.'

They came to the grave and paused some distance away under a tree. There were two gravediggers, a priest, a woman in a black coat and a girl.

'Tanya Voroninova?' Susan asked.

'Yes, and the girl is Morag Finlay,' Devlin said. 'The three women in Harry Cussane's life, together now to see him planted. First, the one he so greatly wronged as a child, then the child he saved at great inconvenience to himself. I find that ironic. Harry the redemptionist.'

'And then there's me,' she said. 'His executioner and I never even met him.'

'Only the once,' Devlin said. 'And that was enough. Strange – the most important people in his life were women and in the end they were the death of him.'

The priest sprinkled the grave and the coffin with

Holy Water and incensed them. Morag started to cry and Tanya Voroninova put an arm around her as the priest's voice rose in prayer.

Lord Jesus Christ, Saviour of the world, we commend your servant to you and pray for him.

'Poor Harry,' Devlin said. 'Final curtain and he still didn't get a full house.'

He took her arm and they turned and walked away through the rain.

What's next?

Tell us the name of an author you love

| Jack Higgins | Go ▶ |

and we'll find your next great book.